The
SECRETS
of
MAIDEN'S
COVE

The

SECRETS

of

MAIDEN'S COVE

ERIN PALMISANO

GRAND
CENTRAL
New York Boston

Copyright © 2025 by Erin Palmisano

Reading group guide copyright © 2025 by Erin Palmisano and Hachette Book Group, Inc.

Cover design by Christa Moffitt/Christabella Designs. Cover copyright © 2025 by Hachette Book Group, Inc.

Hachette Book Group supports the right to free expression and the value of copyright. The purpose of copyright is to encourage writers and artists to produce the creative works that enrich our culture.

The scanning, uploading, and distribution of this book without permission is a theft of the author's intellectual property. If you would like permission to use material from the book (other than for review purposes), please contact permissions@hbgusa.com. Thank you for your support of the author's rights.

Grand Central Publishing
Hachette Book Group
1290 Avenue of the Americas, New York, NY 10104
grandcentralpublishing.com
@grandcentralpub

Originally published in New Zealand and Australia by Moa Press, an imprint of Hachette Aotearoa New Zealand Limited, in 2025

First Grand Central Publishing edition: May 2025

Grand Central Publishing is a division of Hachette Book Group, Inc. The Grand Central Publishing name and logo is a registered trademark of Hachette Book Group, Inc.

The publisher is not responsible for websites (or their content) that are not owned by the publisher.

The Hachette Speakers Bureau provides a wide range of authors for speaking events. To find out more, go to hachettespeakersbureau.com or email HachetteSpeakers@hbgusa.com.

Grand Central Publishing books may be purchased in bulk for business, educational, or promotional use. For information, please contact your local bookseller or the Hachette Book Group Special Markets Department at special.markets@hbgusa.com.

Library of Congress Control Number: 2025930590

ISBNs: 9781538757512 (trade paperback), 9781538757529 (ebook)

Printed in the United States of America

LSC-C

Printing 1, 2025

To my dad, who I miss every day.

Prologue

On a planet with 195 countries and a population of eight billion people, there are a lot of places to see and a lot of stories to tell. For many of those billions, the sun rises and sets, routines take place, and the world exists for each person in a pleasantly expected way. But there are also unexpected moments, joys and sorrows, plans embarked upon, mistakes made, and life becomes a story within a story within a story. Such is life and such is our existence that we live our own beautiful story all the time, every moment of every day.

This particular story takes place in a very small, very peculiar little town called Maiden's Cove, on the Chesapeake Bay in Maryland. It is a very small town because it has a mere 213 permanent residents, and it is a very peculiar town because it is said that Maiden's Cove was home to mermaids. Over the years, history became myth, and myth became legend, and they weaved their way into the beating heart of the fishing town that no longer separates myth from legend and instead embraces both. Though to us, it might seem just a little bit like magic.

The moment this story begins, at 2:36 in the morning, there is a light on in a restaurant hovering on stilts in the water, called Cleary's Crab Shack. If we follow that light inside to the kitchen, we find Della rolling her famous crabcakes and humming a song her mama used to sing, not knowing why she was singing an old hymn about the mermaids of Maiden's Cove that she hadn't thought of since she was a small girl.

She turned when the door opened and saw Georgiana, carrying her big book of secret recipes, going into the baking room to make what she called her "wake me cake"—when she woke with an idea for a dessert and, no matter the hour, had to bake it then and there or she wouldn't sleep again.

Jimbo came through next in an overcoat with a few nets and buckets on his arms, and kissed his wife, Della, before going out to the water where his boat was docked to go hunting in the dark for the night crabs. When, suddenly, it wasn't dark at all. They looked up to see strange lights flickering across the bay, lights they knew and yet didn't know, that were part of the town and yet magic.

"Change is coming," Della said.

"It's already here, I reckon," Jimbo said, and they looked out again at the lights.

If we follow their line of sight across the bay there is a small house called Brixton Cottage on the water and inside, Grace Cleary could not sleep. She stared at her clock at 2:36 a.m., the time that it had been stuck on since she arrived back home to Maiden's Cove two months before.

Grace walked through her screen door and down to the little beach she knew so well as a child, pulling the nightgown over her head and walking into the water, tepid as a cooled bath.

Why is the water always warmer naked?

Because then it knows you belong to it.

Do I belong to it?

Sure you do. Now you're with me.

The voices of the past washed over her as she swam deeper to where she could no longer touch, and she trod water for a little while. There was no moon, no light. She went down then, under the water, to where the noise stopped like the light. Pressing her fingers to her lips, Grace sat on the sandy bottom, remembering the touch of soft lips on hers, her lungs filling with air, the dream of breathing underwater. She gently made her way to shore on her back, staring at the black sky without a moon in it, like it used to be when she was a girl, and there was no sea and no sky, no moon and no reflection, only the realm of possibility and creation.

She gasped as she looked down at her left footprint in the sand, glowing with bioluminescence. She moved her right foot, and the sand glowed around it. She knew it could be the algae, or the presence of something else, something long forgotten by some, something that was legend and myth to others.

But not to Grace. To her, it was familiar, it was her family, her best friend. And just like the first time the bioluminescence found her on the sand when she was but twelve years old, Grace knew that she needed one person right now more than anyone else in the world. She looked down at the sand, glowing in the water, and whispered to the bay, "I need you, Isla."

That light carried that message to where it was destined to be heard, over fifteen hundred miles away in the Caribbean Islands, where Isla was sitting on a beach. Suddenly there were lights around her, though there was no plankton or algae where she was, and she knew they were there just for her.

She knew it was time, time to go home, home to Maiden's Cove. And so our story begins, a story where sometimes the only way back to yourself is by coming home. The story of the magic of Maiden's Cove.

Chapter One

Grace woke with the sun, the light making prisms in her eyes as the sun rose over the bay. She unfurled her body from the love seat on her front porch, marveling again at the fact that her childhood dream home was now hers.

It was old—a charming two-story cottage that looked like it was out of a painting, with white siding and windows framed in blue shutters. A large porch wrapped around the house and faced the little beach where Grace now stood. She walked through the screen door and into the kitchen of yellow wooden cabinets with light all around. Her last home in Phoenix had been decorated by Richard, who loved modern style and blacks and grays. Over the past two months since she and Bayla had moved into Brixton Cottage, she'd turned the beautiful space into a home. It was light and airy, filled with rustic old furniture Grace loved to hunt for at the antique shops. Everything about her home was welcoming and warm and just stepping inside made her feel safe and happy.

"Mom, did you sleep outside?" Bayla asked, putting down an old book. Her eyebrows furrowed as she looked to her mother and the door from where she came.

"I went for a late night swim and fell asleep on the porch," Grace said, winking at Bayla, who looked inordinately pleased by her mother's carefree antics. Ever since they moved to Maiden's Cove, Bayla had been searching for magic in everything. Grace couldn't blame her—she felt the same way every time she looked around her home, or felt the bay breeze that filtered through the always-open windows, smelling like summer. Even the way the water lapped up onto their beach, hinting at a secret beneath the surface—in comparison to their life in Phoenix, it all felt a little bit like magic.

She walked past and tousled Bayla's head, pouring herself a cup of coffee. "Thanks for putting the coffee on, sweetheart."

"No problem," Bayla answered, delving back into the very large book she'd had her head buried in.

"What are you reading?" Grace asked.

The book that Bayla held up looked vaguely familiar.

"Where did you get that?" Grace asked, leaning forward to have a closer look.

"In one of the boxes I got from Gloretta's house. I found it in the basement. It had 'Grace's books 2000' written on the side, so I figured you'd have been about my age and reading it at the time. So, Mom, listen to this and tell me if it sounds familiar." Bayla began to read slowly.

" 'Maiden's Cove's founder was Eyefane Grip-hone.' " Bayla pulled her eyebrows. "Is that right?" She pointed to the name on the page, Ifan Gryphon.

"It's Welsh. You pronounce it like Eevan Griffon," she said, writing it down phonetically. "And the next funny-looking one is said like Kill-drithe Mor-Win-Yon."

"Weird language," Bayla said, and continued. " 'Ifan Gryphon, a fisherman from Wales, founded the town as Cildraeth Morwynion, but over the years the simple fishermen who populated the town translated it into English, and it has been Maiden's Cove ever since.

" 'Ifan was lured into the Cove after his ship had wrecked in the Atlantic by a beautiful woman of the sea, who rescued him and brought him to a forbidden shore. She was cast out by her people for helping the human, and she became his wife on the land for many years, even producing a daughter, as the town began to build and grow with local fishermen. One night, in the year 1714, on the first of June, green lights sparkled on the bay. The whole town saw the lights but knew not what they meant, but in the morning, Ifan, Isolde, and the small girl, Isla, were gone, and never returned. Frightened, the townspeople feared the merfolk had lured them to the water with the lights, calling for their own to come home.

" 'The following year, on the first of June, the new mayor of the town, Ludlow Cleary'—Mom, that's us, right? Cleary?" she asked excitedly.

Grace nodded warily and opened her mouth to interrupt but Bayla continued reading.

" 'Ludlow Cleary began a new tradition, holding the Festival of Lights at the start of each fishing season and the Maiden's Cove Festival at the end. At the Festival of Lights, every Maiden's Cove inhabitant would light a candle to bring the fishermen home, and not be tempted by the green lights that lit the water every year at the same time. It was whispered then that the Clearys could call the mermaids. This is the history of Maiden's Cove and the Festival of Lights.' "

"Your grandad liked to call that story hogwash," Grace said.

"That's a funny word," Bayla said, laughing. "Hogwash." She giggled again. "I wish I remembered Grandad, but I was too little the last time we were here."

Grace sighed, regret and sadness coursing through her. "You were just a toddler then. I wish you would have known him better too, sweetheart."

"It can't be all hogwash though," Bayla said. "The whole town is decorating for the celebration! I can't wait to see the lights tonight. Do you really think there are mermaids out there, Mom?"

Grace laughed. "Well you know what Grandad would say. There are some beautiful lights called bioluminescence—it's algae in the sand and it glows. But you'll see it all summer so you should go to the festival with Sylvie and let me pick you up later. It would be fun!"

"Nope, you promised you'd pick me up after work. Can't I come work at the restaurant with you? Please!"

Grace hesitated. She loved that Bayla wanted to spend her days in the restaurant she herself grew up in, to be a part of the legacy of the Cleary family she hadn't even known until a few months before. She marveled at her daughter, at how adaptable she was since they'd moved back to Maiden's Cove two months before.

Bayla was eight years old and had left her life in Phoenix— her father, school and her friends—without much warning, to cross most of the country to an old and slightly dilapidated but charming cottage in Maiden's Cove. But instead of being sullen or anxious, she suddenly whistled and got up early, embraced a new fashion sense, and seemed overall truly happy.

And the only explanation Bayla had ever given her was a shrug, as though it were obvious. "We are where we belong," she had said when they arrived at the cottage, and began to unpack and put everything away like she'd simply been waiting to arrive.

Grace pulled Bayla in for a hug. "I love it so much that you want to spend the summer at Cleary's Crab Shack. But it's my first summer back in a long time and today is the re-opening of Cleary's since Grandad passed away. Things are not quite as ready as I hoped they would be, and I need to be prepared for any glitches. Maybe next week you can come in and I'll show you the ropes, okay?"

The toaster popped and Bayla put two toaster strudels onto separate plates, handing one to Grace. "Is it still a 'shitshow' in there?"

"Bayla!" she cried, biting her lip to try to stop laughing. "Where did you hear that?"

"When you were on the phone with Cohen," she said. Cohen had been Grace's closest friend in Phoenix and had helped them get the car to drive in the middle of the night back to Maiden's Cove. Cohen had always loved hearing her stories about Maiden's Cove and when she called him crying with the news that her beloved restaurant was in the red and she'd have to close if she didn't get it back on track this summer, he showed up within days of her call to help. For the past few weeks he'd been working tirelessly with her to get the restaurant ready for today.

"Sorry about the bad words," Grace said, and then sighed. "We still don't have a head chef, so that's the biggest problem. Jimbo and Della are holding the kitchen together and Gigi is doing amazing things with the pastry section, but without Dad leading the kitchen team we are still short-staffed. I've done some upgrading as well…" She stopped when she realized that Bayla was listening intently and not eating her breakfast and Grace swallowed guiltily. The last thing she needed to do was add any extra stress onto her young child. "We'll get there, hon. I promise. Don't you stress. You're still a kid, you know?"

Bayla considered the words closely, her eyes shrewd and her head tilted. Finally, she nodded. "Okay. After all, I am eight and I should really enjoy the first day of summer."

Grace laughed. "You should indeed. But it's not actually the first day of summer until June twenty-first. Which is the summer solstice, the longest day of the year."

"In New Zealand, June first is the first day of winter. Did you know that?" Bayla asked. Grace shook her head. "And *December* first is the first day of summer. Their seasons are the opposite. But they also like the first of the month to be the first of the season, so they ignore the solstice and make up their own dates. Uncle Ben has a friend that lived in New Zealand and he says New Zealanders can really do anything because they are so far away, who's going to pay attention anyway?"

"You've been spending time with Uncle Ben?" Grace asked, surprised but pleased.

"Sometimes Sylvie and I pop into his shop. I think she has a crush on him even though he's like, way old."

Grace laughed.

"He tells fun stories and lets me play on the kayaks when it's not too busy. He said he always wanted to travel but never got around to it. I think I might like to travel when I'm a grown up."

"I think you might do anything you want as a grown-up," Grace said, kissing Bayla's forehead.

"Do you think I can be a mermaid?"

⌒

Grace and Bayla walked from their cottage on Chelsea Bay and crossed the little footbridge to the village of Maiden's Cove. The "island" on which the town was built was not actually an island at all, but a peninsula, but during the higher tides the water covered the sand so that it did, indeed, look like an island. It was protected by the mainland with bays and neighborhoods on either side. Chelsea Bay was on the west side of the Maiden's Cove peninsula, their cottage just on the tip so that they had the sunset until the moment it disappeared over the horizon. Grace always thought that Chelsea Bay was the most beautiful place in the world, with its hidden sandy beaches, historic houses like hers, and the long, tall grasses of the marshlands that seemed to sway like they were dancing with the sunset, when the fireflies came out and the sand began to glow with the bioluminescence.

It was said that many things could pass to and from when the tide was in over Maiden's Cove. Even the locals would admit there was something "just a bit peculiar" about it, but they couldn't quite say what.

Or so it was said.

There was already traffic with tourists coming in early to find parking for the Festival of Lights, though the main events weren't until the evening. Grace's heart swelled with pride as they walked through town. While some places decorated their towns at Christmas, Maiden's Cove put on her finery for the summer, starting on Festival Day. There wasn't a streetlight or lamppost that wasn't covered in fairy lights with mermaids at the top that lit up in the night. Shops opened their doors and lined the windows with mermaid souvenirs—wood-carved, glass-blown, hand-painted. Special glowing candles to put in your windows that burned all night to bring the fishermen home. Large seashells that you could hear the ocean in, sea-glass artwork and workshops too, where you could take a guide to the hidden coves and search for sea glass yourself.

Everyone they passed turned and waved to them, smiling and calling out, "Good luck today, Grace!"

In the town square the stalls were being set up for the evening festivities. Food stalls with caramel popcorn and funnel cakes, corn dogs and cotton candy. French fries with vinegar, fried oyster po-boys and massive crab-dip coated pretzels. Then there were the rides—the swings and a Ferris wheel, the Matterhorn and a carousel. There were games—the water-balloon popping and goldfish pinball—and a portrait artist doing charcoals of your face on a mermaid body.

The town was alive, thriving. Bayla's mouth was agape as she pointed out different stalls to her mother, her voice and face filled with joy, and Grace knew she'd made the right decision bringing Bayla here.

"Opening day today, Grace?" a voice called from atop a lamppost.

Grace looked up to see Ole Pete, one of the fishermen from when she was a child who used to bring in fish to Cleary's.

"Dad would have wanted us to be open for Festival Day," she said, smiling up at him. "It was his favorite."

"He'd be right proud of you, Gracey, right proud." He looked at Bayla. "You going to work with your mom, Miss Bayla?"

"I tried but she won't let me. Thinks I should be a kid," she called up, rolling her eyes.

"Ha! Never knew a kid who needed to be more a kid than your momma when she was your age. Spent every day at Cleary's until that friend of hers finally showed up. What was her name again? Henry's girl?" he asked.

Grace's heart skipped a beat. There hadn't been a moment since she'd arrived back in Maiden's Cove she hadn't thought about her best friend from her childhood summers and wished her home in her heart. "Isla," she answered.

Bayla's head snapped back to Grace, her eyes wide. "Like Ifan's half-mermaid daughter? From the history?"

"I think it's called a legend, kiddo," Grace said. "But yes. The same name. It's very popular these days," she finished lamely.

"Well, have fun being a kid today!" Ole Pete called as he turned back to hooking up the lights.

"Thanks! Hey, Mom, look, Uncle Ben is just opening. I can see him pulling out the kayaks. Uncle Ben!" Bayla called, running down to Paddle Cove, her uncle's rental shop.

Grace followed, her stomach in knots. She and Ben had been so close when they were younger. Sure, in their teenage years they'd argued like any other brother and sister, but they were still family, until the year Grace came home after Bayla was born. Ben had seen something in Richard then that Grace didn't at that time. He'd been high-handed and demanding and they'd fought terribly.

That was the last time she'd been in Maiden's Cove. Her dad came out to visit once shortly after, but she was never allowed back home. By the time she realized that she was in a controlled, mentally abusive and unhealthy relationship, she was too embarrassed to say anything to her father or Ben, and too afraid to leave. She and Ben hadn't spoken for years until she showed up two months ago.

"Uncle Ben! Can me and Sylvie take a kayak out today? She's babysitting me while Mom goes to open Cleary's again," Bayla said excitedly.

He smiled at her with obvious affection but shook his head. "It's a big day here too, kiddo, and everything is rented out. All the kayaks, canoes, rowboats and Jet Skis."

"Sounds like business is going well," Grace said with false cheer as she approached. Ben smiled but it was a tight smile, like it had been since she returned. It made her angry and then sad, and then she realized that he didn't know the truth, he didn't know anything, and until she confided in him, their relationship would be tense. But there was nothing tense in the way he spoke with Bayla, and for that she was eternally grateful.

"Everyone wants to be on the water in the summer on the bay," he said modestly. "Hey, did you still need a chef over at Cleary's?" he asked as he started pulling more kayaks down from the racks.

"Yeah. Have you become one overnight and are offering to help?" she asked with a laugh.

"Naw, sorry. Luke just got back home though, from New Zealand. You remember Luke McCann?"

Grace's stomach did an unexpected flip. How could she *not* remember Luke McCann? Her first crush. Her *only* crush until he went away to college and she met Richard. Ben's best friend. She and Isla and Ben and Luke had been quite a group of explorers before they all became teenagers.

"Of course I remember Luke," she said, rolling her eyes when she noticed him smirking. "He was only your best friend for, like, ever. What's your point?"

"He's a chef," he said simply.

"Oh," Grace said, surprised. "Well, tell him to pop in anytime that is not today. Is he any good?"

Ben shrugged. "No clue. Didn't you guys work together at Cleary's?"

"Yes, but he was a bartender then," she said and glanced at her watch. "Shit! Bayla, come on, I'm going to be late!" She glanced back at Ben, who was looking at her like he wanted to say something else but turned instead back to the kayaks. She sighed and started to walk away.

"Good luck today," he yelled to her at the last minute.

She turned and gave him a faint smile. "Thanks."

～

"Whatever is that delightful get-up you are wearing, Miss Bayla?" Sylvie called, as Bayla started pulling on her rollerskates.

"Found it in Mom's old trunk at Gloretta's!" she yelled back. "Isn't it super cool?"

The "delightful get-up" was an old green and blue glittery dress with spaghetti straps Grace had worn to her eighth-grade dance. She'd bought it because it was sparkly like the sand when she'd met Isla the summer before. It caused a stir at the dance and fed the rumors of the "mermaid caller" even more. Grace had been thrilled.

Bayla, who was much smaller at eight than Grace had been at thirteen, wore it with leggings and cinched the dress around her waist with a rhinestone belt. She looked ridiculous but adorable. Richard had always insisted Bayla went to a school with a uniform, and outside of school had strict rules on what was acceptable for each of them to wear. So being able to wear whatever she wanted right now while she was exploring her slightly flamboyant fashion sense made Bayla joyful.

Sylvie turned to Grace, who had brought Bayla's backpack up to the house. "Who's Gloretta?"

"It's Bayla's name for Loretta, her grandmother. Loretta is over the moon to have a cool grandmother name," Grace said wryly. "And be wary—Bayla is obsessed with anything out of her grandad and Gloretta's house. She's confiscated all of Dad's Elvis CDs, Gloretta's lipsticks, and anything and everything from our Cleary history and the history of Maiden's Cove, especially if it's about me."

"Sounds like she's a little curious about where she came from. She must be so excited to come to a home that is all quirky and magical like Maiden's Cove," Sylvie said. "I guess we all take it for granted."

Grace looked out and around, shaking her head. "I never did, you know? Take it for granted. I loved my home more than anything in the world. I never wanted to leave."

"Why did you then?" Sylvie asked.

Grace didn't answer, just stared out at the bay in a reverie until Sylvie cleared her throat. "Sorry, Sylvie," she said, coming back to the present. "Lost in memories."

"I can imagine," Sylvie said.

Sylvie had the kind of mousy brown hair that was neither straight nor wavy, with soft brown eyes and braces, and skin that just hated being sixteen. She was awkward-looking but there was a confidence and humor about her that made you forget the flaws and want to be her friend then and there. Bayla adored her.

"I asked Bayla the other day if she wanted to go to the festival tonight, but she said no, she wanted to be able to see the lights proper," Sylvie said, shrugging. "What did she mean by that?"

"Don't ask unless you want a mythology lesson on Maiden's Cove." Grace sighed. "I'll be back by six, plenty of time for you to get to the festival." She walked down the driveway, catching Bayla on her skates and giving her a kiss on the cheek. "You sure you don't want to go with Sylvie to the festival tonight? I could pick you up later?"

"Nope," she said, wheezing slightly on her skates. "The Festival of Lights keeps the mermaids from coming *in* to the cove, which is exactly where I want them. Apparently from our side of the bay you can see the bio...um...no, the lamination? The green lights, and I want to see them. Also," she said, grabbing Grace to stop her from going downhill on her skates, "someone is coming. I can feel it."

Bayla sped off down the street on her skates as Grace's heart began to race. Did she mean Richard was coming? She opened her mouth to call out but Bayla was already down the road. Bayla still talked to her father on the phone once a week and he knew they were here in Maiden's Cove, but so far he hadn't spoken to Grace and it unsettled her, the way he was making her feel like he'd just let them go that easily, without a fight. No tears of regret for his actions this time. No begging her to stay. Just silence. A shiver went up her spine and she turned quickly, but no one was there.

"Come on, Grace, keep it together. It's Festival Day," she said over and over as a mantra, looking around once more before heading to the restaurant.

Chapter Two

Cleary's Crab Shack was an old building with white wooden shingles and a large deck that sat on stilts over the water in Isolde Bay. It was one of the most famous crab shacks on this side of the Chesapeake, and people came from all over Maryland and the coast to have freshly caught seafood straight off the boats, including, of course, the famous Chesapeake blue crab.

Grace's grandfather had built Cleary's seventy-five years ago with his own two hands. It was a fisherman's wharf at the time, where the boats would come and sell their catch at what was then Cleary's Fish Market. Soon people began eating at the market, so he built the deck and put picnic tables out there and got hold of a deep fryer and steam pot. When Grace's father, Tom, was old enough, he started helping in the kitchen. And when he took over just after leaving school, he began to grow the fish market into something a bit more refined. Grace had always planned to follow in his footsteps when she grew up.

Tom loved his restaurant and he loved food. He and one of Cleary's fishermen, Jimbo, learned how to steam and season the best seafood. They went down South and learned how to do a Southern-style barbecue. He watched videos about smoking everything from pork to brisket to fish. The kitchen grew, the building expanded, the seating turned from plastic to wooden. But what he never changed was the fisherman's wharf, the live catch, and the relationship his own father had built with the local fishermen. Grace remembered her father telling her that Cleary's was not only a staple to the community for its food, but because it bridged the gap that had been part of Maiden's Cove previously, where the fishermen of the Cove were of one class and the landers were of another, better one.

"Here at Cleary's, there are no classes. Just a team of people working together to create a place where anyone and everyone can enjoy good food, good beverages and good conversation," he told her when she was ten years old. "Food is the stuff of life, Gracey. Nothing connects us like food."

When Grace was growing up she was as much a familiar presence at Cleary's as Tom was. She and her brother, Ben, practically grew up in the restaurant after their mother passed when Grace was two and Ben was three. Ben never liked working in the restaurant, though he would sometimes go out with some of the fishermen as he loved being on the water. But Grace never wanted to leave Cleary's. It was like home, it was part of her, just like it was part of her dad.

He had left her Cleary's when he died from a sudden and unexpected heart attack two months ago. Despite the fact that losing her dad was the worst thing that had ever happened to her, it was also the thing that had freed her, that allowed her to see how toxic her relationship with Richard had become. How was it that her daughter didn't know her grandad? How was it that she hadn't been home in over six years? She'd been controlled, she'd been trapped by Richard, and she hadn't even known, hadn't realized. And now her dad was gone. But so too were she and Bayla. Gone from Richard.

What she hadn't realized when she stepped into Cleary's that first day back was that what she'd inherited was a huge amount of unpaid bills and that her beloved restaurant was about to go under. It was barely making enough to pay the staff.

"Oh, Dad," she'd whispered at the books, "what happened?"

"Covid," Loretta, her stepmother, had said from behind her. "Competition. The Eastern Shore is a destination for food in its own right now," she said. "Cleary's isn't the only crab shack on the Chesapeake anymore. You knew your dad, he just wanted to cook and talk to the customers and didn't want to be bothered with rising costs and those things. You should sell the place and go back to that handsome husband of yours."

"I'm not selling Cleary's, or the building, or anything. I will get us out of the red this summer," she'd replied through clenched teeth. She and Loretta had never been close.

"Well, you're going to have to find a chef first, and figure out how to pay them. Your dad did that job and he didn't pay himself a wage."

The determination to save her family restaurant was a driving force. Grace was able to take out a loan with Cohen cosigning so that they could make some necessary changes to get through the summer.

Which starts today, Grace said to herself. *It's opening day. Festival Day, Grace. Keep it together*, she said again to herself, putting on a smile and opening the front door.

"Morning, Della!" Grace called with affection. Della was Jimbo's wife, and they had been at Cleary's since before she and Ben were even born.

Della lifted her head, her warm brown eyes smiling. "Morning, honey. How are you doing today? You feel okay, being here for the first time in so long, and without your daddy?"

For a moment, Grace felt a lump in her throat she didn't know if she could swallow, but Della's arm was suddenly around her and it was as if she was a child again, warm and safe. Della smelled like cocoa butter and deep fryer.

"Close your eyes and taste this, tell me what you think."

She bit down gently into a buttery scallop so fresh she could still taste the saltwater in her throat. The brown butter burst forth and coated her tastebuds and she was overwhelmed with a memory of the first time she'd tasted a scallop. She'd have been around Bayla's age, and it was Della who'd introduced her to what would become her favorite seafood, though she'd made it into a bisque that day.

"Come on, taste this and tell me what you think," Della had said.

"It's like the sea and spices dancing together." Grace had closed her eyes. "What's that new flavor? It's familiar, but different."

"Good girl," Della had said with an approving nod. "With seafood, you should always taste the sea. I made the bisque with the shells myself this time. Takes a little longer to impart the flavor, but it's worth it in the end. You're a Cleary through and through, honey child, I tell you," she added with a laugh.

"Oh my god, this is amazing, Della," Grace said now. "How are you planning to serve them today?"

"Well, you know Jimbo, wants me to wrap bacon around them and throw them on the barbecue. That man would eat pork with everything if he could," she said, shaking her head. "'Psh,' I said to him, 'you stay in your section and I'll stay in mine.' Scallops this fresh only need a quick toss in the pan and some butter. Have to be able to taste the bay in your mouth, remember, honey?" Della said.

Grace did remember. Della had been giving Grace lessons about food since she was three.

"Did Jimbo bring them in?" Grace asked. "We haven't had scallops for a while."

"Some young buck early this morning. Jimbo went out for night crabs and found a few, but look at that pile of shrimp," she said proudly.

Grace looked over to where buckets of shrimp were being dumped on the table, sorted through by Theo and Clarence, Jimbo and Della's sons, who grinned up at Grace.

"He'll have a great time with those, steaming and frying them up too."

"Were there quite a few new boats in this morning?" Grace asked, suddenly anxious. "Or any older, familiar ones?"

"I know what you're asking and she isn't here. Hasn't been for a long, long time. Now come on, it's nearly opening time, and it's going to be a big one."

⌐◡

Grace sunk into the corner booth of Cleary's, took off her shoes, and actually moaned as she massaged her feet. It had been years since she worked hours this long at the restaurant, not since she was a teenager. Festival Day was always a busy day at Cleary's and this year was no exception.

She should have been happy to see so many customers in, and the sales report for the day was the first beacon of hope she'd had in a long time. But at this very moment, Grace didn't know whether to laugh or to cry. The new till system she'd spent weeks setting up to move them to the modern world of computer-ordering froze up just around the first rush of the day. The staff were all used to handwritten ordering but nobody could remember what the new table numbers were since Grace had "spruced up the joint" by changing the set-up. Because nobody knew the table numbers without looking at the computer map, they got creative.

Table Plumber Butt, Table Furry Back, Table Big Tits Magee, were some of the more memorable ones.

"Enough of this!" Cohen said when the front of house team was all in one place for a second. "What if the customer sees their bill or walks by the pass?! Can't you think of nice names for them?"

But his lips were twitching and it was hard not to laugh, especially when Sarah, a young blonde who looked like she'd never had a bad day in her life until today, handed Jimbo a docket that said, *Table with demon child I'd like to drown in the Orange Crush slushie machine.*

The kitchen hadn't done a busy service without her dad for a long time, and with the extra section that Grace had added for Georgiana—who made the desserts and did the baking—the team were tripping over one another and unsure where they were meant to go.

When the deep fryer stopped working, Jimbo had to run out to get a generator and some stand-up fryers they used to use out of storage, frying clams and shrimp and fries outside, creating an entirely new section that had to come out on its own plates.

And when the boats started pulling up to the dock bar, Grace didn't know how the team would make it through. But amazingly, with Cohen's help, they worked their hardest and they *did* make it through the day, together.

⌒

Cohen came down the stairs from the office and flopped onto the bench across from her.

"Good lord that was a stressful day," he said.

Grace had met Cohen Bassett in Phoenix when Bayla started the dance classes Richard had insisted upon when she was five years old. Grace had thought it was adorable when Richard bought Bayla the entire Sylvanian Families Ballet Theatre set that Christmas. He had tears in his eyes when he signed her up for dance classes.

"Mother was a beautiful dancer," he'd said to Grace. "But my father asked her to stop dancing when they married. Bayla will be the great dancer of the family now."

Grace had thought it was so sweet at the time.

"Mommy, no watching!" Bayla had said when Grace stood at the window trying to peek in.

"But you look so pretty, honey!" she'd said.

"Don't you worry, Bayla," a high-pitched male voice came from behind them. "I'll make sure she doesn't stay and watch." The man had turned to Grace. "Hi, I'm Cohen, Daisy's uncle. She's the one over there with the daisies on her tutu. Don't get me started, she's five and already having an identity crisis. Let's go for a drink. They'll be twirling for forty-five minutes." He'd looked at his watch. "Starting now."

As they'd walked into a restaurant and sat at a table, Grace had a realization that she hadn't met anyone new, had any new friends, in years. Was that normal? She had a five-year-old so she talked to other moms, but had she been out at all? No, she'd realized, and found herself staring out the windows, feeling like she was doing something wrong.

She'd quickly learned that Cohen was pretending to study business because his lawyer brother told their father absolutely everything, but in actuality he was working in hospitality as a restaurant manager. He took his niece to ballet each week and always came to Serena's Wine Bar, which is where he'd brought Grace.

"What's your passion?" he'd asked her.

"I generally prefer white wine," she'd said.

"She'll have the chardonnay," he'd said to the waiter. "You'll *love* the chardonnay here. They have one from three different countries. You would never believe in a million years a chablis and California chardonnay were the same varietal, seriously."

Grace had laughed, loving being back with someone in the restaurant industry and with a new person, feeling normal again for the first time in years, like she had woken up somehow. Those weekly nights with Cohen became the highlight of Grace's week.

"So why aren't you training to be a sommelier or something instead of the business you hate so much?" she'd asked a few dates later. "Isn't that something your family would approve, you being of French descent and all?"

Cohen had looked pained. "It's complicated," he'd said, sipping his red wine. "Not as complicated as your particular situation, but complicated. God, seriously, I could just eat this Garnacha with a knife and fork. Can you smell the cooked berries?"

"Cohen!"

"Look, honey, I tell you what. We're going to get you out of what you got yourself into and get you back to Nowheresville, then I'll come and work with you. I want to live in your magical little mermaid village, talk about wine, have a house near the beach. Find some gorgeous man and get cats and grow old and be happy there."

Over the course of the next three years, Cohen had become her closest friend.

Now, after their grand reopening, Cohen threw his head back and groaned.

"Okay, you win," he said. "Your Nowheresville really is Somewheresville. What a day!" Grace groaned too and Cohen leaned forward, grabbing her hand. "I'm so proud of you today, lady."

Grace couldn't help but laugh. "Cohen, it was a disaster. I honestly don't think we would have made it through the day without your militant organization and calmness. I didn't know you had it in you. Seriously. You're like, the opposite of calm most of the time."

"Eye of the hurricane, lady, you know it," he said dramatically, brushing invisible lint from his shoulders. She laughed and shook her head. "You. Are. Welcome," he said. "It will only get better from here, honey."

"Not without a chef it won't," she moaned, putting her head in her hands.

They both turned toward the stairs as the younger staff began to filter out. "I'll leave you to the little Britneys and Christinas coming down now," said Cohen. "Me and Gigi are heading to the festival. I could not possibly convince you to stop being such an old fuddy-duddy and actually join us, could I?"

Grace sat up and slid her shoes back on. "I've got a crazy kid who wants to go home and call the mermaids. You guys have fun."

"Like mother like daughter," he said with a wink and stood, yelling into the kitchen, "Gigi! I'm leaving without you!"

"I told you, it's Georgiana," she said through gritted teeth. She saw Grace and her face softened. "Ya'll right there, Grace? Big day, and not an easy one, I know, but thank you for having me on board. People seemed to love the new desserts on the menu!"

"They did, and I promise I'll have the kitchen and sections sorted better by tomorrow. Thank you, Gi— Uh, I mean, Georgiana. Have fun tonight," Grace said.

Cohen and Georgiana waved and raced out the door when they heard the junior waitstaff team enter.

Nearly every disaster that had happened today was either because of their lack of a chef or because of one of Grace's new changes and she was prepared for her staff to come give her an ass-kicking, so she was surprised when the team came bouncing in, looking happy.

"Grace, are you coming to the festival with us?" Sarah asked.

Sarah was a mainlander, as they called anyone not from Maiden's Cove, despite it being part of the mainland itself.

"Grace never goes to the festival," Todd said, loosely putting his arm around Sarah.

Todd was a local who left as soon as he could and still came back every summer to work at Cleary's. It was hard to beat Maiden's Cove in the summer. A place with heritage houses and small-town charm, where you never technically had to wear shoes or a shirt. A place of myth and legend, where you could see the bioluminescence below your feet when you walked along the beaches, the green lights on the water—the mermaids calling their own home.

Or so it was said.

"Well, I'm very excited," Sarah said, glancing her blue eyes up at Todd. "My first one. But I mean, what is it, anyway? The festival?"

"It's a 'beginning of summer' festival," Grace answered. "The fishing and crabbing season starts, and there's a big carnival down at the docks with heaps of food, rides, all sorts of fun events that really give a bolster to our town as a start of the season. And it brings an enormous amount of tourists, as you have all seen today." They laughed. "There is one at the end of the season too, so you'll have that to look forward to as well, Sarah. You guys enjoy it, and thank you for your hard work today—I promise I'll have those glitches sorted soon."

"I think we did all right," Todd said.

"You all did more than all right," Grace said, standing and heading to the office to do the paperwork for the day. "It was an amazing success. But now is the time for fun, so go and enjoy the festival and I'll see you back here tomorrow."

"Thanks, Grace!" they called in unison as she walked up the stairs, where she found the office door locked and realized she'd left the keys on the table downstairs. Grace walked back down but stopped on the bottom step as she heard the staff still speaking, slightly hushed.

"Why doesn't Grace come? She's a Cleary—isn't this sort of their festival? It's not *just* a summer festival, is it?" Sarah asked quietly. Grace leaned forward to hear.

"A long time ago it started as a local myth," Todd explained, "that by lighting your candle you called the fishermen home and they couldn't be tempted by the green lights on the bay, which were the merfolk. But that was like, hundreds of years ago or something and nobody really remembers that anymore. Mr. Cleary and his wife, Loretta, used to host every year, welcoming in the fishermen and the start of the season. Even though Mr. Cleary just passed, I heard Loretta will still come and light the first light and all that. Tradition."

"So it's only ever been Grace that doesn't come? Why?" Sarah asked.

"My older cousin Fee said Grace hasn't come since she was like twelve," Abby, another waitress, said.

"I heard she was taken by the mermaids then, and they are like, her family, so she refuses to light a candle. She's still trying to get home or something," said Jake, the new dishwasher.

"No! It was her friend Isla. She's apparently the last mermaid. Don't you know the story?" Abby asked excitedly. "Fee said one day, back whenever this girl Isla showed up—some daughter of a fisherman, all wild and feral—people said she was like, *the* Isla from the stories and that Grace called her or something, because Grace was a Cleary. Fee said this Isla girl could stay under water for hours on end and could even breathe into you if you were drowning."

"But that's impossible! Has anyone actually met her, this Isla?" Sarah asked, fascinated.

"Sure," Todd said, sounding important. "If you grew up here you would have met Isla. My babysitter, Daniella, was sixteen when I was five. She used to take me to the Cove on the weekends when my parents were going to be out all day. I was there one day when Isla jumped off the cliff. I swear to god, if you've ever seen that, you'd believe the rumors…that she really was a mermaid. She hasn't been back since before Grace left though. I've been working here the past six summers. Maybe she'll come home this year and we can ask her."

They all began to talk and laugh, and Grace listened as the old myths came pouring out, quieter as they moved farther away from the stairs.

"I hope her friend does come back," Sarah said, as they opened the door to leave. "It must be so hard for Grace. Her dad passing so unexpectedly and coming home alone with a young daughter to your hometown where everyone is staring, wondering what happened to you. I couldn't imagine. She must be so very lonely."

Grace sighed as the door closed again, swallowing the lump in her throat that was choking on the truth of Sarah's words.

Suddenly the low roar of a motor distracted her. Grace followed the sound to the dock outside. The local fishermen and crabbers from the Cove often docked their boat at Cleary's, coming in late at night only to be back at 3 a.m. on the hunt for soft-shell crabs. Her heart began to race as she went out to see who was coming in now. Was it possible? Could Isla have somehow heard her call?

But the boat pulling in was filled with children. Grace smiled and waved. "Hey, you guys. What an entrance!"

"Sorry about that, Grace," Clarence said, docking the little boat, letting out four kids between the ages of five and thirteen.

"Good lord, they're not all yours, are they, Clarence? Hi Leon, hi Rachel!" she called to the two she knew, who were Bayla's age.

He laughed. "Nah, just the two, the others are Theo's. Easier to pick them up on the boat than to drive all the way around the peninsula to the cove."

"Don't I know it. I used to have a friend that would swim it quite regularly," Grace said with a longing in her heart.

"Damn, that's quite a swim." He whistled, tying up the boat. "Dad, you ready to go?" Clarence asked Jimbo, who had appeared from the kitchen. "I'm throwing the kids in the back of your pickup."

"I'll just be a sec," he said. "You kids stop jumping in my truck!" he bellowed in his authoritative voice, and they all quietened down but started giggling. Jimbo was the biggest softie Grace knew.

He looked at her now, his face serious. "How'd we do?"

She sighed. "Sales? It was a good day. A great start. I haven't told any of the other staff about our problems, especially while we're still looking for a chef. I don't want to put that on anyone else."

"Can't say I agree with you, Gracey," he said. "I think you'd be surprised what can come from asking for a little help. Cleary's isn't just yours. It's all of ours."

"That was some catch of shrimp today," she said, changing the subject. "Break any records?"

"Well, I ain't no Bubba Gump," he joked. "But I do all right." He laughed, warm and deep.

Except for the fact that he seemed to grow larger every year, he looked just the same as when Grace was a child. She hugged him tight.

"Uh oh, you not going to break down on me now are you?"

"Can I?" she asked and he chuckled and squeezed her again.

"We'll find a chef, and until then we'll just truck along. The electrician and computer tech guy is coming early tomorrow to fix what's broken, honey," he said soothingly.

"Is there one to fix me?" she asked with a shaky laugh. "The young'uns all just left for the festival telling grand tales of their boss. Highly entertaining." She looked out to the bay over his shoulder, toward her cottage.

"Are you bringing Bayla to the festival?" Jimbo asked.

"She doesn't want to go. I did ask her," Grace said a little defensively.

"Well, if she don't want to go, she don't have to go, that's fair enough," he answered in his soothing cadence. "I'll finish locking up here, Gracey. Go home, the paperwork will be here in the morning."

"Thanks, Jimbo," Grace said, kissing him on the cheek. "Have fun at the festival. Loretta will be throwing a big one this year in honor of Dad. Your grandkids will love it. How many do you have now, anyway?"

"I stopped counting, and just call them all 'honey' so they never know I have no idea who they actually are."

<hr />

Grace sat on the front porch when Bayla finally fell asleep and poured a cold glass of pinot grigio. The only light was the burning candles in the windows of all the houses, fading as the hours passed. It was after midnight, the sky was clear and the stars bright, the second night of this month's new moon.

Grace.

It wasn't a voice, and yet it was. Grace didn't know why she was waiting for Isla, why she was hearing her, feeling her presence. Coming home to Maiden's Cove was supposed to be coming home to her dad. To a Cleary's that was the beating heart of their family, of their town, of her. It was supposed to be coming home to where Isla would be, as soon as the season began. Grace walked the twenty yards down to the beach and waded in, treading water when her feet could no longer touch the sandy bottom. She spun in the water, looking around. She went under, down to the bottom, and sat, opening her eyes and waiting to see if Isla would find her there, touch her finger to her lips, breathe into her lungs. Play games.

But she didn't come. Finally, sadly, Grace swam to the surface.

"Took you long enough," a voice called from the beach. Grace looked up to see a familiar figure sitting on the beach, in jean shorts and an oversized T-shirt. Even though they'd aged over the years, seeing Isla was like coming home.

She stood up when Grace came out of the water. Grace was almost unable to meet her eyes. But Isla walked over and gently took her chin, turning her head so that Grace could do nothing but meet the green eyes of her childhood best friend, that seemed to see every single moment of her life in the years since they'd last met. Isla let go of her chin and Grace turned away, feeling suddenly both bereft and relieved.

"Go dry up and grab that bottle of pinot grigio you were drinking. I'll be on the porch," Isla said.

Grace walked into the house and dried off, then pulled her pajamas back on. She went to the refrigerator and grabbed the bottle of wine and saw that her hand was shaking. Even though she'd been hoping for Isla to come back since she returned to Maiden's Cove, and longing for the best friend of her youth, to see her now, here in the flesh, threw Grace completely. The person who was her other half most of her childhood, her summer soul sister, her everything, until they grew up. And here they both were now, adults, in Maiden's Cove together. It was terrifying and confusing and yet so completely right.

Grace grabbed another glass and went back out to the porch. Isla was already there, her leg tucked under her like she always used to sit, like she was ready to jump up at any time.

Grace poured them both a drink and they sat, not sipping or speaking, but glancing in each other's direction when the other wasn't looking.

"I love that you moved into Brixton Cottage. You always said you were going to live here when you were young," Isla said finally, glancing at the house.

"My dad bought it for me. He knew how much I loved it and he knew I needed a way back home. And then..." She paused, swallowing. "I found out the cottage was in my name when they read the will."

"I was so sorry to hear about your dad, Grace."

"When I got the news I was devastated," she said, her eyes filling. "I remember sinking to the ground with my phone in my hand and I don't even know the sound that came out of me, it was between a scream and a sob. My daughter, Bayla, heard me and ran into the room. When I told her what happened, she said, 'Oh, Mommy, I'm so sorry. I wish I would have known Grandad.'" Grace took a deep breath. "She'd only been here and met Dad once, when she was still a baby. She didn't remember, of course. I couldn't believe it. She's *eight* years old. And suddenly I realized I hadn't been home in over six years. That Richard—"

"Richard?" Isla asked, her head snapping up. "Richard Monroe, from that summer?"

"My husband," Grace whispered, as tears slid down her cheeks. "Suffice it to say that that was finally the moment I had the strength to leave a relationship that was…"

"That was what?" Isla asked.

But Grace shook her head. "I don't want to talk about that right now."

"Is that why you never answered any of my postcards?" Isla asked.

"What postcards? I never heard from you, not those years I was still here or after I left," she said, confused.

Isla remained quiet a long time. "That last summer I left hurt and angry and you're right, I didn't come back or call. But then one day I was sitting on a beach in Thailand and I saw this postcard that said 'From The Sea' and it made me think of us," Isla said, and Grace smiled a bit, wiping her tears. "I sent it to your dad's place and he called to tell me you'd moved and gave me your address in Phoenix. I was so shocked. I never thought you'd leave Maiden's Cove and Cleary's, let alone live away from the water. I started sending them to you from every new place I went."

"I never got any of your postcards," Grace said softly, realization coming over her. "When Richard found out I'd been sent an invitation to a wedding back home one year, we suddenly stopped getting mail at home."

When Isla opened her mouth to say something, Grace spoke quickly. "He had it diverted to a PO Box, but—"

"You don't want to talk about that right now," Isla finished. It wasn't a question, and for that Grace was grateful.

"So where have you been?" she asked instead.

Isla smiled. "All over. Thailand, the South Pacific, Indonesia, Mexico. Teaching recreational free-diving if you can believe it. I came here from the Caribbean."

Grace smiled with actual joy. "Who would have ever guessed you could make a living using all that mermaid magic of yours?"

"Funny, never once mentioned on those possible career quizzes we used to take in *Seventeen* magazine," Isla mused.

Grace laughed outright now and relaxed in her seat, sipping her wine. Isla reached out her hand, which Grace took.

"I know you have regrets," Isla said softly, "and I am sure you'll tell me everything when you're ready, but you're home now."

"And so are you. What brought you home, Isla?"

But she just shook her head and looked at the glowing bioluminescence on the beach. "I forgot how bright they are here."

"Brightest on the island," Grace said, taking her hand. Suddenly it was like every moment of their shared friendship came together right at that instant and not a day had passed.

"It's almost as if Maiden's Cove stood still and we're twelve years old again," Grace said, taking Isla's hand. "Gracenisla. One name."

Isla smiled. "One soul, reunited."

" 'One from the land and one from the sea. Summer soul sisters forever shall we be.' "

Chapter Three

Summer 2002

G race sat in her windowsill and stared out to the bay. She was twelve years old, and so lonely it felt like there was a hole inside her she thought she'd never fill. But this year, she thought determinedly, was going to be different. She was going to the festival tomorrow and she was going to find a friend. A best friend.

The night was hot, so she quietly slipped outside and walked down the little path behind her house to the beach where she liked to wade at night. She took off her nightgown and walked into the bay, which was warm like bath water. She dived under, holding her breath until she had to touch her toes to the bottom and shoot herself back to the surface. It felt like electricity was pulsing through her—all the loneliness and the aching sadness of not having her mother, of not having a true friend.

There was no moon and it was getting darker and harder to see. She decided to go into shore, and a faint light on the beach guided her back. She'd never seen any lights in the sand before and wondered if there was algae or plankton on this side of the bay this summer.

When she stepped onto the shore, suddenly the sand around her foot lit up spectacularly.

"Oh my gosh," she whispered, laughing as she took another step. It was amazing. The lights under her feet glowed, and Grace began to dance. Every time she took a step and the bioluminescence glowed, a green light on the bay winked at her. She knew this instinctively. It winked. Not glowed, not blinked. Winked.

Grace sat for a long time, and the green light stayed too, until finally, right there on the beach, she fell asleep.

"That's the last one this morning, Jimbo," Grace said. "Restaurant's about to open."

"Just wait, Gracey," he said. "There's one more."

Sure enough, what looked like a very small wooden boat came into view on the horizon, but Grace had to squint to see it.

"He's paddling," Grace said. "He must have lost the engine. Come on, Jimbo, he must be so tired to have rowed all the way back into shore. Let's go help him."

"Them," Jimbo corrected.

"What?"

"There's two."

"I can't see another fisherman in the boat," she said.

"It's not another fisherman," he concurred. "There is a fisherman and a little girl. Looks like she might be your age."

"A girl?" Grace breathed. "How can you see that from here?"

"I got good eyes," he said, walking to the end of the dock and picking up a long rope. "Get ready, they're coming in faster than they look."

Jimbo was right. By the time Grace looked back up after letting the rope loose, they were nearly at the dock. And now her eyesight was as clear as Jimbo's. Rowing was an older man of an age impossible to gauge. Like most fishermen, he was so tanned and lined he could have been thirty or sixty and you'd not know. But standing behind him was a girl, and she was clearly around Grace's age.

The man smiled and caught the rope she tossed, pulling their boat in until they reached the dock. Jimbo helped him in, the girl lifting the coolers filled with ice and fish with spectacular strength and agility.

"Thank you for letting us in so late in the morning, and my apologies," the man said in a slow drawl. "I'm Henry, we just moved to the Cove yesterday and didn't have time to come in before now." Jimbo shook his hand as Henry handed him papers.

"What have you got here, Henry?"

"Well, we've got some bay scallops, and some shrimp too. Saw some oysters but they seem to be spawning so we left them alone. But the soft clams looked too good to pass up so we brought some of those too. Can you use them?" Henry asked.

Jimbo lit up. "Where on earth did you come across them at this time of year? They're hidden deep. Only divers can find them now."

Henry smiled. "I've got a diver right here. Isla, honey, come on up and introduce yourself." He helped the girl up onto the deck. "This is Isla, my daughter."

Grace felt something funny stir inside her as Isla stepped onto the dock, something almost familiar.

The girl was her age, of that she was certain. But there was something different about her than other girls, something feral and restless. Her hair was red and tangled and curly, the top bleached blonde in the strangest way. Her skin was tanned with freckles everywhere, and her eyes were a murky shade of green like moss had grown on top of them. Grace was mesmerized.

"I'm Grace," she finally said, and smiled at her.

Isla met her eyes and lit up suddenly. "Oh, good, you're here."

"It seems impossible that summer is over and you're leaving in two days," Grace said, as they were floating on their backs in the water.

"I know, I wish I could stay," Isla said longingly.

"You can't?"

"Season's finished, have to move onto the next one," she answered with a sigh.

They were quiet for a while until Grace said, "Why is the water always warmer naked?"

"Because then it knows you belong to it."

"Do I belong to it?"

"Sure you do. Now you're with me."

It was a new moon so there was no light in the sky, and the bioluminescence was bright and clear, but they were floating on blackness. It was like they were living in magic and filled with possibility.

"Hey, Isla?" Grace asked.

"Hmm?"

"You remember the stories I told you about Maiden's Cove? The myths?"

"Yeah," she said, turning over to look at Grace. "About the mermaids?"

"And," Grace said, blushing, "the mermaid caller. The Cleary."

Isla was quiet for a minute. "Yeah, I've been thinking about it too."

"You have?" Grace asked, getting excited. "Because you know, the night before I met you, a couple months ago, I was on this beach and I saw the bioluminescence for the first time, and a green light out on the water. I thought...maybe, like, I called a mermaid."

"Oh my god, Grace, that was me!" Isla cried. "I was out on the sandbar diving and I saw these lights. So I started shining mine back. I always have to carry a locator beacon light with me when I night dive. It's how you get found if you're lost."

"What?! It *was* you?"

"Yes!" She laughed, and then they were both laughing.

"Do you think that maybe, like, you are a real mermaid caller, and I am a real mermaid? Not, like, I grow fins or anything, but that, like, I belong to the sea?"

"One from the land, one from the sea," Grace mused. "I love that. It feels so right."

"Like we are two parts making a whole," Isla said. "One from the land and one from the sea. Summer soul sisters forever shall we be."

Chapter Four

When Grace woke, the sun was shining through the open window, a soft bay breeze blowing in. She smiled. She and Isla had stayed up talking on the porch and, when it got late enough, went to Grace's bed to lie side by side and whisper in the dark until the sun came up, like they did when they were girls. She'd told Isla she was not quite ready to delve into details about Richard, but she would—today. And hopefully Isla would tell her why she was back after all this time now. Something happened, Grace could feel it. Something that had brought Isla home too. And now they were here, together in Maiden's Cove.

Grace hopped out of bed and pulled on her slippers and went down to the kitchen to find Bayla, who would likely be listening to her music playlist and eating toaster strudels. But as

Grace reached the bottom step she heard two voices. Curious to hear her daughter and her best friend's first interaction, Grace sat and listened.

"Did you want to listen to some music?" Bayla was asking tentatively.

"Sure thing. What's your favorite breakfast music?"

She heard Bayla run into the living room then shuffle back dragging a bag and wheezing slightly. Grace stood up.

"You okay?" she heard Isla ask. "That doesn't sound good. Here, let me take that." A pause and laugh. "Good lord, where on earth did you find this?"

"It was Mom's," Bayla said, struggling for breath. "I found it at Gloretta's last week when she let me look through the stuff in the basement." As suddenly as it came on, the wheeze cleared and Bayla began chattering away at her usual speed. "Gloretta said it was her old 'boom box' or something and it used to drive her mad when Mom was a teenager."

Isla laughed. "Gloretta, huh? That's some name for her. It suits. And yes, this was our boom box and we literally used to play music all day and night when we were young, and jump on the bed, dancing. I imagine it must have driven her crazy, but at the time that was sort of the point. Do you have our old CDs too?"

"Yeah, but I like Grandad's music better so that's what I've been playing. This one's my favorite."

"Oh wow, the number one hits, Elvis Presley. Double gold album. Your mom bought it for him for his birthday one year. Never seen a man so happy in my life," she said fondly. "Well, go on, put it on."

Bayla started the CD but turned it down low so she could keep talking to Isla.

"How did you get here last night?" Bayla asked. "I don't see a car. I bet you swam here, didn't you? I've been reading all about Maiden's Cove and you can hold your breath for ages, like a real mermaid!"

Isla chuckled but Grace felt something off about it. How *had* she got here last night? She used to swim from the Cove all the time when they were younger but Isla had been dry when she arrived.

"Do you like living in Maiden's Cove?" Isla asked Bayla instead of answering.

"I love it! We're new here. Did Mom tell you we just *escaped*? Well, it feels like it anyway. Girls like us did not belong in Phoenix. There's no water anywhere. And my dad was kind of…"

Grace stiffened on the stairs. She'd never heard Bayla talk to anyone about Richard. Not even her. She thought they escaped? Had Bayla felt threatened in a way Grace hadn't been aware of? She held her breath.

"Kind of what?" Isla asked nonchalantly, though Grace could hear the tension in her voice.

"He liked everything to be in its place, even if it was the wrong place," she said, as if she was trying to figure out what she meant to say. "And he was kind of mean sometimes, so I'm glad we left. Now we're in Maiden's Cove which is where we've always belonged. I can tell."

"Well, it was very brave of you girls. Did you swim back here too?"

Bayla let out a half laugh, half sigh. "No, we drove, almost the whole country though! But Mom said we definitely crossed the Bay Bridge and I know that I had this dream when we were crossing over it that there was a mermaid in the water that had us in this protective bubble that nobody but me could see."

"Super cool," Isla said.

"Yeah," Bayla gushed. "Once I got here, people started talking to me like I should know something because I'm a Cleary. They kept asking if I could see the green lights. So I started reading about the history of Maiden's Cove," she said proudly. "But the history is all based on a myth and now all the traditions are from these old mermaid stories. And even though it seems like a silly bit of magic, I'm not so sure. I've heard people say that my mom is a Cleary and that Clearys can call the mermaids, and that she called…well, you. When you were kids."

Isla didn't seem to know how to reply so Grace took that moment to step into the kitchen.

"The green lights are the bioluminescence I told you about, the algae in the water. They say the algae comes in on the new boats, that is why it's only here in the summer and not every summer," Grace said, leaning against the doorframe, smiling at her two favorite people.

It almost hurt to look at the mixture of disappointment and relief in Bayla's face. She was so young, she deserved to believe in a little bit of magic and myth. But it scared her—Bayla was born needing the world to make sense.

"Are you a fisherman then?" Bayla asked Isla, and then blushed. "Fisherwoman I mean, sorry."

Isla smiled at Bayla. "I was a fisherman's daughter. I came in every summer on the boats for the season with my dad, Henry. I used to go fishing with him sometimes, mostly diving."

"Their house is on the Cove," Grace said.

"Did you swim all the way from the Cove? That's very far," Bayla said. "Why didn't you just drive here like a normal person?"

Isla laughed and grasped Bayla's chin. "Now what fun is there in that?"

"That's true," Bayla conceded. "I couldn't swim that far. I've got a little lung, you see."

Isla glanced at Grace, who nodded imperceptibly. "Well then, I suppose you'll just have to grow some gills."

"Gills!" Bayla laughed. "But fish have gills, not girls!"

"What about mermaids?"

Bayla opened her mouth to answer, but closed it, thoughtful suddenly. "Do mermaids have gills? Is that how they swim underwater?"

"No clue." Isla shrugged. "But they certainly can't use their lungs because lungs use oxygen. So if you've got a small lung, and you're a mermaid, who cares?"

~

"It suits you here. Being home, the cottage, being a mother," Isla said a few hours later as they walked to Cleary's, Bayla on her rollerskates up ahead.

"Not too fast on the hills, Bayla!" Grace called out. "The cars never stop at the stop signs."

"What hills?" Bayla yelled back and Isla laughed.

"Seriously, what hills? We're on the flattest marshland ever."

"Oh, shut up and put a pair of flip-flops on," Grace said. "You're going to get a splinter." They grinned at each other and then followed Bayla in silence, but Grace could feel Isla glancing at her, waiting.

"He didn't beat me," she finally said, and she could see Isla relax slightly in her peripheral vision. "I mean, once or twice he may have pushed me up against a wall or up the stairs, but I would like to think I'm the kind of woman who's strong enough to have left if it had been the norm." She paused and lowered her voice. "It was slow. So slow and so subtle you don't even know it's happening. Postcards that never came, calls that were intercepted. He knew my every movement, where I was at all times of the day. He even policed my clothes—what was acceptable and not. I should have known earlier. Richard idolized his father, Earl, and looked down on his mother, Sandy. She's the sweetest person you'd ever meet. And Earl—he's charming. Very charming. And controlling, abusive. But you'd never know it, not at first.

"The first time Richard cheated on me, I was devastated. I packed my bags and was ready to take Bayla home. When he saw I was leaving, he broke down, begged me to stay, to help him become a better man than his own father was, a better husband. We were so young, you know? It was amazing for months after that. I lost track of time. They say it's like that, in a long-term abusive relationship. That it's like little pieces of you are chipped away, bit by bit, slowly and steadily, so that you don't even notice you're not you anymore." Isla raised her eyebrows. "Cohen made me go to some meetings," she said sheepishly.

"Cohen?"

Grace smiled. "You'll meet him at Cleary's. Just now actually," she said as it came into view.

Isla smiled as she saw the familiar restaurant. "Gosh, I missed this place. How's it going?"

"Wow, that was fast!" Bayla called as she caught the railing outside Cleary's to stop her from flying into the street on her rollerskates.

Bayla took off her skates and pulled on her sneakers to run into the restaurant. Isla went to follow, but Grace put a hand on her arm.

"Nobody but Cohen and Jimbo really know what's going on, but it's an absolute mess. Cleary's has no chef to run the kitchen and the entire restaurant is in the red, Isla," Grace said in a low voice.

"Oh my god," Isla gasped. "How? This place is a Chesapeake icon."

"All the usual things. High costs, low margins, stuffed economy. And you knew Dad," she said with a shake of her head. "He wouldn't have wanted to change things for the worse, like raising the prices or cutting staff hours. He always said that Cleary's was the place—"

"For everyone to come, enjoy 'good food, good beverages and good conversation,'" Isla quoted. "I remember. Henry told me once that Cleary's was not just a restaurant, but a pillar that stood for something more. It made everyone a part of the community through our love of food and this place.

Henry thought your dad was a really fine man, Grace," she said softly.

"This never would have happened if I'd stayed here, not married Richard—or if I'd come back earlier. The first time I came home with Bayla, when she was just two, I could see the relief in Dad's face. He was so happy to have me home.

"I didn't come back, and now it's my life's mission to get Cleary's out of the red this summer and back to what it used to be. I will not let Dad down, not again," she said determinedly. She didn't say it out loud, but Grace kept thinking that if she could fix this, if she could fix Cleary's, maybe she could fix herself too. "Come on, let me introduce you to the team. Wait until you see who I've hired to do the desserts," she said with a grin. "And be nice." She pulled the door open. "Ooomph!"

"Oh sorry," said a deep voice as Grace bumped into the large figure of a man and stumbled backward into Isla. "Grace?"

She looked up and recognized the face of Luke McCann in front of her. Her eyes raked over him and she shook her head at how *Luke* he still looked. Tan skin, curling brown hair with streaks of blond that fell a little too long under his baseball cap. Jade green eyes, a nose just a little too large and crooked but that sat perfectly over his cheeky smile that had the hint of a side bite.

Her first crush. Luke McCann. Ben's best friend and the man she daydreamed about marrying a million times over. She shook her head in suspended disbelief that this was really happening, and then remembered Ben said he'd just come back from New Zealand and was a chef. What were the odds?

"Luke McCann," she finally said. "Well I never."

He grinned at her. "Hey, Cleary," he said, saying her name the way he did her freshman year of high school when he started flirting with her. They stared at one another overly long, smiling, reminiscing in some unspoken way.

"Wow, it really is a reunion," Isla said from behind Grace. Luke's eyes widened as he laughed and picked up Isla, giving her a bear hug.

"Mermaid!" he said fondly. "I was thinking of you a couple weeks ago trying to teach my niece to wink. She's nearly as bad as you were. Did you ever learn?"

Isla looked perplexed. "What do you mean? You taught me that summer." She blinked as if to prove it, still using both eyes. Grace pressed her lips together to keep from laughing. She and Ben had never had the heart to tell Isla she didn't get it right.

But Luke just laughed good-naturedly and said, "That was perfect. Damn it's good to be home."

Cohen's voice shouted loudly from the other room. "Britney! Christina! We've been waiting on you."

"Why do you keep calling us that?" Abby asked as she and Sarah came in from the staffroom.

"Because you're young blonde teenyboppers. You know, Britney Spears and Christina Aguilera?"

"Jeez, how old are you, Cohen?" Sarah laughed. "You could at least call us Taylor and Selena instead."

Cohen opened his mouth to speak but closed it. "Noted. Okay, team, feedback essential." The whole staff had come out of the kitchen by this stage, including Della and Georgiana. Luke hovered by the door, clearly unsure whether to stay or go.

"Okay," Todd said, stepping forward. "I know we put new systems in and now that they're running right we're definitely modernized. But I guess what I've been wondering is why change it at all? I've been working here every summer since I was a busboy at fourteen. I mean, it's Cleary's, man, you know? Classic, iconic. It doesn't need to move with the times."

Jimbo cleared his throat and looked at Grace, his eyebrows raised. Then he caught a glimpse of Isla hiding behind her and his grin widened enormously. "It's time, Gracey," he said. "Now you got the whole team here." He winked at her and Isla.

Isla squeezed her hand as Grace took a deep breath. Now they were here, together, she felt stronger, filled with more hope.

"Because," Grace said, answering Todd's question, "even though it seems busy, and even though the reviews are always good, and even though it's been running like a machine for years, the restaurant is in the red."

"What?" they cried in unison.

"What does that mean? Is Cleary's going to close?" Todd asked.

"Not if I can help it," Grace said. "I have to start by saying it wasn't anything Dad did wrong. But ever since he passed away, we have been missing the most important person in the restaurant—a head chef. Competition is fierce and the truth is we need to be a lot busier than we've ever been to get through this. In order to keep Cleary's open for the long term, I needed to make some big decisions. You guys are, like, on season one of a reality show," she said, and they all laughed. "I have ideas. Obviously, this restaurant has been my home since I was born, but I need help. So what about you guys? Any ideas?"

It was silent for a minute as reality sunk into the staff that Cleary's was actually in danger of closing. Grace thought perhaps Jimbo had been wrong and she made a mistake in telling them so early in the summer, but then Todd spoke up.

"We should have an outdoor bar for when the boats come in," he ventured. "Small menu, just orange crush and beers and a couple wines."

The whole bar team muttered support. Cohen nodded his head to them encouragingly.

"I know y'all are always yelling at me for being on my phone," Sarah said, "but I love taking pictures. I could start us an Instagram. Grace, we need to be on social media."

"Great ideas. Really great," Grace said, smiling.

"You still finish the season with Tommy's Cook-Off and a guest chef?" Luke asked, stepping out from the wall.

Grace started. She'd forgotten about that for a moment, but now remembered that she and Isla and Luke had all been working at Cleary's the year her dad had started the tradition, which had eventually landed him and Cleary's on his favorite television show. She started to answer but Isla beat her to it.

Isla grinned. "Did you see Tom on *Diners, Drive-Ins and Dives?*" she asked Luke.

"Yes! My roommates and I watched it in cooking class in college. I felt like I knew a celebrity or something. It was awesome," he answered.

Isla turned and smiled at Grace. Tom had been obsessed with that show and had appeared on it in 2018. "Never been so proud in my life as I was that day."

"The cook-offs stopped over Covid for about three years," Jimbo said, "but I reckon now would be a good time to start them again. Especially since Mr. Tommy isn't with us any longer, we could have one at the end of the summer in his honor. Invite a whole lot of folks. But of course, we'll be needing a chef." Jimbo turned to Luke. "Gracey, I was just chatting with Luke before you came and he's got skills. I'm proposing he come in and be our head chef for the summer."

Luke stepped out in his white T-shirt and green shorts. "I was here the first two years of Tommy's Cook-Off," he said reverently.

"Best years of my life. It'd be an honor to be part of the Cleary's family again this summer, Grace, if you, Isla and the team will have me?"

Suddenly the young team fell into a hush.

"Isla!?"

"The mermaid, holy shit!"

"Wow, you seriously just stole all of my thunder," Luke said under his breath. "I've been back ten minutes and I'm already forgettable. You're back ten minutes and you're already famous. Again."

Isla scoffed. "Don't be ridiculous. You don't become famous again, you just never stop being famous." She turned back to the team. "Excuse me," she said, putting her hand out to shush them. "I happen to be the best busgirl and dishwasher Cleary's ever had. So no slacking this summer." She turned to Grace. "Let's make Tommy proud and get Cleary's back on track."

Grace turned to Luke. "You in?" she asked.

He smiled and took her small hand into his warm one, sending tingles through her arm. "I'm all in," he answered.

⁓

Isla skipped barefoot along the old path. "Luke McCann! Can you believe it? Did you, like, dream up this summer or something? I swear you wrote this in one of your letters when we were young. Remember when we used to write letters to each other as our future selves?"

Grace shook her head. "Don't get any ideas in your head, Isla. It's awesome timing that Luke has come back and happens to be a chef. And yes, I am finding it slightly hard to believe, but I'm grateful that you're here, and Luke too. I need all the support from my old friends that I can get."

"Oh, come on, you crushed on him for so long, you seriously don't have any romantic feelings seeing him now? He was never my type but he's definitely turned out pretty hot," Isla said.

Grace couldn't deny that. "It doesn't matter. After what I've been through and what my kid is going through with our life changes, the most I can offer of myself to anyone is friendship."

Isla put her arm around Grace. "I understand that." She laughed then and started skipping like they used to when they were young. "I honestly can't believe that after all this time these kids still have the mermaid thing going. They are so much younger than us, how do they even…Ouch! Oh my god, are you kidding me?"

Grace ran over to Isla, now sitting on the ground. "What? What's wrong?!"

"I've got a splinter." The look of utter shock on Isla's face was enough to put Grace into a peal of giggles.

"Oh, come on, don't be a baby. You had plenty over the summers you were here."

"No, but I haven't had one since that last day and it really hurts!"

"Come on, the pharmacy is right around the corner."

"No! What's that stuff we used to have as kids? The magic stuff?"

"You can only get that at Paddle Cove, but—"

"Oh, look! It's still there," she said, hobbling over toward the rental shop.

"Isla, wait! You don't want to go in there!"

But Isla was already through the front door and it was too late for Grace to tell her that the current owner was none other than her brother. She did not know if either of them was prepared to see the other after all this time, especially when Grace was pretty certain that Ben was one of the reasons Isla never came back.

~

This was the quiet part of the day for Ben. The shop was always quiet on Tuesday mornings and it gave him too much time to think. He was staring out to the Chesapeake Bay and thinking of his dad and missing him so much it hurt his very soul. But Grace was home, finally. She'd left that terrible man Ben knew had hurt her. And he had a niece now. Bayla was like a beacon of light in his life that he hadn't even realized he was missing. It suddenly felt like life had a purpose again, meaning, and that perhaps he could fix some of the mistakes he had made, the regrets, the things he'd missed out on. Of course, there was one person he could never get back, he knew that. And yet she was the one person he'd not stopped thinking about since the moment Grace walked back into Maiden's Cove.

The bell on the door of his shop rang suddenly. Ben sat at the front desk looking through sales and figures and sipping his coffee.

"Excuse me, can you please help?"

Ben jumped up from his seat and ran to the woman who'd just hobbled, hunched over, through his door. He took her elbow so she could lean on him. Then she lifted her face and Ben started, releasing her elbow, so she lost her footing and dropped onto the floor.

"Thanks a lot," she muttered.

"Isla?"

"Ben?"

Ben stared at the girl from his youth he'd just been thinking about. It had been more than ten years since he'd seen her, when he was young and in love, when Isla's very breath both filled and took his away. She was a girl of the sea, and there had been a point where he thought he'd leave Maiden's Cove forever, with her.

Her frizzy reddish gold hair fell in waves down her back, the crown bleached from the sun, as if she'd spent her days with just the top of her head above water. Her skin was still tanned and freckled in all the right places, her eyes still that murky shade of greenish brown with flecks of yellow that she used to say allowed her to see in the dark. And at this moment she was sitting on the floor of Ben's shop, looking up at him with those eyes, and he wanted to leave with her right then.

"What are you doing here?" he managed to say, trying to quickly rebuild the walls of his heart.

Isla lifted her foot. "I've got a splinter and I was just looking for that salve we used to use ... you know, that magic stuff that drew splinters out? Grace said it was here but ...".

"But?"

"She didn't say you were."

They looked at each other for a long moment. Finally, Ben turned and walked into the back of the shop. It took him a few minutes to calm the racing of his heart at seeing the girl he'd never stopped thinking about, the girl he'd always wondered about, the one he'd always loved. Why was she here now? Was there any chance for them? Any hope?

Stop thinking nonsense, Ben, he said to himself. *Just be a professional.*

He strolled back into the shop and sat down beside Isla, lifting her foot into his hand.

"Didn't my sister tell you not to walk barefoot?" he asked as he rubbed the salve onto her foot and sat it in his lap.

"She's been telling me that since we were twelve."

"Maybe after a couple decades you'll finally listen." He smiled faintly and glanced at her again. "So, really," Ben said, "why are you here?"

Isla blushed. "Grace wants me here, isn't that enough?"

Ben looked away. "I guess I mean, why now? Why not then?" His expression was pained, as if he already knew the answer. Shaking his head, he returned his attention to her foot. "Almost there now."

"I wasn't expecting to see you," said Isla. "I always thought you'd leave here, leave Maiden's Cove."

"I was planning to."

For a moment they said nothing, but the longer nothing was said, the more attuned they became to the fact that their breath moved in and out at the same pace, drawing them closer and closer to one another. Ben was the first to pull out of their spell. And with it came her splinter.

"Ow!" she yelled. "You didn't have to pull the skin! You did that on purpose, Benjamin Cleary!"

"Splinter is out," he said, standing up and releasing her leg. "You can go now."

Isla rubbed the bottom of her foot. They both looked up at the sound of the bell at the door as Grace entered, appearing a little too innocent. Isla stood and hobbled to Grace, who handed over her flip-flops, which she put on with a scowl, then left through the door, slamming it behind her.

Grace glanced toward the back of the shop to the door her brother had passed through, still swinging. When he didn't return, she finally left and met a stony, irritated Isla outside.

"Do you still...?"

"Shut the hell up, Grace."

Chapter Five

Tom Cleary hadn't been a trained chef. In fact, he learned almost everything he knew about cooking from Jimbo and Della, and later from visiting restaurants around the country, and a lot from watching programs like *Diners, Drive-Ins and Dives*. He never claimed to be a chef, he only claimed to love food, and to love his restaurant and the customers. So it shouldn't have been such a shock to the business to lose him from the kitchen, and yet it was Tom's passion, innovation and constant desire to learn new and exciting dishes that the restaurant was feeling in his absence.

The appointment of a head chef looking to change what Cleary's was famous for would have been a disaster, but instead,

Luke McCann simply reintroduced himself to his former Cleary family and asked them to show him the ropes.

"I remember one summer," Luke said to Della one morning as they prepped for the lunch service, "you caught me in the linen closet kissing Annalise Duncan."

Della laughed with a loud hoot, making Grace smile from the other room where she'd been going through her invoices. She stood and glanced in the kitchen, keeping herself unseen. It was easy to admire Luke from here.

Luke and Ben had become best friends when they were twelve years old, the first year of middle school. Grace was only ten then, a young girl, but she always wanted to stay up later and watch movies and play games with the boys. He was always so nice to her, even when she was the annoying little sister.

It didn't take long until Grace fancied herself completely in love with Luke when she was twelve, the same summer she met Isla and they all became fast friends. But he always treated her like a younger sister, even when he was kind and helped her through high school. Even when they worked together at Cleary's. There had been a time when he was a senior and she was in her sophomore year where he started flirting with her. Really flirting, like he was finally seeing her not just as his best friend's little sister anymore. That was the same summer she had also caught him kissing Annalise Duncan in the walk-in fridge, and she'd cried on Isla's shoulder for two weeks.

She smiled now as she watched Della laugh and shake her head. Luke McCann would have kissed any girl anywhere and they would have kissed him back. Such a charmer. It was hard not to have some of those old feelings creep up when she looked at him now. But that couldn't be. Not now, not after Richard.

"Was she the blonde or the brunette?" Della asked, still laughing.

He grinned. "Redhead." Della threw her head back. "You probably don't remember, but you pulled me outside by my ear and told me to get my 'grubby-ass bartender hands' away from your crab meat."

"Did I?!" Della asked in surprise. "I sound like a right mafia boss or something. Tell me more."

"Then you told me since I was on a break and obviously had nothing better to do than grate on your nerves, I could help you cook. We made your famous Maryland Crab Soup."

Della's jaw dropped. "The one where I made the stock from the shells myself?"

"Yup," he said, putting extra emphasis on the "p." "You made me crush them for an hour."

"Oh, boy! What are you doing here again after that?"

Luke gave her his sideways smile that Grace had always loved. "That was the day I knew I wanted to be a chef." He dipped his spoon in the sauce he'd been making and put it to Della's lips. "What do you think?"

Della took a small sip and closed her eyes, the silence of the room deafening as Grace found herself waiting to hear her verdict. Finally, Della put her fingers to her lips, smiling softly, eyes still closed.

"Tastes like the sea."

"Then you taught me well," Luke said.

Grace left them to their cooking, feeling lighter, more vital, alive. And her body was humming.

~

"So I was thinking," Grace said to Isla a few days later, "that it might be fun for us to have a cookout tonight, here at the cottage. Bayla deserves a fun night. We haven't had many of them since we've been back. I'm afraid I've been highly unsociable outside of the restaurant and Bayla is a very social creature. It can't have been easy on her, leaving like that, and she's handled it so well. She's dying to show you off to her new best friend, Mape."

"Mape?" Isla asked. "What kind of a name is that?"

"Short for Maple, but that's all Bayla ever calls her and the only name you'll ever hear Mape call Bayla is Bay. You should see them together—they remind me of us."

Isla smiled. "That sounds good. Maybe don't invite too many though? Being at Cleary's every day is a social workout!"

"Isla, you work in the back and refuse to talk to customers just like you always have," Grace said. "Though to be fair, the staff do want to talk to you all the time."

"I am extremely popular with the Taylors and Selenas," Isla said, mimicking Cohen's high pitch. "*Please* don't invite them!"

Grace laughed. "Just family and close friends. Do you want to dive for some scallops and crabs? I know you'd be terribly offended if I got them from someone else."

"Oh, I…I can't, sorry. I was actually just heading into town," Isla said quickly, looking around and slipping into her flip-flops. "Don't want to get another splinter," she said breathily with a fake laugh.

"*Okaaay,*" Grace said, not pushing it.

"Hey, I've got an idea. You should get Luke to bring scallops and crabs from Cleary's! I bet since he just got home he'd love some social time with old friends."

It was Grace's turn to flush. "He's working. But maybe after? I mean it would be rude to invite Jimbo and Della and not him, right? Especially if I'm asking him for food? That would be rude, right?"

Isla raised an eyebrow. "Exactly, repeato girl." She started to walk toward the road instead of the water, her usual form of travel.

"Where are you going?"

"Oh, just for a walk, a few things to do. Busy, you know?" Isla said, waving behind her. "Grab some corn on the cob from Gail's stand," she called back. "And do you think you could convince Della to make her famous potato salad? God, I still dream about it. You know, the one with the dill and stuff?"

"Sure," Grace yelled, rolling her eyes. "Are *you* going to bring anything?"

"I'll grab heaps of wine on my way back! Promise!" And she was gone. Grace had never once, in all the years she'd known Isla, watched her leave on foot. And definitely not wearing shoes. Something wasn't right.

⌒

"Grace!" Cohen gushed when she walked into Cleary's. "I cannot wait to update you on all we've managed in the past few days. Honestly, that little pep talk the other day seemed to really make the difference. The team is all on board and seems to be making magic happen to get Cleary's to its best."

"I don't know if it was me." Grace laughed.

"Of course not! It's all Luke McCann, believe me. Though they do seem to love having the token mermaid on board," Cohen said, rolling his eyes playfully. "As my best-friend competition, I am jealous of course. And I must challenge her to a duel."

"Well, you'll have the opportunity today if you want," she said. "I'm here to invite you to my place after your shift for a proper Maiden's Cove cookout. I thought it might be nice for Isla and Bayla to have some friends around and enjoy the summer evening. Will you come?"

Cohen placed his hand to his heart in earnest. "I would be honored. What can I bring?"

"I'm going to ask Luke for some scallops and crabs. Isla thinks I should invite him too. What do you think?" She put her head in her hands. "I really don't know what I'm doing."

"Oh, honey, you're doing just fine. And I reckon Luke will be happy you asked him for anything, but he'd be even happier if you actually invited him to drop in after work," he said with a wink.

"Cohen! After Richard? You of all people know there is no place for another man in my life for a long time," she scoffed, but she was blushing and he noticed.

"Hey, there's no rush, honey, but even though you've only been here for two months, that relationship with Richard was over in your heart years ago and you know it. It might be nice for you to invite Luke tonight—just as friends, of course. Plus, come on, wasn't he, like, your great love in high school or something?"

"Anyway," she said, ignoring his words. "I've got to pick up some corn on the cob, but first I must beg Della for her potato

salad. I might risk being thrown out of my own home if I don't," Grace said.

"Naturally." Cohen nodded. "I'll bring the most beautiful rosé sangria recipe I can put together quickly. How many people?"

Grace blushed. "Just you and Isla so far. And I'll invite Della and Jimbo of course. Honestly, I wouldn't really know who to invite except for you two."

Cohen just smiled and squeezed her shoulder. "Georgiana is in the back with Della and Jimbo. You know she'd be stoked. And of course, much as it pains you, you'll have to invite ole Gloretta." Grace grimaced but nodded. "And your brother, Ben? He must be coming, especially if Luke is here?"

"I'll invite him, yes. Coming? I don't know." She sighed at Cohen's raised eyebrows. "It's complicated," she said, thinking of Isla and Ben and also of her own rift with her brother.

"What about Aunt Lou? She'd be a hoot."

Of course, Aunt Lou. Grace didn't know why she didn't think of her before. Isla loved Aunt Lou. Everyone loved Aunt Lou. "I didn't know she was back."

"She's just back in town from her secret rendezvous over the bridge. I'm convinced she has a lover," Cohen said.

"Ew," Grace said, but hugged Cohen. "And thank you. That's exactly what I needed. Your sangria sounds perfect. Shall we say four o'clock?"

"My favorite hour," he said.

"Every hour is your favorite hour."

"I moved from the desert to an island—I love island time," Cohen said staunchly, "so don't rain on my parade."

"You know it's not really an island, right?"

"Raining!" he yelled.

"Leaving!" she yelled back, smiling.

⌒

The kitchen smelled divine as Grace ducked into the back. "Hi, Gigi!" she called, as the beautiful blonde shrieked.

"Jesus Almighty, you scared me to death. And you know I hate it when you call me that."

"Sorry," Grace said. And she was. Georgiana used to go by Gigi back when she was one of the Feathers, the mean girls at school who had tortured Grace before she met Isla.

When Grace got Cohen into Cleary's and placed an ad for a pastry chef, thinking that their dessert section was another area that could be expanded with the right person, a resume came in from a Georgiana Glover.

Along with her resume, Georgiana sent a pastry plate, and it was like unwrapping your favorite present ever on Christmas Day. The pastries were so good that Grace begrudgingly offered an interview. So she was surprised when the Georgiana that showed up was lovely and full of self-effacing humor. She was passionate about baking, and she was good at what she did. Cohen loved her. Even Grace was charmed, and she never thought she might be friends with any of the Feathers as adults.

"I'm glad you're here," Georgiana said. "I've got the most pressing conundrum. What do you think, biscuits or sponge cake?"

"I'm going to need a bit more information than that, Gi— sorry, Georgiana."

She laughed. "Oh right. Well, come, look at these."

Grace followed her to the back where a huge pile of beautiful strawberries sat on the bench.

"Oh my god," Grace said, reaching out to take one and bite into it. It melted in her mouth, still warm from the sun.

"I *know*. Came in today, fresh and hand-picked from the farm. I just knew straightaway it had to be strawberry shortcake, but I can't decide whether to go all Southern and do ladyfinger biscuits, or Northern with sponge cake. Maryland is such a tough state, so divided. I feel like I'm always going to offend one or the other. Why couldn't we have just picked a side during the damned war?"

"Are you putting it on the menu tomorrow?"

"Planning on it. That okay?"

"Of course!" Grace said. "I'm having a few people around this afternoon for a cookout for Isla and Bayla. Why don't you bring the dessert with both the biscuits and the sponge and we can all vote for our favorite? It could be fun."

Georgiana smiled. "I'd love to, but you have to promise not to tell Isla that we used to call her the fisherman's daughter," she said. "I'd completely forgotten about her until she showed up with you last week."

Grace was momentarily stunned. She had forgotten that that was what everyone called Isla when she was young. But more than that, Grace couldn't believe that anyone could ever forget about her. She was such a force, Grace assumed everyone remembered Isla the same way she did, like she had shaped the life of all of Maiden's Cove because of the mermaid lore, not just hers.

"Why did you guys call her that?" Grace asked, curious.

Georgiana shrugged. "Probably started as a Feather-ism. That girl who was always in the water, diving from the highest cliffs, and was sort of feral. Someone probably said she was cool, and Monica likely said she was just a local fisherman's daughter, jealous of attention anywhere but on her—especially once you guys became famous for being the mermaid caller and the mermaid," she added, laughing.

"She'll love that story," Grace said.

"No! You promised you wouldn't tell her!"

"Wouldn't tell who what?" a deep voice said as Luke came through the kitchen with a plate of fish.

Grace thought she would never, ever trust a man again in her life, but sometimes she couldn't help wondering what it would be like to run her fingers through Luke's beard, which looked so soft to touch, or find out how far the tattoo that just peeked out below the sleeve of his T-shirt actually went up his arm.

His jade eyes crinkled as they smiled at her. Being around Luke made Grace feel like she wanted to flirt, to laugh, like she was a girl in school again. And every time she tried to be cool, something went wrong. She stumbled, or he did. She figured it was fate trying to remind her that, after Richard, she shouldn't trust anyone. At least not for a long time. She had to find herself first. But Luke did light her up from the inside, and she wanted to at least be his friend again, like they used to be.

She took a deep breath. *Not your first rodeo, Grace,* she thought. *And also, just friends. No pressure.*

"I'm having a few friends around this afternoon," she said to him, trying to sound nonchalant. She was starting to feel hot in her face. "Would you like to come? I know you're working, but maybe after?"

"I'd love to!" he said enthusiastically.

"Oh! Okay, great. See you later then!"

She turned and left, got into her car and was halfway down the road when she realized she hadn't actually asked him for the food she needed. "Oh god, I'm such a disaster," she said, putting her head in her hands and turning back.

Luke grinned at her when she walked back in.

"Would you by any chance have two pounds of scallops and a bushel of crabs in the back?" she asked casually.

He laughed and went to check, coming out a few minutes later. "Plenty to spare. Should I send them over later with Jimbo and Della?" he asked.

"Yes, please," she said. "So I'll see you later I hope?"

He smiled. "I'm looking forward to it, Grace Cleary."

She was halfway to Ben's when she realized he'd used her maiden name.

~

Grace sent a Facebook message to Aunt Lou on her way to Ben's shop. Everyone who met Aunt Lou called her Aunt Lou, but she was actually Ben and Grace's true great-aunt. Tallulah Cleary knew every tale, every story, every myth and legend in Maiden's Cove. She was older than their father, who remembered Aunt Lou as Aunt Lou, even when he was a boy. She had white hair that shimmered almost like blonde that she always wore in a long braid down her back, and had done her whole life. But no one knew how long that life had been, let alone Aunt Lou herself. Which was interesting, considering she knew everything else about herself and everyone around her.

The only way to get a response out of Aunt Lou was to message her on Facebook. And the only response she ever gave was in a meme or a GIF. Aunt Lou had 6,172 followers on Instagram and on Facebook. No one knew why.

Barbecue at mine, 4 p.m. Isla's home, Grace messaged.

Within seconds Aunt Lou had sent back a black and white GIF of Zac Efron shirtless over a grill. Grace laughed as she pushed through Ben's door.

"What are you laughing at?" he asked.

"Aunt Lou's last GIF." She showed it to Ben. He smirked.

"She's got to be nearly a hundred. Why does she always use Zac Efron?"

"She's in love with him, she told me. He was kind of funny in the *Baywatch* movie."

"Why are you here, Grace?"

"Wow, that was faster than usual. Generally you at least attempt about thirty seconds of small talk with your sister before you dismiss her completely. Well accomplished, Ben." She turned to leave.

"I'm sorry. I'm sorry, Grace. It's just…"

"Save the excuses, Ben. I just wanted to invite you to my house for a small barbecue with some friends later today. Even Luke is coming. I know you won't come, but it would be really nice if you considered it. I am your sister, and we don't have Dad anymore."

Grace turned and left, feeling momentarily guilty that she had just invited her brother into a situation that neither he nor Isla might be ready for.

Chapter Six

That afternoon, Della was at Cleary's making her famous potato salad for Grace's cookout. Her salad only worked with new season fingerlings, as they needed to be sweet enough to entice, small enough to keep the flavor, and bold enough to hold it all together.

Before she did anything else, Della made her salad dressing. Using a mortar and pestle she ground together fresh garlic, Dijon mustard, red wine vinegar and celery seeds into a paste, adding olive oil tablespoon by tablespoon. Once creamy, she seasoned it with salt and pepper, whisking in her own homemade Old Bay seasoning—the secret ingredient.

Della boiled the already-scrubbed fingerling potatoes in a large saucepan until tender. While they were cooking, she chopped celery, shallots and pickles into a bowl. When the potatoes were done, she tossed them in, along with dill, parsley and her special dressing, adding last the soft-boiled egg, and placing the bowl into the fridge while she cleaned up.

She pulled her cloak around her, the familiar feeling of comfort engulfing her. The cloak was made by her great-great-grandmother, sewn together from bits of a quilt from the Underground Railroad, which her family helped start on the Eastern Shore to free the slave trade in the 1850s.

She smiled to herself thinking of the year Grace, Isla, Ben and Luke came to her asking questions about the tunnel they found when they were teenagers. Della had shown them the patchwork quilt of her cloak.

"Many of the slaves from the South ran away and made their way North," she'd explained to them then. "They followed tunnels, paths and transportation routes to freedom, with some help along the way. The quilts were coded, you see. To help the freedom seekers keep safe and make their way to their destination."

Della's mama was bought by the Cleary family just when she thought she'd escaped, but it turned out the Clearys were sympathizers to the cause and were helping to fund the Railroad. Even when freed, Della's family, like so many others, stayed on to help the changing world of the Eastern Shore.

Of course, it wasn't a fairy tale, and she left most of the horror out of the story, but it was why Della's family, and Jimbo's too, were still on the Shore and did not leave. They were part of the veins that changed the world here with the help of the Cleary family.

Gracey's face that day, Della remembered, had never been more proud. Grace was a Cleary through and through, she felt every part of her heritage and it meant something to her to be a Cleary. Della also remembered little Isla's face that day. Isla was one of a kind and she rarely displayed the moody silences of others her age. But that day, Isla looked at Grace with a burning in her eyes. Not anger, no. Jealousy? A bit. But more that she wanted to understand what it felt like to know where you came from and who you were. Della reckoned that was just about when Isla moved into the Cleary's residence full time.

And then there was Ben. Who didn't look proud, who didn't look thoughtful.

He only looked at Isla.

They didn't see much of Ben these days, even though he lived in Maiden's Cove and worked so close. But she thought of him often and wondered why he never left with Isla the way she knew he'd wanted to. She wondered if now that Isla was home, things might be different for Ben too.

"You coming to Gracey's barbecue, my love?" Jimbo wrapped his arm around Della now, pulling her out of her reverie. She still felt the shiver of their union even after forty years.

"You know I am. Just had to make Isla's favorite potato salad first. It's just chilling down now, then I'll be right 'round." She leaned into him for a kiss.

"I'm taking the steamer with me. I'll see you there soon, honey."

Della packed everything and stepped outside, looking up as the wind shifted. Isla was here, and that always made the tide turn. But something was different this time, something vital. Something had changed.

⌒

Cohen and Georgiana pulled up to Grace's cottage after work.

"Oh my god, this place is adorable," Georgiana said, looking at Brixton Cottage as she got out of the car.

"I know," Cohen said longingly. "I want one."

"Still renting?" she asked.

He nodded.

"Me too, and I'm from here. Housing market, right?"

"Seriously," Cohen said. "You okay with that box?" he asked as Georgiana lifted it from the trunk. "It looks heavy."

"It is heavy, Cohen," she said, "but I've got about ten pounds on you so why don't you grab that little box there and show me where to go?"

They both chuckled and Cohen led Georgiana through the small yard to the porch. "Grace!" he yelled, seeing her over at the shed pulling fold-out tables from storage. "You need help?"

"No, I'm all good," she called. "Kitchen is yours. I've cleared the island for you and Gig— Uh, Georgiana."

They set up in Grace's kitchen side by side, as if at work. Cohen took out a large bowl and started pouring bottles of rosé into it. Georgiana laid out her trays—sponge cakes on one and the ladyfingers on the other. She began to cut the fresh strawberries, so red and juicy they were bleeding into her fingertips. Cohen started taking them from her crate.

"Hey! Those are my strawberries!" she said, smacking his hand.

"You want my sangria?" he asked.

"Yes."

"Then share your strawberries," he said with an air kiss.

They shared an amiable silence preparing their dishes until Georgiana said, "What is your story, Cohen?"

In the short time he'd been in Maiden's Cove, he and Georgiana had become friends, and he genuinely liked her. They were work friends, their conversations never straying further than shoptalk and friendly banter. But Cohen had moved here for a reason, and at this moment he realized he did want to be friends with Georgiana, very much. Genuine friends.

"Grace and I were very different people when we met in Phoenix three years ago," he said, looking out the window to where Grace was shucking corn with Isla and laughing like she hadn't a care in the world.

"I know Grace doesn't talk about it, nor would I ever even think to delve into her private life, but I have been under the impression that Grace left a bad situation back in Phoenix," Georgiana said carefully.

"That's her story to tell," Cohen said gently, "but what I can say is that she is almost like a new version of herself. Dresses differently, moves differently. The only time she was like that—" he nodded his head toward the women in the yard, "back in Phoenix was when she was talking about Maiden's Cove, and it entranced me. I promised her, as a friend, that once she freed herself of her situation and went back home I'd be there for her in a heartbeat. But I secretly started dreaming of Maiden's Cove myself. A cottage like this one, the soft lapping sounds of the bay, the sunsets and the bioluminescence. Cleary's Crab Shack, and the people. I started thinking that if I could live here, somewhere so magical and warm and inviting, that maybe I could be different too. Be a version of myself that lit up and stopped hiding."

"Who were you hiding from?" Georgiana asked.

"Probably myself, in the end. My family have very specific ideas about what kind of life is good enough for my brother and I," he said with a sigh. "And the truth is, I love them, and I hate disappointing them. I mean, I'm gay—not the first disappointment but probably the biggest one, though I expect it was entirely unsurprising.

"I hated disappointing them so much that I agreed to go to business school even though I was working as a restaurant manager. Hospitality was never good enough," he explained, "just a job to get you where you were really going."

"I know, right?" Georgiana said, spooning her strawberries into the sponge cakes. "When I say to people, 'I work at a restaurant,' they say, 'Oh, and what else?'"

"Exactly," he said, laughing and pouring ice into two glasses. "I had my family and I had Grace and I had work colleagues, but the truth is, I was lonely. And I realized I couldn't meet someone and share a life with them until I could accept myself honestly and truly, and I was too afraid to do that around my family."

"So, when Grace called…" Georgiana guessed at the rest.

"It's hard to be brave alone," he said quietly. "I never let Grace be brave without me, and she didn't ask me to be brave without her. We gave each other the courage we needed to free ourselves."

"So how is Maiden's Cove living up to your expectations so far?" Georgiana asked.

"Well, there's never a dull moment! A restaurant in the red, a mermaid in the house, a town of crazies. I love it," he said fondly. "I'm still renting until I find my perfect cottage, and it's certainly not easy meeting men in a town this small."

"Tell me about it," Georgiana said with a long sigh.

"How and why are you single anyway?" he asked. "You're beautiful, funny, and your baking is a thing of the gods. Surely you can sweeten the men."

"Oh I sweeten a lot of men, honey," Georgiana said with a chuckle. "They usually get sweet on me for a little while and then move on. But I'll never give up hope of finding love. My expectations are pretty low. He just needs to be attractive and kind, and to love food as much as I do. You know," she said, glancing at him sideways, "when Luke McCann walked in the other day I thought, well, hey now, mister. But then he opened his eyes and saw Grace."

Cohen bit his lip. He, too, had seen that look and wanted Grace to open her heart to Luke McCann, despite how adamant she was to not date again for a millennia, if ever. But he liked Georgiana and he wanted to see her happy too.

"I see that look out of the corner of my eye, Cohen," she said, "but I assure you it was only a passing thought. I wouldn't mess with another woman's man, even if she hasn't claimed him yet.

It's only a matter of time. And I deserve better than being second best. So, nope, I'll just keep waiting and dating. Now pour me one of those drinks, for goodness' sake."

Cohen had finally mixed the perfect amount of rosé, triple sec, mint and fresh berries, and used a ladle to pour it over a glass of ice for each of them.

"Thank you," said Georgiana, raising her glass.

Cohen followed suit. "Tell you what, Georgiana. If you never find a man, and I never find a man, we can grow old, fat and happy together, with cats in a cottage here in Maiden's Cove. What do you think?"

"Why, Cohen," she said, clinking their wineglasses together. "That doesn't sound too bad. Not too bad at all."

~

Bayla Monroe was born with one lung smaller than the other. She didn't remember being born this way but she always thought that maybe it made her special. Just a little bit. Like when she noticed things that a girl her age with two normal lungs wouldn't. Like the fact that her Aunt Isla, who wasn't really her aunt, was different from other people. It wasn't just the myths, even though Bayla was happy to pretend it was. But, for instance, the moment Isla touched her shoulder the other day when she was wheezing, it got better. She could breathe easier.

So, whether it was instinct or magic or her little lung, Bayla reckoned she could smell Aunt Isla now, like what her science teacher called a pheromone, even though apparently humans don't have pheromones and that was a myth just like the mermaids. But she wasn't necessarily sure that Aunt Isla *was* a human. Anyway, whether there were pheromones or not, Bayla could smell Aunt Isla, and she smelled scared.

She and Isla were sitting in the backyard peeling corn for the barbecue. They didn't use any knives. Gloretta had been teaching her the Chesapeake way, which was to peel the corn by hand and drink wine and talk for hours in the slow afternoon heat, which she shared with Isla now. Bayla was too young to drink wine, so Aunt Isla decided it was probably okay for her to drink enough wine for two of them. She poured something she called a "peeno greejo" and they sat on their chairs with a trash bag in front of them and slowly peeled two dozen corn husks, while her mom pulled out picnic tables and started cleaning them, preparing for their first house party since they'd left Dad in Phoenix and come to Maiden's Cove.

Bayla was glad they'd left Phoenix and come to this place that was truly home. She loved him because he was her dad, and he loved her because she was his daughter, but he was a mean man to her mom, even though she hadn't seen it for a long time, and he did not belong where they did, which was here in Maiden's Cove. Sometimes when he got mad at her mom he took all the air out of the room. Bayla's small lung got smaller when he was around and got bigger when he went away, so she thought maybe he was bad air.

"Do you think they'll like me?" Isla whispered to Bayla, glancing through the window to the kitchen where they could see Cohen and Georgiana talking and laughing. "I've only worked with your mom's new friends a few times."

"Why would anyone not like you?"

"Because nobody knows me," Isla said.

"Nonsense," a voice came from the door, "I know everything about everyone and you are certainly no exception to that, Isla."

"Aunt Lou!" Bayla yelled, running to the old woman and hugging her tightly.

"Duckling!" the older woman called, giving Bayla a squeeze, before holding her back and looking at her intently. Aunt Lou always did this, like she was looking for something in your very soul and no matter how many times you looked away, or how many times you thought there was nothing to see, she saw it anyway. But just as she was about to say something possibly profound, Aunt Lou tilted her head. "Your new haircut is just terrible."

Bayla laughed. "Aunt Isla cut my bangs this afternoon."

"Next time ask her to do it in the dark. Her vision is better then." Aunt Lou looked over to Isla and they smiled at one another.

Bayla thought it was the kind of smile between two people who had known each other their whole lives, even though Aunt Lou was the oldest person in Maiden's Cove—so old that nobody knew how old she was. And Aunt Isla was her mom's age which was somewhere near thirty.

Mape walked through to the backyard at that moment and Bayla ran to meet her best friend.

"Mape!" she called. "Hurry and come meet Aunt Isla!"

⌒

Grace looked around and realized that for the first time her lawn was filled with people. But not just people—friends. Something warm and tingling began to set in.

Jimbo brought his steamer and was seasoning the crabs with Della's Old Bay seasoning, while Della opened the scallops that Luke had sent with her. Georgiana and Cohen came out from the kitchen with glasses of the rosé sangria for everyone. Aunt Lou was sitting in the middle of a row of chairs, shucking the corn with Isla, who finally seemed to relax now that Aunt Lou was here.

By early evening Grace had brought her fold-up picnic tables outside and Mape was showing Bayla how to line them with old newspapers from Loretta's. Gloretta couldn't make it to their cookout, Bayla said, because she was staying at home "moping." Bayla said she didn't know what that was, but Isla and Grace had met eyes and giggled like girls.

"But why don't we just use a plastic tablecloth?" Bayla asked.

"Beats me, Bay, this is just the Chesapeake way," Mape answered, and they taped the newspapers down on the picnic tables.

Grace and Isla, Aunt Lou, Georgiana, Cohen, Jimbo and Della, and Bayla and Mape, sat outside next to the little beach in front of Brixton Cottage and had a true Maryland feast. They ate the scallops first, which Della had sautéed in the kitchen in butter, allowing them to relish the taste of the bay in their mouths. When the crabs came out of Jimbo's steamer he dropped them in the middle of the table to a collective cheer. They were full in-season blue crabs, doused in Old Bay.

Jimbo was teaching Bayla and Cohen how to properly eat crabs.

"Okay, first thing, you break off the little legs. Hold your hands close to the base though, so you can get some meat out."

Bayla broke one of hers, and a big chunk of crabmeat came out. She squealed. "Mape, look!"

"I can't believe you haven't picked crabs before," Mape said, doing hers professionally.

"Don't really grow crabs in Phoenix," Bayla said.

"Mine has nothing in it!" Cohen complained. "My crab's empty."

"It's not empty," Aunt Lou said, "just means all the good meat is still in the body. You'll get there, don't worry." She patted Cohen's knee.

"All right, now take off the big claws the same way," Jimbo said. "Then, you break them in the middle and suck out all the meat from the claws. Go on then."

Even the seasoned crab eaters followed his instructions.

"And now, we get into the body. Pull that little flap back and take out all the grainy stuff," he said. "Then break it in half and go to town!"

It was a feast from there. Eating crabs, Della's potato salad, coleslaw and corn on the cob, it was a perfect day on the Eastern Shore of Maryland.

Grace realized while looking around at her friends and family that she was truly home. She was healing, and Bayla was finally getting the chance to live her best life. She glanced around to blow her daughter a kiss. Bayla and Mape had been sitting with her just moments ago, but Grace realized they were now missing.

"Where did Bayla and Mape go?" she asked casually. Grace heard a loud scream and a splash, and suddenly Isla ran past her toward the water.

"Bayla?" Isla called loudly. "Bayla, where are you?"

"What's wrong?" Grace asked, running to Isla in a panic and looking out. But there was nothing wrong. Bayla and Mape were splashing in the water, screaming and laughing like little girls.

"Come on, Mape, let's mermaid swim!" Bayla said, and they started swimming with their feet together.

"Aunt Isla!" Bayla called from the water. "Are we doing it right?"

But Isla didn't answer straightaway. She was breathing heavily, looking like she was going to cry with relief. Finally she looked up, asking, "Doing what right?"

"Mermaid swimming! Watch us!" Bayla and Mape did a few mermaid dives in and out of the water.

Grace turned to Isla and smiled, squeezing her hand. Isla gave her a tremulous smile in return.

"Perfect!" Isla called, turning and walking back to the table.

"Will you come swim with us?"

"Not now, girls," she called. "I just…"

Suddenly her eyes went wide as she looked across the yard. All eyes followed her gaze to the one person none of them had expected to see, least of all Isla.

Ben.

"I just have to go," Isla said.

Ben watched her leave with his heart in his eyes.

Suddenly, Grace realized what had been strange since Isla had been back, the little link she hadn't figured out until right now.

Isla hadn't been in the water since she'd come home to Maiden's Cove.

It was after dark when Grace began to clean up. Cohen had just left with Georgiana after a detailed conversation about wine, of which they had both consumed more than their fair share. Bayla and Mape had so much saltwater up their noses and in their eyes from mer-swimming that they'd both fallen asleep on the bean bags outside hours ago, and Jimbo had picked them up, one in each arm, and carried them to Bayla's bedroom.

Jimbo and Della left just after that, taking Aunt Lou off with them. Ben had stayed for an awkward drink, looking up constantly to see if Isla had returned, but she didn't come back and eventually he left too.

Grace was alone doing the dishes when she heard the back screen door open.

"I brought wine," Luke's deep voice said from behind her.

She turned around from the sink and looked at the boy she'd loved as a girl and realized the man was even more handsome than she would have imagined he'd become. The laugh lines around his eyes, his tanned skin from the New Zealand sun, hands just a little rough from working so long in a kitchen. Her mouth was slightly dry as she turned back to the sink, blushing, as if he'd just read all of her thoughts. "Anything good?"

"Well, Bayla informed me that you and Isla drink 'peeno greejo,'" he said, pronouncing it in Bayla's voice, which made Grace laugh. "But when I asked Cohen, he quite adamantly told me to buy a bottle of this. Chablis, it's called."

"Did he give you the full spiel?" she asked, drying a plate.

"About the chardonnay grape and how you'd never believe they were the same wine?" Luke laughed. "Yup. I'm sorry I'm so late, but you'll be pleased to know that Cleary's had a great night."

Grace lit up. "That's fantastic! I wasn't sure if opening on the weekend nights, instead of just during the day like we always have, was going to be a good idea or not."

"If we can guarantee a sunset like tonight's, I reckon those Friday and Saturday evenings will book out faster than we can seat it," he said. "It was a cruisy first night, but we only had me in the kitchen with Theo and Clarence and Todd running the front of house, so it was perfect. No more parties for you though, taking all my staff," he joked.

"I'm so sorry!" Grace cried, but she could tell he was teasing her.

When Luke put his hand on her shoulder and squeezed, she wanted to melt into him, and the knowledge of that made her tense up instead.

He pulled his hand away. "I'm sorry I missed the party. Should I go?"

"No, stay for a drink," she said, picking up two clean wineglasses. "Shall we sit outside? The mosquitos shouldn't be too bad with the citronella we had out all night."

They walked out to the porch and sat, Luke pouring two glasses of the chablis. He looked out to the calm of the bay, gently lapping into the small beach. The bioluminescence was faint, but it was there.

"I didn't realize how much I'd missed it here until the moment I crossed the Bay Bridge," he said. "It was like..." He seemed to be searching for words.

"Magic," she said.

"Exactly," Luke replied.

"And," she added slowly, "relief."

He glanced at her, his eyes encouraging her to go on.

"That's how I felt when Bayla and I crossed the Bay Bridge two months ago. It was like the last ten years were on the other side, and then I was home. I think the bay sighed with me when I saw Maiden's Cove come into view." She took a sip of her wine.

"I was surprised when I heard from Ben you'd moved to Phoenix. When you were younger you swore you'd never leave," he said. "Well, unless Isla dragged you off to the Caribbean or to some mermaid layer in the depths below."

Grace's laughter came in a burst, and she covered her mouth to keep the wine from coming out. She appreciated the way Luke could still read her, even though they hadn't seen each other for so long.

"I wouldn't talk," she said. "New Zealand, huh? How on earth did you end up there? Though I hear it is beautiful, don't get me wrong. But isn't it on the other side of the world?"

"It most certainly is," he said with a smile. "Which is probably why it's still so unspoiled and majestic. I went to a school called Johnson and Wales University in Providence, Rhode Island, for college, did you know that?"

"I did," she said. "Remember we had a big party for you guys at Cleary's that last summer before you went off to college?"

"That was the first year of Tommy's Cook-Off," he said and Grace grinned. "Your dad and Della were the ones who made me want to be a chef, and it was during a time I was applying for colleges. I wanted to go to a specialized culinary institute, but my parents wanted to make sure I had a well-rounded education and all that, so they made me promise I'd go to a normal university where I had to do all the undergrad classes just so I could make a choice. JWU is one of the best culinary schools on the East Coast, but it's still an undergrad degree, so they agreed. Anyway, I worked at this restaurant in Providence and met a girl there, a Kiwi girl named Emma."

"Of course you did," Grace said, smiling.

"Hey! What's that supposed to mean?" he said in mock defense.

She raised her eyebrows and didn't answer, so he put up his hands in surrender.

"Okay, so maybe I was easily smitten by a lovely lady. What can I say, I'm a romantic."

Grace laughed.

"Emma was great and I was so in awe of what she was doing," Luke went on. "She was living in another country! And that was, like, normal for New Zealanders. I thought, jeez, that'd be kinda cool. Ben and Isla always talked about traveling everywhere and, to be honest, I'd never really thought about it until then. So I went to visit her after we graduated and got a job cooking at this restaurant on the South Island on a working holiday visa, and then they sponsored me and I got to stay."

"And Emma?" she asked.

"I catered her wedding this past summer." He grinned. "I think we dated for like a week after I moved there and then she went back overseas, and I stayed in New Zealand. I've always been a guy who liked to stay put, you know?"

"I really do," she said, shaking her head. "Wow, New Zealand. Poor Ben must have been so jealous. I was sorry you missed him tonight. I wonder why he never went to visit you?"

Luke shrugged. "I invited him out once or twice early on, but with opposite seasons it never really worked for either one of us. His business is doing really well though. I know it wasn't the exact life he wanted for himself, but he doesn't seem too miserable."

Grace raised her eyebrows.

"He waited for her, I think," said Luke. "For more years than he remembers. I wonder if now she's home…"

"It's funny, isn't it, all of us home this summer?" said Grace. "And yet it feels like it was always meant to be. Do you remember when we were just Gracenisla, a unified being? I mean, I don't even think I had a real name from the ages of twelve to sixteen," she added. "Gracenisla, the mermaid caller and the mermaid."

Luke laughed and topped off their wine. "How did that all start anyway? Something about the green lights? I remember you guys talking about them but I never really knew what the hell you meant."

"It's the algae," she said.

"The bioluminescence? That's what the famous lights are?" he asked, disbelieving.

"To be fair, there were accounts of lights on the water. But nobody ever saw them. Well, almost nobody."

"You? It actually was you?"

Grace blushed. "Festival eve, 2002, I danced with a green light winking at me from the sea. Isla arrived the very next day. I was at the restaurant, and Isla came in on a boat with Henry. She said something I never forgot. She just looked at me, relieved, and said, 'Oh good, you're here.' My whole life changed that day."

"So that's why people think she's the last mermaid?"

"And that I called her," Grace said, "because I'm a Cleary. But she's just Isla, my best friend. We were more than just best friends though—we were summer soul sisters, we used to say. I think that kind of connection stays with you forever, no matter what else happens."

"What was the green light?"

She laughed heartily. "It actually *was* Isla, I found out at the end of the first summer. On a sandbar, diving with her beacon light."

Luke laughed. "Man, it's great to be back here. I missed Maiden's Cove." He turned to her. "I missed Cleary's. I missed you, Grace."

The glass of wine paused at her lips and she met Luke's eyes as they delved into hers. "I…"

He was just inches away from her face, so close that she could smell the wine on his breath. He did not pull back, nor move closer, but he did look into her eyes, searching, questioning. She could feel her breath quicken, and for the first time in longer than she could remember, Grace felt passion burn inside her. A desire she couldn't even name. And she wanted him to kiss her, to feel his warm, full lips finally on hers, which she knew would be gentle, yet filled with heat and desire.

His nostrils flared slightly, and his eyes darted to her lips. She was sure he could feel the shift in her, just as she could feel it in him.

And then she pulled back. "I can't, Luke, I'm sorry."

He immediately moved and gave her space, but that space was filled with longing.

"Don't ever say sorry," he said. "I'm always here for you, as your friend."

She relaxed immediately, and yet at the same time she was disappointed. Some part of her wished he would have just kissed her, but he seemed to know she wasn't ready.

"Thank you again for inviting me," said Luke. "Shall I walk you out?"

He was leaving? She *had* upset him. And then, confused, she said, "Walk me out? But I live here."

"I think someone out there might be needing you," he said quietly, nodding his head to where Isla stood, staring out at the bay.

"Thank you, Luke," she whispered, and without turning back to him, Grace went to Isla.

~

She walked out onto the beach where Isla stood staring out to the water. They stood side by side, not saying anything for a long time.

"You *are* the reason I came back," Isla said. "One night, I was sitting on the beach in the Caribbean and I heard you call my name, saw bioluminescence in the sand, and I knew you needed me. In my heart I knew."

"That's one reason. What's the other?" Grace asked.

Isla took a deep breath, looking at the water. "I nearly drowned," she finally said, quietly.

Grace kept her expression emotionless, and somehow managed to keep her breath from catching. But she was shocked. What she wanted to really ask was, *You?!* But instead she asked, "When?"

"Three months ago," she said. "Do you remember that time we went to Henry's, and you made my fake birth certificate?"

"Yes," Grace answered slowly. She and Isla were thirteen and they were out exploring with Ben and Luke in the Cove when Isla took them to the house where she lived with Henry. The memory was clear in her mind now.

"Her name was Rebecca," Isla had told them. "She would have been my adopted mom I guess." She'd lovingly touched a photo she'd taken off the shelf of Henry and Rebecca. "They adopted me when I was a baby. Then Rebecca got sick shortly after and died so I don't remember her. Henry doesn't like to talk about her much—he was so heartbroken. We got on the water after I was old enough and followed the fishing seasons, and it's been me and Henry ever since."

"What about your birth certificate?" Grace had asked.

Isla had shrugged. "I just have my adoption certificate with adoptive parents Henry and Rebecca Dupont, daughter Isla Dupont. Closed adoption."

They'd all remained silent for a moment, not knowing what to say.

"You know," Grace had said thoughtfully. "Maybe it's not a coincidence that you came to Maiden's Cove. Maybe Henry brought you on purpose!"

"What do you mean?" Isla had asked.

"Well, you are named Isla, just like Ifan and Isolde's baby," Ben had said.

They'd all nodded thoughtfully.

The next time they were all together, Grace had passed her a piece of paper.

"What is this?" Isla had asked, looking at the handwritten page and reading it aloud. "Parents, Ifan and Isolde, daughter, Isla."

"Your very own real birth certificate. For who you might really be," Grace said, and Isla had hugged her tightly.

"I think, in some way," Isla said now, "I took that with me for a long time, longer than was healthy to do make-believe. That's probably why we grew apart as teenagers." She glanced at Grace. "I still wanted Neverland."

"And I wanted to grow up," Grace said, her heart filling with regret. "I wish I'd never wanted to grow up so fast. Look at what happened to me."

"And I should have grown up more," Isla said. "I think there was a part of me that wanted to believe that maybe it was all true in some weird way." Her voice shook and tears filled her eyes. "I never really had a home before Maiden's Cove. Never had friends, let alone a best friend, a soul sister. And then I had one. I knew what it meant to be home. I longed for it all year until summer came and I was home again. I'd never been happier. I belonged somewhere. I found my identity in us, in our magic, in our myths. I didn't realize I didn't know who I was without it, until that day."

"Tell me what happened?" Grace asked gently.

"It was like any normal day. I was in the Bahamas exploring a new dive. Found a cave, went in, and then I got lost. I couldn't find my way out. I'd never been under that long before, and at first I thought it would be kind of like an adventure. But then...then I knew that I was going to die. That I wasn't magical or special, that I was just a girl who was going to drown and die, and that I was going to do it alone. All I could see was your face, and Ben's, and Maiden's Cove. I think a part of me hallucinated in the end and thought you were breathing into me the way we used to."

"Oh, Isla," she said. "So you haven't been in the water since?" Grace asked, her heart breaking for her friend. "But that's where you feel the most you."

"I still swim," she said. "I am just too afraid to go deep or far and I avoid places with a strong current."

"How did you get out?"

"It was very dark in the cave, so I just literally followed the light," said Isla. "Swam with everything in me and once I saw a hole big enough, I kicked as hard as I could to the surface. I wasn't actually that far under, but I must have passed out or something because the next thing I knew I was in the back of a pickup truck with some local fishermen driving me to the hospital."

She sighed deeply. "Being back here has been my greatest gift. But seeing Ben...I don't know. I think I always wanted him to see me the way I wanted to be seen—as something slightly mystical, slightly out of reach. Something just a little bit not real."

"But why?"

Isla turned to her. "Because I have no idea who I am. Or why I'm here. Or if I have any purpose at all. I only know that I almost died and I was alone, because I was too afraid to be real."

"Ahhh," Grace sighed, and Isla sighed with her. "And now you're home. To the only home you've ever really known."

Isla took Grace's hand again. "To the only family I've ever really known."

They stood for a long while.

"Isla?"

"Yes?"

"Let's go for a swim," Grace said, taking off her clothes.

"I...I don't know if I can."

"Of course you can."

Grace waded in the water until she couldn't touch the sand anymore and waited, until finally she heard Isla behind her. "You belong to it."

"Are you sure?" Isla asked, tears in her eyes.

"Sure you do," Grace said, switching their childhood roles. "Now you're with me."

Chapter Seven

Summary 2004

Dammit!" Grace hissed, running the familiar path from Cleary's back to her house. She was late. Late for Isla.

She arrived at their beach out of breath, but it was empty. The bioluminescence was faint in the sand, but no winking green light came from across the water.

"No, no no," Grace cried. She'd been having doubts but now that the night was here, the idea of Isla not coming back was making her start to hyperventilate.

Suddenly she saw a dull light out in the bay. It was not like the bright winking green light from years before—that had been much closer. This was a couple of hundred feet away, perhaps less, but way too far to swim.

Grace was suddenly flooded with relief, and sat on the sand waiting. But the light didn't come closer, it just hovered, illuminated in the bay, beckoning her.

"Dammit, Isla, I can't swim that far without you," she whispered to herself, shrugging off her shorts and top and just leaving her red bikini on. But as she walked to the edge of the water, she realized she was a lot closer already and the bay had yet to lap around her ankles. Low tide. She could probably make it in low tide—she wouldn't have to start swimming for another fifty feet or so.

In another few minutes she was swimming slowly toward the light, which was starting to grow brighter. Eventually, after about ten minutes, her foot touched sand. It was a sandbar, and it was alight with bioluminescence, a floating island of light in the bay. Grace laughed and lay down on the sand and waited.

"This one's new," Isla's voice startled her from behind.

Grace turned and grinned. Isla was holding onto the edge of the sandbar like the side of a swimming pool, her long legs slowly kicking behind her.

"Wasn't here last year."

"We've had a couple of good storms lately, must have stirred things up a bit," Grace said, rolling onto her stomach so she and Isla were face to face.

"I like it," Isla announced. "It's like our castle, mine and yours. Where the one from the land and the one from the sea could both live, together!"

Grace rolled her eyes and forced a smile, feeling mildly uncomfortable. Were they going to keep this going again all summer even though they were fourteen now, she wondered?

"Yes, in low tide," she said pragmatically, "but what about in high tide?"

"You're right, of course. 'We're gonna need a bigger sandbar,'" she said in a deep voice quoting *Jaws*, a favorite of theirs.

Grace laughed genuinely this time, lightening.

"Hmm," Isla mused, then snapped her fingers. "I've got it!"

"A bigger sandbar?"

"Way bigger. An island, duh," Isla said at Grace's perplexed look. "Think about it! We turn eighteen, we go down to the Caribbean where it's warm year-round, live on the islands, get awesome jobs. I've only been a couple of times but you'll love it."

"We'll meet heaps of gorgeous guys!" Grace enthused.

"We'll have coconuts for breakfast..."

"Rum punch for lunch..."

And suddenly, with relief, Grace realized that they were Gracenisla still, and summer began.

"What are you doing back here, honey child?" Della asked Isla one day in July.

"Waiting for Grace," Isla said, not meeting Della's eyes.

Della sat beside her. "Why don't you go out there, honey, and wait with her? Make some new friends. I've never known Miss Isla to be shy. Or scared?"

Isla scowled, but not at Della. "I'm not shy or scared. I just haven't seen Grace all day. I went to go out and it was like she didn't even know I was there. And she was acting...I don't know, like she's laughing all weird. And at *Luke*."

Della laughed. "I think it's called flirting, honey. You and Grace are fourteen. You're both turning into beautiful young girls and growing up. It's supposed to be fun, starting a new job and meeting new people, especially boys, at your age."

Isla's face flushed as deep red as her hair.

Della wanted to chuckle at the angst that could come out of such a young girl for such a small reason, but she stopped. Being fourteen was the worst.

"That's why I became a chef," Della said, smiling at Isla. "There isn't any place better to hide than in a kitchen. I was shy as a little girl, real shy. But I had a special place I lived in every day, a place that was comforting, a place I loved to be. In the kitchen. I didn't start out in the kitchen here at Cleary's. I have the clearest memories from when I was young. Coming home to our house in the Cove, sitting in the backyard with my mama and my aunties. All the boys were out in the bay. The babies were all asleep. And us women were in the kitchen, rolling crabmeat, slicing fish, laughing, gossiping, telling stories. Best time of my life. By the time I grew up, everything'd changed. Everything except the food. Food brings us all together, makes us connect. Come on, honey child. I'll show you how to make my famous oyster chowder."

~

"This is impossible," Isla groaned a week later, throwing her pen at Grace and dropping the notebook in her hand. She rested her forehead on the window in Grace's bedroom. "I hate the rain."

Grace rolled her eyes with a smile and threw the pen back at her. The rain always made Isla grumpy and petulant. She poked her tongue at Grace now. They were writing notes to each other as though they were twenty-five-year-olds, a game Grace was loving, surmising what life would be like as a grown-up, how many possibilities there were for where her life was going to lead. She was already four or five notes in, and Isla couldn't write even one.

"How can it be so difficult? It's just a game, Isla. Here, I'll read one of mine, okay?"

Isla rolled over onto her stomach and nodded, listening intently.

"Dear Isla, just heading to Cleary's for the day to film *Celebrity Cook-Off* with Dad. And guess who I have a hot date with after? Luke McCann! He's just back from college and I hear he can fly his own helicopter, so maybe we'll end up in Manhattan for the night making love on a rooftop. Drinks tomorrow? Love you! Grace."

Grace looked up with a wide grin but faltered at Isla's expression.

"But this is Maiden's Cove," Isla said, incredulous. "What about the Caribbean? Rum punch on the beach?"

"Well, yeah, I mean for holidays and maybe, like, a winter or something. But I never want to leave Maiden's Cove permanently," Grace said. "This is my home. And Cleary's—I want it to be mine one day. Dad and I have such great ideas! And I know the Caribbean is surrounded by water too, but here, the Bay? I just love it. It's home. I don't think I could ever live anywhere else."

"I'd be too restless," Isla said, "staying in one place."

"You sound like Ben," Grace said with a laugh. "Hey, you know, maybe you two should run off together to the Caribbean? Making sweet love in the lapping sea…"

"Ew, gross!" Isla yelled, throwing a pillow at her, but Grace saw that her face was bright red and she knew that Isla had thought about Ben in that way, even if she never told her.

Isla scribbled away quickly on the notepad and threw it at her. "Here!"

"Dear Grace," she read, trying to get through Isla's awful left-handed writing. "One from the land, one from the sea, summer soul sisters forever shall we be."

Isla stopped trying to fight her and sagged back into the window again, looking out to the rain. "Stupid, I know."

Grace stepped off the bed and gently handed the notebook back to Isla, wrapping her arms around her forlorn friend in the window. "Not stupid. Perfect."

Chapter Eight

Look what I found in one of the boxes Bayla brought back from Loretta's," Grace said to Isla a few days after the cookout, handing her a small shoebox.

"What is it?" Isla asked.

"Open it and look," Grace said, glancing back at Isla. She wondered if Isla would feel the same way she did when she'd stayed up all night reading them.

Isla gasped and let out a soft breath of laughter. "Our letters to each other from when we were our make-believe twenty-five-year-old selves? I cannot believe you kept these!" Isla read through the first couple, smiling and shaking her head. "How old were we when we started writing these? Fifteen?"

"Fourteen," Grace corrected.

Isla reached out and picked one up at random. On it she had drawn a beach with a piña colada on one side, and colored it with bright magic markers, writing *Caribbean* across the top like a postcard. She smiled fondly, grazing the letters with her fingertips, and turned it over.

"Dear Grace," she read out loud, "I've got the spare room of the beach house all ready for your visit. Pick you up at the airport on Saturday, and I'll have piña coladas on the porch waiting for us. Together forever till death knocks us out. Love, Isla."

Grace smiled and watched Isla's face as she experienced a wave of nostalgia.

"Good lord, I had terrible handwriting," Isla finally said, and Grace laughed. "And to think this was one of my more interesting letters. You were so much better at them than I was. Here, listen to yours.

" 'Dear Isla, I'm all packed for our weekend together and can't wait to see you in Saint Barts! I keep joking with Luke that we're going to be wining and dining with celebrities on their yachts the entire time, and he pretends like he's not bothered, but I think he actually *is* a little jealous. Which is thrilling. Can you believe we are getting *married* this year?! Ah! I did tell you that you're my maid of honor, right? I mean, I figured it was obvious, but if I didn't—you are! I mean who else would be, but my one and only summer soul sister? X Grace.' "

"You just had all the details and imagination so clear. I swear in one of these letters...didn't you send me a packing list?" Isla asked, flipping through them.

"Yup." Grace grinned. "Five bathing suits, one for every day, and room for two new ones for the weekend that we'd buy there."

"Gosh, we were young," Isla breathed, looking through the letters. "We thought at twenty-five we'd have everything we ever wanted."

"The reality of twenty-five for me was so different," Grace said with a sigh. "That was the year I met Cohen and I realized I hadn't been anywhere new in over five years. I had a schedule that I had to stick to. Bayla and I both. I was trapped in a life of someone else's making and I didn't even know it. And in Phoenix! The *desert. Me.* Who never even wanted to leave Maiden's Cove."

"Oh Grace," Isla whispered. "Whatever happened with Luke? And how did you reconnect with Richard after that last summer anyway? I thought he was going away to be a hot shot Wall Street guy with that guy Matt's dad?"

"Luke just treated me like he always had—like a little sister. I mean, I couldn't blame him. When I met Richard that summer, it was like I was finally really seen for the first time. As a woman. And you have to admit, he was gorgeous and charming."

"I never thought he was charming, as you well know," Isla said slowly, "but I can see how you did. That kind of charisma and sex appeal was exactly what you were wanting as you got to that age. I know it was hard for me to understand then, but I do now. And yes, he was attractive. And boy did he know it."

Grace shook her head with a deep sigh. "Yes, he did. He did go to New York, but he still came in over the summer with Matt's family those couple of years after high school. We got pretty hot and heavy over those summers," Grace said. "Dad started taking me on trips with him to talk about the future of Cleary's and keep me involved, but now looking back, I can see that he was trying to keep me grounded when he could see that there was only one thing I was really focused on, and that was Richard Monroe. I was such a romantic, and Richard seemed so…perfect. My ultimate summer romance. The reality was even better than the way I'd imagined it would be then."

"But how did you end up married? And so young?" Isla asked, wrapping a blanket around Grace, who was shivering.

Grace raised her eyebrows. "I'll give you a few guesses, but you only need to look at my kid and do the math for the answer. I was twenty-one. We had this, like, all-summer romance fest. And then summer ended and I found out I was pregnant. Well, I should say Loretta found out I was pregnant. I had no idea. I was sick in the mornings, but I just thought I had a bug. It was Loretta who knew and took me to the doctor."

"Oh god, of all the people to have found out!" Isla gasped. "She must have been a nightmare. Did she tell your dad?"

Grace looked up thoughtfully. "No, actually, she was great. I didn't realize it at the time, of course. There was so much bad history between us. But she swore she'd never tell anyone without my permission and sat with me while we were given the options. I didn't know what to do, but I knew I had to at least tell Richard. So I called him, and it was so weird, he was *over the moon* about it."

Isla looked perplexed.

"I told you about his dad, Earl?" Grace asked. Isla nodded. "Richard grew up watching his father abuse his mother, who he adored when he was a child. Ridiculing her, belittling her, watching her wilt away to a sheer version of the woman she once was. He told me that when he was young he would stick up for her, and he would get the brunt of it instead. By the time I met him, however, he was a man out to prove to his father that he was good enough, who somehow had grown to hate his mother for her weakness. He didn't want to become like his father, though, and I think he saw becoming a husband and a father as a way to break himself of the inevitable fate that he thought was his.

"He came to Maiden's Cove and was the perfect gentleman. Asked Dad's permission to marry me. We had the wedding at Cleary's like I'd always wanted and he promised we'd always stay close. And then he got a job in Phoenix, and I was pregnant and twenty-one, married, and suddenly living in a baking, landlocked city with no friends or family, only a husband I was crazy about.

"It was great at first," she said. "He was attentive for the first year or so, and he tried really, really hard to be a good father, I think. And then he started drinking—whiskey, just like his own father. Suddenly, out of nowhere, he would lose his temper and get mean. That started just after the time I brought Bayla home to Maiden's Cove, when Ben begged me not to go back to Phoenix." She paused for a moment before continuing. "A few months later, I found out about the first one. April was her name."

"What do you mean, April was the first?" Isla asked, frowning.

"Then there was Samantha, then Kristy. It was the same every time. It usually started with some sort of work stress or finances, or a conversation with his father. Suddenly I would see the whiskey glass in his hand on the porch, and despite his good mood earlier, as it went on, he would get more mean. Had more control over us that I didn't see. And then when..."

"When what?" Isla asked.

"When I found out about my dad passing I tried to leave with Bayla for the funeral. Richard told me that we couldn't leave. That we couldn't leave him."

She took a breath. "I know I told you he didn't beat me, and he didn't. But that day I made the mistake of laughing at him.

Told him he was being ridiculous. Our relationship was already over at that point. He had a new girlfriend and wasn't even sleeping at the house anymore, which was a relief. But he didn't like being laughed at. He pushed me down the stairs. I must have got knocked out because it was Bayla who found me," she said, tears now freely falling. "My own daughter, Isla. I told her I'd fallen. I looked at her and said, 'Oh sweetie, look how clumsy Mommy is!' and laughed. But she saw through me. I could tell she didn't believe me. At the hospital they told me I had a broken rib and a concussion from such a bad fall. We left a week later, in the night, with Cohen's help."

"And he hasn't tried to contact you?" Isla asked.

"He talks to Bayla once a week, but he's never asked to speak to me. He was in love with his latest girlfriend when this happened. Raine," she said, laughing bitterly.

"That's her name?"

When Grace nodded, Isla snickered, and they both started to chuckle.

"Ten years of controlling you and no word at all?" Isla asked. "That worries me."

"Me too. But I'm just trying to hold onto the hope that we are all in better places—happier now—and that this is a good thing."

"Yes. But best to be careful," Isla said, closing the curtains.

Grace nodded. "I know it's not over. Not yet. I just hope that being here in Maiden's Cove protects us somehow."

"It will, because we are all here, and we won't let anything happen to either of you girls," Isla said, putting her arm around Grace's shoulder.

~

Grace was in the restaurant every day now, usually with Isla in tow, who worked any job necessary without complaining, so long as she didn't have to talk to the customers. Bayla was dropped at Mape's most days since Sylvie was on vacation with her girlfriends for a couple of weeks. Sometimes she went with Gloretta, but occasionally Bayla was allowed to come into Cleary's for an hour or so and help bring in the boats, like Grace did when she was her age. It filled Grace with great joy to watch this transition to the next generation take place, though with a deep sadness, she wished she'd have come back with Bayla earlier and have had her dad experience it.

"He knew," Isla said from behind, as if she'd heard every thought in Grace's head. "Just like Henry knew."

"Knew what?" Grace asked.

"That we loved them," she said. "And ole Tommy'd be so proud of you. Look at this," she said, nodding to the full restaurant. "Keeping the dream alive with all your hard work and ideas."

Grace sat back from the computer and sighed. "And yet it's still not enough."

"No difference?" Isla asked, her face falling.

"Definitely a difference, just not enough. Not yet. Here," she said, turning the computer screen. "Look at this email from Genevieve Hull from *Food and Travel* magazine. She wants to do an article on the restaurant, and I've said yes. Something like that could help, right?"

The effort everyone was putting into making sure that Cleary's remained one of the best crab shacks on the Eastern Shore was astounding. Todd's new tiki bar, outside where the boats docked, which he manned himself with only one waitress, was growing their numbers tremendously.

"Hey, Grace," he called from the bar where he was pouring tap beer and orange crushes. "Come try this new drink, my 'Oh Mama Colada.'"

She took a small cup from him. "How on earth do you have time to make a piña colada, or anything else, with all these fans of yours?" she said over the music. There were probably twenty people around the bar—all women, she noticed.

"Pre-made recipes. I mix them when I am either opening or closing out, and then voila," he said, holding up a bottle. "Cocktail in a bottle, ready to go. Glass, ice, pour. Drink. Tell me what you think."

"Wow, brilliant," she said, as he went back to the ladies, giving them a charming grin. Grace laughed as she walked into the kitchen sipping the drink. "Damn that's good!"

"Oh Mama Colada?" Georgiana asked. Grace nodded.

"Boy genius over there has raised our alcohol sales by twenty-five percent overnight. And god he's pretty," Cohen said, resting his chin in his hand.

"He reminds me of you, Luke," Grace called into the kitchen, winking at Georgiana. "Do you remember Luke in high school, Georgiana?"

"Oh my god, you are so right! Senior boys," she said with a sigh. "What is it about senior boys?"

"It's a pragmatic woman thing!" Luke yelled from the kitchen, poking his head out. "We're about to leave town for the better part of a year and you know you won't have to deal with us again until Christmas."

They laughed.

"Don't make me tell you girls to stop gossiping and get back to work," Jimbo said as he came into the baking section, winking at Grace.

"Oui, chef!" Grace, Georgiana and Cohen said at the same time, and laughed when he guffawed.

Grace had just taken another sip of her drink when Luke snuck up behind her and touched her waist ever so slightly.

She squealed, and the drink came out of her nose and dribbled down her chin.

Isla walked in just at that moment carrying a polybin of fish. Her eyebrows pulled together and she mouthed, *What's wrong with you?*

I don't know! Grace mouthed back silently.

"Thank you for picking this up, Isla," Luke said with his crooked half-smile.

"Boys didn't bring enough in today?" Jimbo asked.

"They did, yes, but I didn't want to compromise the menu and I want to try a new dish tonight after service. You got the extra crabmeat too?" Luke asked Isla.

She nodded. "What new dish?"

Luke pulled off his baseball cap and ran his fingers through his hair. "It's not new actually. It's old. Thought I'd try to recreate Tom's Rockfish and Crab Imperial dish, the one he did with you and Della," he said to Jimbo, "on *Diners, Drive-Ins and Dives.*"

There was a murmur of approval, and Luke seemed to breathe a sigh of relief. He looked at Grace. "I know it's something really special to you and Cleary's so I'd love you to make sure I'm doing it right?" he asked.

"Oh!" Grace said, blushing. "I'm sure Jimbo or Della would be much—"

"Grandkids tonight," Jimbo said, picking up the polybin and walking away. "Right, Della?"

"Oh, right," she said, looking confused but grabbing the crabmeat. "Grandkids. Sure. I'll pick this out for you, Luke honey. Might want to grab punnets next time," she suggested.

He put his head in his hand. "So obvious, sorry, Della, and thank you." He turned back to Grace. "So?"

"Kid. Bayla," she finished, shaking her head. "I've got Bayla, sorry."

"I can take Bayla!" Isla said brightly.

"But—" Grace started.

"Perfect!" Cohen said, loudly interrupting. "Grace, this will be a perfect recipe and story for that *Food and Travel* magazine article you were just telling us about!"

"Yes but…"

Before Grace could finish her sentence, they all disappeared into the kitchen, leaving her and Luke alone.

"You know, I think your friends are trying to set you up with me," Luke said mischievously.

"Friends? What friends?" she asked.

He chuckled. "Don't worry, I will aim to keep my charm at bay. All that 'senior boy' charm, that is," he said.

"Luke, you couldn't hold back that 'senior boy' charm of yours if someone handed you a check for a million dollars," she said with a laugh.

"Are you offering? I could at least give it a go for that much money, though of course, it would be hard in such close proximity to you," he teased.

"You are relentless, Luke McCann!"

"So you'll stay tonight then?" Luke asked, somehow making it sound sexy.

Grace gave up arguing. It wasn't as if she wanted to argue anyway, not really, she had to admit to herself. "Of course," she said, holding out her drink to him. "Oh Mama Colada?"

"Is it as good on the way out of your nose as it is on the way in?" he asked.

Grace groaned, putting her head in her hand. "I'm a mess."

"I think you're a fine mess, Grace Cleary," Luke said, tilting her chin and heading back into the kitchen through the swinging door.

Grace watched his figure disappear with admiration before swinging the opposite door open. Cohen, Jimbo, Della, Isla and Georgiana all stood there with wide grins.

"You do know we still have an entire service to get through and you're all just standing there with those ridiculous looks on your faces, right?" she asked.

"Oh, shit!"

"Righto, sorry, boss!"

Jimbo just chuckled his deep, soothing laugh.

Isla looked at her with a cheeky smile. "Kinda reminds me of some of those old letters of ours."

"Shut up, Isla," Grace said, her face as red as Isla's hair.

~

Grace and Isla walked together to pick Bayla up from Mape's, where the girls begged to spend just one more night together.

"Please, Mom!" Bayla cried.

"Please, Ms. Grace," Mape pleaded at the same time.

"Girls, stop," Grace said firmly, putting her hands in the air. "Not tonight. Aunt Isla is watching you, Bayla, and…"

"Oh, Aunt Isla, please! Pretty please, Aunt Isla!" Bayla and Mape said at the same time, turning to Isla, who looked overwhelmed.

"Fine!" Isla finally relented. "Yes, Mape, you can stay. Jeez. Go pack a bag and let's go," she said, then turned to Grace. "Did *we* do that?"

Grace laughed. "Did you ever ask anyone if you could do anything, ever?"

Isla grinned. "Nope. Wait, what do I have to do anyway? I don't have to cook for them, do I? You know I can't cook."

"I remember very clearly, don't worry," Grace said, recalling the time she tried to teach Isla to cook scrambled eggs and she'd melted the plastic spatula into it, making them all sick. "I brought home all the leftovers from Cleary's. You'll just need to heat it up."

"How do I do that?" Isla asked.

"Don't worry, Aunt Isla, I know how to cook," Bayla said, out of breath from helping Mape pack her overnight bag so quickly. "We're ready."

Suddenly Isla looked nervous. "Okay, me too then." She didn't move.

"Aunt Isla!" Mape cried, laughing, "Come on!" She took one hand while Bayla took another and they dragged her back to Brixton Cottage, Grace looking on in amusement.

But once they were out of sight, she was suddenly incredibly nervous as she walked back to Cleary's. She trusted Luke to keep their relationship on the "friends and coworkers only" level. They were having fun, and she appreciated the way he was not only helping her business, but also becoming her true friend again. Sometimes she wondered, though, was he just being Luke—charming and flirty Luke McCann—or was he starting to see her as a woman he was interested in?

Whatever his motivation was, their attraction was mutual, and it was very real. And Grace was nervous to go back to Cleary's because she didn't necessarily trust herself not to act on that attraction, especially one with such a long, deep-rooted history of infatuation with him when she was younger.

The sun was turning the sky brilliant colors over the bay as she made her way back to Cleary's, and it relaxed her, as the humidity of the sweltering night enveloped her.

"Hello?" Grace called out when she arrived at the restaurant, having slipped through the back delivery door. There was a light on in the kitchen but the restaurant was dark otherwise. Grace followed the light and the music that was playing.

Luke was leaning over the stainless-steel bench and prepping some mixing bowls. The album he was playing brought her back to her childhood.

"*Soul of the Sixties*, I believe," Grace said, coming up to the iPod and turning down the music as Luke turned to look at her. "My dad's favorite."

Luke smiled and put his knife down. "Your dad, Della and Jimbo let me stay behind late nights and help them prep. This is the only music I know for cooking."

"You must have been a great hit in New Zealand," she teased.

"I did have to overrule Taylor Swift once or twice."

She raised her eyebrows. "You're not a Swiftie?"

Luke held up his hands. "Isn't everyone? I just need my 1960s mojo when I create new dishes."

Grace laughed and turned the music back up, coming up beside him. "So."

He looked down at her. "So."

Grace stood next to him, their arms touching as tingles spread through her.

"What...uh...what are we making first?" Her face was tilted up to Luke's and his down to hers. She stared at his lips, full and with a soft beard growing around them, the same dark brown as his curled hair. When she looked back at his eyes, she found that they were focused on her lips as well.

Her phone dinged a text message alert and Luke turned back to the recipe in his hand.

"Sorry," she muttered, and looked at the text.

Did he kiss you yet? Isla's text said.

There will be no kissing. Aren't you supposed to be watching my kid?

What? What kid? Oh, shit...

Isla!

Just joking.

Her phone said Isla was still typing when suddenly a photo came in of Isla, Bayla and Mape outside on the beach, the bioluminescence beneath them.

Gotta show off a little bit.

Grace laughed and put down her phone.

"Everything okay?" Luke asked.

"I'll let you know in the morning if Isla manages to keep my daughter and her best friend alive for the night," she answered. "Where were we?"

Luke smiled and handed her an old piece of paper. "Della's original Crab Imperial recipe."

"There are a lot of notes written on here," she said.

He laughed. "I know, and I recognize the handwriting. This is your dad's while he was playing with the recipe. This is Jimbo's trying to correct his overly excited attempts to change it. And this here is Della's again."

"What does it say?" she asked, squinting at the tiny handwriting.

" 'Ignore all other notes, ya fool' is what it says," Luke said.

Grace laughed. "I get it, I get it! So we just use Della's original recipe and don't touch it, right?"

"Right," he said, picking the recipe back up and gathering the ingredients he'd already taken out from the dry store. "First we're making Della's Old Bay seasoning by hand."

"But why not use the seasoning we have already?" Grace asked.

"Because for the magazine, we have to have made the entire thing from scratch to be published. Including any rubs, herbs or sauces. Plus, I've always wanted to learn Della's secret recipe, so I coerced it out of her this way," he said with a grin.

"I am surprised you chose this particular dish. It's so…"

"Classic?" he offered.

"Old school," Grace corrected. "It's a very old-school dish from the nineties, and I'm not really sure anyone even orders Crab

Imperial anymore, let alone a magazine that specializes in food and travel showcasing it," she said honestly.

"But that's exactly why I chose this dish. Cleary's is a Maryland 'old school' classic crab shack. I want us to bring it back to its glory by showing off what made it famous in the first place: Maryland classic recipes and Maryland classic people that represent what your dad, and all the Clearys before him, gave to this community. That is what all of us—the chefs, bartenders, waiters, fishermen—have fallen in love with. This summer is a celebration of seventy-five years of Cleary's. I want to bring that love back. For Maiden's Cove. For the fishermen. For the staff. For you, Grace."

His words made the hair on her arms stand on end. The way he spoke of it was the way she felt about it. Somehow she knew that, together, they could do this. They could keep Cleary's alive.

She nodded, her lips pressing together as her eyes became glassy with unshed tears. "Okay. Let's do it."

They started a clean page in the recipe book using Della's Old Bay recipe, for which no notes had ever been given, perfect as it already was and would always be. Working in unison like they'd been in the kitchen together their whole lives, Grace dumped into the bowl the celery salt, smoked paprika, black pepper and cayenne pepper, while Luke added in the allspice, dry mustard, nutmeg, cinnamon and ginger. They bumped into one another just as they both reached the bowl, and Grace picked it up to stir, their faces close.

"We're missing something," she said, tilting her head into the bowl to smell it, her eyes closing.

Luke leaned in too, and their foreheads pressed together. Suddenly he reached his hand up and ran his thumb over her bottom lip, gently, softly. Grace closed her eyes and moaned softly. It was the most intimately someone had touched her for years. She opened her eyes and his jade ones were delving into hers, his full mouth moving closer to where his thumb was still on her bottom lip.

"Bay leaves!" she cried suddenly.

"What?" he said, pulling back.

"It's missing the bay leaves."

He sniffed. "You're right. What's next?" he asked, stirring the Old Bay.

Grace looked down at the recipe, barely able to make out the words and wondering what was happening between them. Her heart was racing, her blood pumping. They'd nearly kissed—three times now. She and Luke. *Luke.*

"Um…" She licked her lips, which were dry. "Mix the parsley with more mustard, pepper, lemon juice, butter, a good deal of mayonnaise, and the homemade seasoning." She glanced up as he did those things. "Gently stir in the crabmeat and bread crumbs…Hey, wait."

"What is it?" he asked.

"Della never uses bread. Her secret recipe uses saltines instead," she said with a smile.

"Are you sure?" Luke looked at the recipe as if it had secrets it should tell him.

"Positive, though I might be the only person on the planet who knows that."

"Ha, sneaky Della," he said. "I'll go to the dry store to find them."

Grace watched him go, admiring him from behind before looking down at her phone, which she'd turned on silent. She started to laugh at the series of pictures the girls had sent. It seemed at first that Isla was taking selfies and sending them to Grace, which was strange. But then Grace noticed Bayla and Mape were in the background, pretending to drown, or jump up as mermaids, all sorts of crazy antics that "Aunt Isla" wasn't paying attention to. Her heart was so full, having Isla home with her daughter.

There was a loud crash from the back, followed by a yell.

"Grace!" Luke called out. He sounded pained.

She dropped her phone and went into the dry store. "Luke?"

"Down here," he said, on the floor, covered in pounds of flour that had fallen on top of him.

"Oh my god," she said, holding her hand over her mouth to keep her from laughing. "What happened?"

"Della hid the saltines. Seems she doesn't want anyone to know her secret," he said, sitting up and brushing himself off. Still, he was covered in flour. Grace couldn't stop chuckling. "Is it that bad?" he asked.

But when he sneezed, she was lost. "Oh my god," she managed, "Luke, you…" But she couldn't get the rest of the words out.

He sneezed again and began to laugh as well until they were both on the floor, unable to stop. Finally, about five minutes later, they exhausted themselves.

"Oh, a tea towel," Grace said, finding a bag of laundry beside her. "Here, let me try to get some of this off your face so you can stop sneezing."

He sneezed again. Grace snickered, but reached his face, gently wiping the flour aside as to not get it in his eyes, nose or mouth. In a few minutes he was mostly clean, and when they met eyes, suddenly nothing was funny anymore. Suddenly, there was nothing but their breath, their lips, their hands, and for the first time in her life, Grace Cleary felt the warm lips of Luke McCann upon hers.

~

Bayla and Mape were convinced that if they stayed up late enough they would find out the truth about Aunt Isla. Whatever that might be.

They stayed out on the beach so long they fell asleep there, and when they woke up, the moon was bright and Aunt Isla was asleep in the hammock she'd tied up just off the porch, snoring.

"She snores really loud for a mermaid," Mape whispered, yawning.

"Maybe it's because she needs water and not oxygen?" Bayla whispered back, her eyebrows raised. Mape shrugged. "Or maybe she knows we're watching and she's *faking it*," she said, getting louder.

Isla woke with a start. "What the?"

Mape rolled her eyes at Bayla. "Sorry, Aunt Isla. Bay was being hi-*lar*-ious. We were just going to bed."

"Oh, okay," Isla said, rubbing her eyes. "Sorry I fell asleep. Is your mom home?"

"Not yet," Bayla said. "Did she text you?"

Isla looked down at her phone, a faint smile forming. "Yes. She'll be home soon. Go on then, go to bed, girls, or she'll never let me babysit again."

"We're going!" Bayla said, and she and Mape ran to give Isla a kiss on the cheek. "Night, Aunt Isla!"

"Oh!" Isla said, touching her cheek as she blushed. "Goodnight."

They skipped brushing their teeth and went to Bayla's room, Mape hopping into bed and snoring nearly as loudly as Isla had been within seconds of lying down. Bayla waited as the moon moved to the other side of the trees, the sky getting darker and darker, but Aunt Isla never moved from the hammock and her mom still hadn't gotten home. Bayla's eyes got heavier and heavier until she could no longer keep them open and she drifted off to sleep.

She didn't know how long she had been asleep when she heard a splash and jolted awake. It was black, both inside the house and out. There was no moon reflecting on the water and the bioluminescence was faint at best, though it looked as though there were traces of green light, like two small footprints, just before the water rushed into the beach. Bayla pressed her forehead close to the window, trying to get her eyes to adjust to the darkness. Outside was starting to become clearer. She wiped the fog of her breath from the glass, and suddenly she saw it.

She'd never know exactly what "it" was. And she never knew for sure if she was still asleep and dreaming, or if it was real.

But what she saw, or thought she saw, was something not of this world, green and brilliant, that lit up the sand and splashed the water—a tumble of wild red hair following.

Chapter Nine

Though only 213 permanent inhabitants lived in Maiden's Cove year round, in the summer the crowds came in hordes on the weekends. By the end of June the town was full, the B&Bs and historic inns at capacity, and in that little town on the Chesapeake Bay there was never a weekend when there wasn't a festival or event of some sort. Summer solstice was no exception. Every year on June 21, the longest day, the Maiden's Cove Crab Festival was held.

"What do you want to do at the festival, Bayla?" Grace asked the evening before as they sat outside eating dinner. She had made rockfish burgers with some offcuts from the restaurant, crumbed and served with lettuce and tomato on fluffy kaiser rolls with tartar sauce that Luke had made for them.

Bayla bit into hers and looked through the events schedule. "Evwyfing," she enthused, her mouth stuffed with food.

Grace sat beside her and looked through the pamphlet, taking a bite of her own sandwich, which was delicious. "Hmm, I don't think everything is possible unless you can be in two places at once," she said. "Look, the Crab Race is at the same time as the Crab-picking Contest."

"Crab Race," Bayla decided. "Do I really get to pick a live crab and make it race to the finish line?"

"Yup. Weird, isn't it?"

"So weird." She laughed. "But much better than picking crabs. I got lots of little cuts when we ate crabs at our cookout and Old Bay got in them and it hurt so bad."

"I know, I've never liked that part either. Uncle Ben used to say it was the price for being awesome," Grace said with a smile.

"Will Uncle Ben come with us tomorrow?" Bayla asked.

"Oh he'll be so busy, hon. Look here." She pointed out a passage on the pamphlet to Bayla. " 'Paddle Cove's guided kayak trips will be one of the best parts of the festival this year,' " she read out loud, feeling proud. "That's Uncle Ben's own business. Pretty cool, huh?"

"Super cool," Bayla agreed. "Can I call him and invite him to come see us later after work?"

"That's a great idea," Grace said. "Did you and Mape finish decorating the buoys that we'll tie the crab pots onto?"

"Yes!" she cried excitedly, jumping up and running inside, leaving the screen door wide open.

"The mosquitos, Bayla!" Grace called after her.

"Sorry," she said, out of breath but back already, carrying out three plastic buoys, not an inch of them not covered in bright paint. "Look what Mape and I did."

Grace shook her head, impressed by the work the girls had put into their designs, which were all filled with the mermaid lore of Maiden's Cove. They were beautifully done.

"This one is 'The Mermaid Caller,'" Bayla said, indicating the painting of a girl blowing into a large seashell, the bay behind her. "And this one is just called 'Mermaid.'" It was painted as though from behind, and depicted a large rock, long red locks and just the hint of a fin.

"These are really good, Bayla," Grace said.

"The designs were my idea but Mape drew and painted them. She's going to be an artist," Bayla said.

Grace thought that Mape would go far in that dream if she kept up with this talent. "What's that last one?" she asked, pointing to the third buoy.

Bayla giggled and handed it to her. "Aunt Isla's. Took her ages to even think of something to paint on it and she was getting really frustrated. Finally she just started writing stuff. Is her handwriting always this bad?"

Grace turned the buoy in her hands and read the graffiti-style words.

Summer Soul Sisters. One from the land and one from the sea. Together forever till death knocks us out.

She smiled. "Yes, it's always been this bad." She turned back to the events schedule. "Okay, so that's the Crab Race at eleven. Then we can go get some lunch before we head out on the boat."

"Me, you, Aunt Isla and Mape, right?" Bayla asked.

Grace nodded. "Isla said she'd bring Henry's old boat, *The Maiden*, for us. The crabbing competition gives you an hour on the water, then we'll come back while the judges tally up the crabs that were in the pots and announce the winners for the most decorative buoys, which you girls will surely win," she said. "So, crabbing competition, Crab Race, and buoys. Is that it?"

"Only if you miss the most important part of the entire day," Bayla said, pointing at the program with her eyebrows raised.

Grace looked down. "The Mer-swimming competition," she said, shaking her head. "Of course."

～

In the morning, Grace, Isla and Bayla walked together from the cottage to pick Mape up from her house, which was just shy of the footbridge to get to town. Grace was in a sundress, sunglasses perched on her nose, and a wide-brimmed hat to keep the sun from burning her fair skin. Isla, as per usual, was in jean shorts and an oversized T-shirt that covered her bikini, flip-flops in hand as she walked barefoot. Bayla had decided to wear the same spaghetti-strapped sequin dress from Grace's eighth-grade dance and a hat of Loretta's she found, adorned with bright peacock feathers.

"Hi Grace!" called Linny and Bill, Mape's parents, stepping out of the front door just as the trio were walking up the drive. "Are you sure you're up to having the girls all day?"

Grace looked at Linny and Bill and couldn't help but laugh. They were dressed normally from the neck down—shorts and flip-flops and T-shirts from last year's Crab Fest. But on top of their heads they each wore a hat with a large crab carrying a crown, saying, "Winner, Crab Fest."

"I'm sure! After all, you have a crown to hold onto!" said Grace.

"We are fierce competitors for the Crab-picking Contest," Linny explained. "Won the last three years, so we've got a title to uphold. Maple, honey, come on. They're waiting for you!"

Mape ran out and closed the door behind her, grinning at Bayla with her arms wide. She wore the same peacock-feather hat that Bayla did, and what looked like it might have been one of her dad's sleeveless undershirts, but covered in sequins and sparkles so that it matched Bayla's dress.

"She's been working on it for weeks," Linny said to Grace, smiling at Mape.

"You've got a little artist there, that's for sure," Grace said. "I promise we'll take good care of her today. Good luck with the contest!"

"Thanks! And thanks for taking her out on the boat too, Isla. We don't have one so this is her first year getting to do the crabbing competition." Linny kissed her daughter. "Honey, have fun today, be good, and we'll be there at 4 p.m. for the Mer-swimming competition."

"Promise?" she asked.

"Wouldn't miss that for the world, honey," Bill said, kissing her forehead.

The foursome made their way over the footbridge with all the other locals and tourists excited for the day. In addition to the fairy lights and mermaid decorations, there were now large posters of crabs and blow-up Maryland Blue Crab floats. The carnival that had been there for the Festival of Lights was doing its three-month tour through Maryland and the tri-state area before it came back for the end of the summer festival, so today the square was filled with local vendors from town selling their food and memorabilia. There was a stage for the awards ceremony at the end of the day and for the music and dancing that would follow.

A massive tent with long tables had been set up for the Crab-picking Contest, and there was a little galley set-up that looked like a mini bowling alley for the Crab Race.

"All right, go pick your crabs for the race, girls," Grace encouraged. "Isla and I will just be here watching. Good luck!"

"Do you remember the year we entered?" Isla asked Grace as the girls ran inside.

She snickered, which made Isla follow suit, and suddenly they were laughing just as the judge called for silence. "You mean the year I entered as the racer, and you—"

"Entered as the crab!" Isla finished, nodding, tears of mirth coming down her cheeks.

"SHHHH!" they heard from the galley, but lost it again quickly when they turned to see a bunch of young people running after blue crabs fleeing for their lives.

"How on earth did we ever leave all this?" Isla asked.

Grace reached out and touched Isla's hand, clasping it within hers. "We're home now."

Ainsley Beach was packed with people signing up for the crabbing competition and getting safety checked before hopping into their boats.

"Aunt Isla," Bayla said, "your boat is so far out in the bay! How will we get to it?"

"Don't worry, the anchor is dropped in the shallows. *The Maiden* has just been pulled out by the tide," she said. "I'll go pull it in, easy peasy."

"Easy peasy, lemon squeezy, my mom always says!" Mape said cheerfully, grinning at Bayla, who grinned back and started skipping behind Isla.

"Easy peasy, lemon squeezy," they sang with each skip, holding hands.

Grace followed them down to the busy beach, lining up to sign the paperwork for the competition.

"Hi, Grace," a familiar voice said from behind her.

"Luke!" she exclaimed, surprised and, at the same time, warm all over. Just seeing his face reminded her of their kiss in the pantry the other night, covered in flour, while stealing Della's hidden saltines. "What are you doing here? I thought you were working today."

"Jimbo wants to take Della out for a special anniversary date tonight, so they're doing the lunch shift and I'm working the night with Clarence and Theo," he explained. "I was on my way out for the crabbing competition, but my date fell through."

"Your date?" she asked. "Oh, who was she?"

"My favorite girl in the world," he said, "the little traitor."

Grace's mouth opened to speak, but she had no words.

"My niece Ruby decided she wanted to hang out with her friends and not her uncle," said Luke. "So now I'm partnerless. But seeing as I had the afternoon off and haven't been since I left for New Zealand, I thought I'd stay and watch for a bit. Are you and the girls going out with Isla?"

"Yes, she's just pulling *The Maiden* in now," Grace said, playing with her sunhat nervously. Someone handed her the form to fill out.

"I'll be cheering for you girls out there," he said to Bayla, Mape and Isla as they came to join Grace and have their life jackets certified for safety.

"Thanks, Mr. Luke!" Mape and Bayla said together.

"We don't have Cohen cooking today, do we?" Isla said, turning around so Grace could use her back in lieu of a table to fill out the form.

"Better him than you," Luke teased, and Isla grinned.

"Who are you going out with, Mr. Luke?" Mape asked.

"I'm just here as a cheerleader," he said. "My date fell through."

"Why don't you come out with us?" Bayla said cheerfully. "Mom, can't he?"

Grace flushed but looked apologetically at Luke. "Sorry, we only have four life jackets, even though this one over here," she said, pointing her forehead toward Isla, "will throw hers off the second we get out of view—making a terrible impression on my daughter, by the way."

Isla chuckled sheepishly.

"But they're pretty strict about the boating rules," said Grace. She started signing the form but Isla suddenly moved away from her.

"Actually, Luke, you'd really be doing me a favor if you could take the girls out today instead of me," Isla said, so innocently it was hard to tell if she was being genuine.

"But Aunt Isla!" Bayla cried. "What about—"

Isla leaned down and whispered something into Bayla's ear, and then Bayla whispered it to Mape.

The girls lit up and started jumping up and down, turning to Grace. "Oh please, Mr. Luke, come with us? Please say yes!"

"Ms. Grace, please, please?!" Mape pleaded.

"Isla," Grace hissed desperately, but Isla remained looking completely innocent until Luke and the girls turned their heads, then she wiggled her eyebrows and gave her best friend a wicked grin.

"You devil!" said Grace.

But Isla only laughed. "I really do have something I need to... practice. Unless you really don't want Luke to join you," Isla said, dropping her voice to a whisper, "and if you really don't, just give me the sign. But maybe you really *do* want him to and you're just scared?"

Grace looked over at Luke. He was relaxed and chatting with the girls as they showed him their buoys, which were being checked in as well. She nodded at Isla almost imperceptibly and Isla's face lit up.

"It's settled then. Luke, you'll take my place today on *The Maiden*!"

"Well, isn't that just lucky then?" he said with a bright smile. "Here, hand me the buoys, girls," he said, helping them onto the boat. "There are some pretty good fishermen out there today, so we'll need some real luck, and I reckon these will be just the thing."

"We don't believe in luck though, Mr. Luke," Bayla said, as he started the engine. "We believe in magic."

As they pulled away from the shore, Grace watched Isla. She was looking out to the water, waving at them, but Grace knew her mind was elsewhere. She did truly seem like there was somewhere else she'd rather be, somewhere that Mape and Bayla seemed pretty thrilled about. So she decided to relax and enjoy the day, and let Isla do what she needed.

~

"Mape," Luke said, as they found a spot in the middle of the bay to turn off the motor, "you're probably the most seasoned of all of us crabbers. Any advice?"

Mape blushed at the compliment but shook her head. "We don't have a boat so I don't get to go out crabbing, I only take some chicken necks out on a string sometimes into the shallows and try to catch a couple that way."

"An excellent method, but with these crab pots we can catch a lot more, and drop them a bit deeper, with the same bait," he said.

He took the leftover chicken bones that Grace had brought from Cleary's and dropped them into the bait trap of each of the three vinyl covered pots. Bayla and Mape were to cut some rope to attach to the pots so they could lower them to the bottom and lift them back out.

"How long should the rope be?" Bayla asked.

"About as tall as you, standing on top of yourself three times," Luke said.

When Grace looked over, Mape was measuring Bayla with the rope and folding it three times. A few minutes later they had finished.

"Now what?" Bayla asked.

"Now," said Grace, "we tie one end to the crab trap, and on the other end we tie the buoy."

"Not that it wasn't fun to paint them," Mape said, "but why not just use a normal buoy?"

"Well, what fun would that be?" Grace answered with a wink, borrowing one of Isla's favorite phrases.

"It will probably take a while," Luke said as he and Grace pulled back up to the crab pots twenty minutes later. He turned off the engine and dropped the anchor.

"We only have an hour for the competition, which narrows the margins a bit," Grace said.

She glanced back at the beach they'd let Bayla and Mape play on, just twenty feet behind them, then relaxed and leaned back into the seat on the boat. She closed her eyes, feeling the sun on her face, and started to chuckle softly.

"What?" Luke asked.

She didn't open her eyes, but could hear the smile in his voice, could feel him looking at her.

"I was thinking about how funny it is that I haven't been crabbing since I was about eight years old," she said.

"What?!" he exclaimed. "How is that possible? *You?* You run a crab shack. Your best friend is a friggin' mermaid!" he finished.

"I know! Maybe it's because the water has always been so magical to me. The bioluminescence we shouldn't have in this part of the bay, the myths and legends... Isla. After I met her, I always wanted the water to stay a magical place," she said. "That probably sounds really stupid."

"No, it doesn't," said Luke. "It sounds like Maiden's Cove. It sounds like *you*. How *did* you end up landlocked in Phoenix for so long?"

"A lot of things happen that you don't see clearly until you're out of it. That's a scary thing," Grace said.

"I can imagine," Luke replied. "Grace, I don't want to be a scary thing for you. But I do want to be a thing for you, if you're willing. And I can go slow, so slow we don't even have to turn the motor back on today. But only if you say yes."

Grace sat back, looking at him, and her eye caught on his tattoo. She reached over and touched the intricate design, unlike anything she'd ever seen.

"What is it?" she asked.

"It's a Māori design. I had it done in New Zealand," he replied hoarsely.

She leaned forward and lifted the sleeve of his shirt until suddenly, she was face to face with him. "Sorry, I just always wanted to see how far up your tattoo went." Her mouth was dry, her lips so close to his she could feel his breath on his lips when he spoke next.

"I can show you," he said, leaning in to kiss her again, right as the "Mermaid Caller" buoy started bobbing up and down.

"Oh my god!" Grace cried. "Look, the crab line is going down, I think we caught something!"

"This quickly?" Luke grabbed the oar and paddled them over to the bobbing buoy. He lifted up the line as the same noise and movement started from the "Mermaid" buoy.

Grace squealed happily. "Come on, let's pull one up." She began to lift the closest crab pot, but it was so heavy Luke needed to help her. It was still a few feet under when they saw it. "Luke! It's full!" she cried.

"How did this happen?" he asked incredulously a few minutes later as they pulled the second full pot into the boat.

She started the engine to go pick up Bayla and Mape, and the last crab pot, with Isla's graffitied buoy. "Must be all that mermaid magic down there."

⌒

Ben glanced at his phone as his Siri timer went off. His business partner and colleague, Mike, looked as frazzled as Ben felt.

"Fifteen minutes without anyone walking in the door," Ben said. "I think we're in the clear."

The Crab Festival was always one of the busiest days of the year for Ben's shop, and this year had been especially bustling since Lance, one of Ben's summer hires from the mainland, suggested they offer guided kayak trips through the day to experience the festivities from the water. It had been a great success, but with Lance out all day with the guests, Ben and Mike had been extremely busy.

"Are you heading to any of the festivities later?" Mike asked.

Ben's lip quirked. "My niece called this morning and asked, if I got out early enough, if I could make it to the Mer-swimming competition. But it starts at four, so I'll probably just stop by later and check to see how she did."

"Nah, man, go watch. Little Bayla will be stoked to have you there," he said. "Lance will be back with the last group soon and we can close up here together."

"You sure?" Ben asked. "It will be a big job."

Mike raised one of his eyebrows and Ben knew that his partner saw right through him. Mike didn't know much about what had happened between him and Grace, but Ben realized this summer that the tension between them would be obvious to anyone. It ate at him with guilt, and yet still he couldn't bring himself to talk to her. But this couldn't continue. Not now. Bayla was suddenly in his life, and without even knowing how it happened, he was completely enamored with his niece and found himself wanting to mend things so that he and Grace and Bayla could have a normal family relationship. And then there was…

"Isla will be there, right?" Mike asked, as if reading his thoughts. Ben scowled and Mike chuckled. "Go, man."

"Thanks," Ben muttered.

He quickly changed out of his work uniform into a clean T-shirt and flip-flops and walked to the bay where they'd set up the Mer-swimming. There were a dozen or more sandy bays around the town peninsula alone. Ainsley Beach was closest to town and a great swimming beach in the summer, but it was used as the base for the boats in the crabbing competition, so the town council set up the Mer-swimming for the younger kids at a smaller beach on the east side of the peninsula, just near the Cove.

It was crowded, but mostly with parents there to watch their kids, so it was easy enough to spot Grace in her floral dress and floppy hat. It gave Ben a sense of relief seeing her dressed the way she did when she was younger, to see the way her shoulders were relaxed, unlike the last time she'd come home to visit. Ben cringed inside with shame and guilt thinking back on his behavior then.

Grace had been so young, only in her early twenties, and Bayla was two. They'd been living in Phoenix for two years and the family was losing touch with her. Their dad had been trying to get Grace and Richard to bring Bayla home for a visit for years, and finally sent plane tickets to the three of them.

When Grace showed up with just Bayla, Ben had been filled with relief. He'd never liked Richard, and he had an instinct that Grace was being hurt by her husband. As soon as he saw her, he knew it was true. There were no bruises, no. And she and Bayla seemed happy enough. But she was *different*. Cautious. She dressed differently too. Neat and tidy and conservative, completely unlike his sister a few years before.

And his suspicion was confirmed the next morning when Richard knocked on their door and he saw the look on Grace's face—she was afraid of him.

"You shouldn't go back with him, Grace," he'd said to her the next day.

She was packing after they'd had breakfast that morning and Richard had announced they were all going home that day. Ben had stood in the doorway to her room, practically blocking her way out.

"He's my husband and Bayla's father. And I love him," she'd said.

"You need to leave him, and you and Bayla need to stay here," he'd said forcefully. "If you go back there with him today you can consider yourself out of this family."

Her eyes filled with tears of hurt, betrayal, and something else he didn't recognize at the time but knew later was desperation.

"Get out," she'd said.

"Grace…"

"Get out!" she'd yelled. "I am going home with my family."

"You *are* home with your family," Ben had growled.

"Apparently I'm not," she'd said, slamming the top of the suitcase.

That had been the last time Grace came home to Maiden's Cove, and the last time they spoke to one another until their father passed away. It was time, he knew, to mend their relationship.

Ben drew closer to where Grace was sitting at Ainsley Beach and touched her shoulder from behind, noticing the way she jumped and put her hand to her heart as she turned, noticing the way her eyes filled with relief to see him. Not only relief, but happiness. He smiled, genuinely, and after a moment of surprise she smiled back, and they both turned to the beach.

"Let me guess," he said, "Bayla's the one in the rhinestone bikini?"

"Actually that's Mape. There's Bayla," Grace said, pointing. "The one in the green and blue swimming dress."

He laughed. Bayla's swimming dress looked like a mermaid costume of sorts, with frills on the shoulders and a skirt over the bottom. She was jumping around, shielding her eyes from the sun like she was looking for someone.

"Who's she looking for?" Ben asked.

Grace shrugged. "Isla, probably."

Ben flushed. "I thought you were going out on *The Maiden* with her today?"

He noticed Grace flush now. "She said she had something else to do and the girls seemed quite enthusiastic she do it, so Luke took us out instead." He felt her glance at him. "Is that okay?"

Ben didn't know why he was surprised. Not that Luke and Grace were connecting, but that she was open to it, and that she was asking him. He took his sister's shoulders and turned her to him.

"Of course it's okay," he said. "Grace, I—I'm sorry." It felt so good to say the words, he said them again. "I'm so sorry. I felt helpless and worried and angry and I didn't know how to help you, so I pushed you away instead. And then I never came after you. I never came after you and I'm sorry I let you down," he choked.

Her mouth opened in surprise, but she closed it and pressed her lips together as her eyes filled with tears. "I was so ashamed," she said. "I was so ashamed of the way I didn't listen to you. By the time I knew, I felt it was too late."

"We're family, Grace," he said. "It's never too late." He pulled her in for a strong hug and they both choked back their tears.

A horn sounded loudly from the beach and the crowd hushed. Ben and Grace laughed and sniffed as they withdrew from their hug and turned to the beach to watch, but Ben noticed they were both instantly more relaxed, both lighter. Both happier.

Ben and Grace caught Bayla's eye and waved, and she lit up and waved back at them, jumping and mouthing something, pointing up to the Cove.

"Good afternoon, ladies and gentlemen," a voice sounded from a megaphone at the water's edge. "And welcome to the Mer-swimming competition! As usual, all our lovely little Mer-children will be judged on both their Mer-swimming technique and on their ability to hold their breath. I'd like to thank our judges who will be kayaking alongside the swimmers for safety—Katie and Izzy." The crowd clapped. "This year, we also have a special guest judge—please give a warm welcome to our own Maiden's Cove mermaid, Isla Dupont!"

Ben and Grace both gasped as everyone pointed up to the highest point of the cliff, to where Isla stood in her green bikini. Even in the distance, Ben could see that she was stiff and uncomfortable. Which would be normal if she was standing in front of a crowd, but not normal for where she was most confident.

"Oh my god," Grace whispered, "I can't believe she's doing this."

"Is she okay?" Ben asked, but Grace had clamped her hands over her mouth like she was holding her breath.

"She's doing this for Bayla," she said in a muffled voice.

"She looks—"

"She's terrified," Grace said, dropping her hands from her face and clutching them to her chest.

And Ben finally saw what he'd not seen since Isla had been back: fear, vulnerability. He didn't know why but he could feel Isla even from here—could hear her heart, her breath, like his own was hitched too.

Isla, I'm here. I believe in you.

Ben didn't know why he thought that, but he did, and despite the distance he could see her turn her head to the beach, and her body relaxed as if, impossibly, she'd heard him.

And then she dived off the cliff.

~

"I can't believe Fiona Murchison won the Mer-swimming," Bayla said that night. They were making s'mores over the grill Jimbo had left at Grace's cookout.

Grace, Ben and Isla chuckled. It was just the four of them tonight, which felt right, somehow.

"Well, you and Mape did win first prize for your decorative buoy designs," Grace said. "And we did come in runner-up in the crabbing contest."

"I know," Bayla said with a pout. "I'm not complaining."

"Ya win some, ya lose some, kiddo," Isla said, pulling Bayla onto her lap for a quick hug. "I'd better turn in. Been a long time since I've done a swim like that."

"You were so cool, Aunt Isla," Bayla said, and yawned. "When I saw you underwater making faces at us I almost laughed water into my little lung." They all laughed, Grace and Ben remembering the way Isla did that with them as children. "How long were you under?"

"Three minutes and two seconds," Ben said, starting to extinguish the fire. "Not your best."

Isla pretended to scowl but it was more a smile.

Grace noticed the moment between them and faked a yawn. "Wow, I'm tired too. Bayla, why don't we go brush our teeth and fall asleep watching *The Little Mermaid*?"

Bayla jumped up. "I can sleep with you?"

"Like a slumber party," Grace said with a smile. "I'll put on popcorn."

Bayla raced to the house and then turned at the last minute. "Will you be in our slumber party, Aunt Isla?"

But Grace nudged her inside. "We'll see, kiddo."

Isla started to clean up, taking the plates and glasses to the kitchen, and coming back out to pick up the unused marshmallows, graham crackers and chocolate. The fire was extinguished, so Ben picked up the chairs and followed Isla to the house. Suddenly he and Isla found themselves standing on the porch, in the doorway to the kitchen, close but not too close. That was dangerous, Ben knew.

"I'll be going then," he said, grazing his hand down her arm. "Isla..."

But he didn't finish. He didn't know how.

Isla waited a long moment and then leaned in and kissed his cheek, whispering into his ear, "Thank you."

"For what?" he asked.

"Believing in me."

Chapter Ten

Summer 2005

Isla looked across the boat to Ben, who was laying back against the seat, arms crossed behind his head, hat pulled down slightly over his eyes, which were closed. He looked relaxed, languid, as if he were enjoying the lulling rock of the boat the same way Isla did. She took the moment to study him closely, something she wasn't able to do normally, what with them living in the same house all summer and being friends, *and* him being the older brother of her best friend.

She'd known him for four years now. At fourteen he'd been a skinny boy, that gangly look boys sometimes get at that age when they shoot up overnight and the rest of them takes a few years to catch up. Isla was thinking that Ben had done a very nice job indeed of catching up, now that he was seventeen. He shared Grace's dark glossy hair that waved when it got longer, which it always was in the summer, but his eyes were a darker blue than Grace's, and he had thicker and prettier lashes than hers.

Isla flushed at the thought, feeling guilty. What would Grace think if she knew that Isla was having these feelings for her brother?

She probably wouldn't even notice, Isla thought now. Bitterly for a moment, and then sadly. She was losing her best friend. She could feel it and it broke her heart. She didn't know what she'd do. Coming back to Maiden's Cove every summer to Grace was coming home.

"Gonna scare all the crabs away making that face," Ben said, and when she turned his eyes were open. He smiled at her. Ben almost always smiled with his lips closed, and it made his eyes crinkle in the best way. She loved that smile. "Shall we have a look?" he asked.

Isla nodded, so Ben pulled one of their buoys closer and began to lift the rope on the crab pot up. Isla swallowed as she watched the veins in his forearms bulge, muscles flexed from the weight. He was still slim, but sinewy and muscular now.

She cleared her throat. "Anything?" she asked when they could see the pot.

"Nope, still chicken wings," he said, and let it back down to the bottom. "So what was the face for anyway?"

She shrugged. "Just thinking about all the places I'm going to go when I'm old enough to go on my own," she said with false cheer. It wasn't what she was thinking about, but she thought about it enough that it was at least a lie she could talk about. "Grace and I are going to go to the Caribbean when she graduates high school. I can take my GED when I'm sixteen," she said. She'd tried school before but much preferred being on the sea with Henry, traveling with the seasons, so he let her study on her own.

"You know Grace will never go with you," he said, not unkindly.

"She said she will, and she's my best friend," Isla said quietly. But she knew he was probably right.

"I, on the other hand," he said with a rare toothy grin, "am applying for my passport the second I turn eighteen. And then I'm outta here."

"Where do you want to go?" she asked, leaning forward.

"I was thinking Southeast Asia. Have you been?" he asked. She shook her head. "Oh man," he said, suddenly animated. "So you know the shop at the port, the one where you can rent the kayaks and do water sports and stuff? I was there the other day waiting for an interview for a job, and there was this magazine, *Lonely Planet*, the travel guides, you know?"

She nodded enthusiastically. Whenever they went to the library she hoarded *Lonely Planet* books.

"So I'm flipping through and there are these amazing pictures of underwater dives and beaches in the Philippines, so I thought maybe I'd start there. Look," he said, pulling out his flip phone and showing her a photo he'd taken of the magazine page.

It wasn't a great image but even she felt moved by the crystal clear waters, the colors of the fish in the water, the white powder of the beach. "Wow," she breathed.

"Yeah," he agreed, and she realized that they were so close she could smell his spearmint gum. "Over seven thousand islands, can you believe that?" he said, snapping his phone closed and leaning back into his seat across the boat. "Wonder if we're getting any crabs yet?"

Isla was so flushed, so confused, so excited, she had to cool off. She quickly threw off her top and dived into the water, hearing Ben's "Whoa!" behind her as she rocked the boat.

Under the water things all made sense. The way the noise of the world silenced, the way she was just there, herself, nothing around her but the water, which she was both invited into and yet somehow a part of. She swam down to the bottom to the pots, which were still empty, so she found a few crabs and ushered them into the pots herself. Once her heart was back to a normal rhythm, the dive relaxing her, she looked up and saw the underside of the boat, the sun glaring beside it, and the moving silhouette of Ben leaning over and looking down for her. She knew he couldn't see her. The Chesapeake was brackish and often brown or dark in places, unlike those pictures of the Philippines. Or the Caribbean.

She was about to run out of breath but stayed staring at his silhouette another few seconds wondering... would Ben, perhaps, one day come with her?

"Grace? Grace, are you awake?"

"I am now." Grace yawned, rolling over to look at Isla, who was sitting up on her side of the bed on her knees. "What's wrong?"

"Let's go for a swim," she whispered, a hint of desperation in her voice.

"Now?" Grace yawned again but got out of bed and followed Isla quietly down the stairs and out the back door. They'd traversed this little path down to the beach hundreds of times over the last four years. Grace wasn't surprised that Isla wanted to get out and swim, they often did this in the middle of the night. But there was something different about her tonight. Something restless and desperate.

When they arrived at the beach, Isla promptly dropped Grace's hand, took off her oversized T-shirt and underwear and dived naked into the bay. Grace left her underwear on but followed, walking in until she could just barely touch the bottom, and started treading water. Isla hadn't surfaced yet. Suddenly, but not surprisingly, something yanked Grace's foot and dragged her to the bottom of the bay. She held her breath until she couldn't anymore, and then felt Isla's hand pinch her nose and breathe into her mouth, filling her lungs with air. Isla had taught her this game the first summer they met, and Grace was fascinated with how long they could stay under together, laughing and playing, only occasionally coming up for air. It had been a couple years since they had done this, and it confused Grace. She put her feet on the bottom and kicked her way to the surface, Isla surfacing shortly after, laughing.

"Why is the water always warmer naked?" Isla laughed, floating on her back.

Grace flipped onto her back too. "Because it knows you belong to it," she answered automatically.

Isla was quiet for a moment. "Remember what we used to say? One from the land and one from the sea..."

"Summer soul sisters forever shall we be," Grace finished, smiling.

"We're still going to leave together when we're eighteen, right? End of the summer, me and you?" Isla asked.

"Yes," Grace said, after the slightest hesitation. They'd always said that and they always meant that. Gracenisla together forever.

"You hesitated," Isla said.

"I did not," Grace quickly answered. But she had hesitated. She was fifteen. Isla was only here for the summer, and Grace was no longer the simpering shy girl she used to be, who needed her best friend and nobody else. She did need Isla—but Grace also wanted to have real friends, not just summer ones. And she wanted the boys to see her, really see her. Luke McCann especially. Isla didn't really seem to understand that part.

Grace wondered again if it wasn't that Isla didn't want to meet any boys, but that she only wanted to be around one. There were times when Grace would feel jealous of Ben, or when she'd feel exhausted by Isla, who wanted to never grow up. She'd wonder, for just a moment, what life would be like without Isla.

But then she'd feel sick. Not guilty sick, but physically sick at the idea of not having Isla in her life. Isla was like the twin part of her soul. Grace didn't actually think she could breathe without knowing Isla was there.

Isla's hand reached out and grabbed hers as they floated on their backs, as if she heard every one of Grace's thoughts.

"I'm confused too," Isla said softly. "It's different for you because you live here, and you have a life here in between the time I leave and the time I come back. But I don't really come alive until I get back here each summer. So when things change—you, Ben, Cleary's—I feel a little lost trying to keep up. I look down and know I'm different too. And I feel different. I start questioning things I never have before."

"Like what?" Grace asked.

"Like where I come from. Like where I belong. Who am I, really? And what do I want? Who do I want to be and grow into? Am I pretty? Am I ugly? Will anyone ever look at me like I'm a woman, in that way?"

Grace had never heard Isla speak like this before. She had to ask. "Isla? Are you in love with Ben?"

"No!" she shouted, swimming away, her feet kicking so hard she was creating a whirlpool and Grace had to turn and paddle to keep her head above the waves.

"Do you think maybe Henry can help you to find your family and where you came from?" she called out, trying to change the subject.

Isla didn't answer for a long time, but the splashing stopped. "Maybe. I'd never want to hurt the old guy's feelings, you know?"

"Maybe when we turn eighteen, we can go look for your family. Together."

Isla swam over and grabbed Grace, hugging her tight. "I love you," she said.

Grace felt whole and complete again and hugged her back. "I love you too. Together forever?"

"Till death knocks us out." Isla nodded, and they swam to the shore. "Grace?"

"Yeah?"

"I kind of maybe might be a little bit in love with Ben."

Grace laughed and soon so did Isla, and as the girls swam to shore, the whole beach lit up beneath them.

Chapter Eleven

This summer reminds me of when we were twelve," Isla said one evening.

"You mean those 'hot summer days and hotter summer nights'?" Grace quoted one of their old mantras as she grabbed a bottle of rosé from the fridge.

"And the fact that I live at your house," Isla said.

"Still haven't been back to Henry's?" Grace asked.

Isla shook her head. "Only to pick up the boat and drop it back off. I haven't been inside. But soon. I can feel it's time." It was eight in the evening and the sun was still high in the sky. "I can't believe it's already past solstice and the longest day of the year. It feels like the sun will go on forever this year." She paused to consider Grace. "You seem good. More relaxed."

Grace sat. "I am. Now that I'm back here in Maiden's Cove and now that you're here. The broken world I lived in with Richard just seems further and further away. I was terrified for a while, based on his silence, that he was going to show up and do something crazy. But now it just seems like...I don't know. Like he can't touch us here or something."

"Maybe he can't," Isla said, taking the rosé and pouring a glass for them both. "Maybe this place is for you like it is for me. Home has its own sort of protection that nothing else does." She sipped the wine. "Mmm. One of Cohen's is it?"

"This one he imported himself from France. He bought an entire case for the Fourth of July."

"Wow, the Fourth already. I feel like I just got here and its already time to leave."

"Why do you have to leave? You just got home. We're building a life, a real one, with family and friends. You can't leave now." Grace knew she sounded like a child.

"Let's not talk about it tonight," Isla said. "I promise I'll stay through the summer. Let's talk about the Fourth. What are we doing?"

Grace bit her lower lip but let it drop. "Bayla has had it all in her short time here. All the magic and myth and legend, all the stuff that makes Maiden's Cove what it is. I want her to run around with sparklers, and get bitten by mosquitos, and swim and get sunburnt and go 'Oooh' and 'Aaaah.'"

"Sounds like a Sandy Bay kind of moment," Isla said, smiling.

"I was thinking that too," Grace said. "We could invite everyone, all our friends, I mean."

"All our friends like your totally hot new boyfriend who was your great childhood crush Luke *McCaaaannnn*," she said, making kissy faces.

"Oh stop," Grace said, blushing and laughing. "Luke is amazing but—"

"But what?" Isla asked.

She sighed. "I don't know. I thought I had it once, you know, when I married Richard. I don't know if people get a second chance when they mess it up so badly."

Isla leaned in and pulled Grace to her. "Oh, honey, there isn't a number on how many chances we have. We get as many as we're willing to give. And I think in some ways that's what this whole summer is, for all of us, Grace. A summer of second chances."

Grace smiled. "Who's the romantic now?"

"This summer, it just might be me," Isla said.

There were many fireworks displays around Maiden's Cove, but the greatest was over the water outside of Saint Michaels, the main tourist town on the Bay. Thousands of people drove to Saint Michaels, but the locals knew a secret spot, a beach they named Sandy Bay, aptly, for it was a bay, and it was, in fact, sandy—warm golden sand, almost like the Atlantic beaches thirty minutes away.

Only the fishermen and Maiden's Cove residents knew where it was because Sandy Bay was tidal and had a sandbar nearby that often caught even the locals unawares. Myth said the mermaids used the sandbar to lure fishermen, who thought that they'd come to a beach. But now, no one talked about the sandbar, almost as if it didn't exist—the locals still came every year on the Fourth of July to Sandy Bay, though.

The unlikely group of friends met at Cleary's at 4 p.m. as they closed for the day.

Della had spent the morning making shrimp salad with Jimbo's hefty catch. When she got shrimp that good, they were steamed with the tail on and cooled, and the tails were picked off later. She cut green onion and celery and chopped the cold shrimp into it in large chunks. It was then seasoned with heaps of Old Bay, salt and pepper, celery and garlic powder, fresh parsley and lemon juice.

Georgiana had made fluffy brioche rolls and now she packed them into ziplock bags as Della ice-packed her shrimp salad. Grace and Isla locked up the restaurant and made their way to the parking lot, where Jimbo had just pulled up with his grandkids, Leon and Rachel, in the back of the pickup truck.

Bayla and Mape, who went to school with them, jumped into the bed of the truck and started chatting away.

"We aren't all going to fit into that truck, even if we squeeze in the back. Which," Cohen pointed out, "is completely illegal I might add."

Grace laughed. "Don't worry, I'd never put my kid in the back of a pickup truck if it was going on a real road. It's only beaches and back roads."

"This is a Maiden's Cove tradition, Cohen. Don't be scared," Georgiana said. "But don't worry, you can take my seat in the front with Jimbo and Della and the rest of us will go with Luke. He's here now."

Grace's heart fluttered as she saw Luke's blue 1984 Chevrolet Silverado pull up. He joked that it made him look a little "back country," but it was his grandpa's and he loved it too much to get rid of it. Grace thought it only made him look more attractive.

She felt Isla's finger on her cheek, and she turned.

"Sorry, had to get that drool off your face."

"I'm not drooling!" Grace hissed, blushing and wiping her cheek self-consciously, but Isla only laughed before greeting Luke with a smile and a wave.

"Hi, Luke!" Bayla yelled.

"Hey, kiddo." He waved then turned to the others, opening the back of his truck. "I seem to be carrying the catering but there should still be plenty of room. How many are coming with me? I'll clear some space in the back."

"Good lord, what did you bring, Luke?" Georgiana asked as she saw the piles of boxes he was moving. "We've only got Della and Jimbo's shrimp salad, rolls and a few snacks."

"I brought my famous deviled eggs," a voice called from the front seat.

"Aunt Lou?" Isla said, surprised, and Lou poked her head out. "I didn't know you were coming!"

"That's because you didn't ask me," she snapped.

"Isla!" Grace admonished. "You promised you'd call Aunt Lou."

"I did!" Isla turned to Aunt Lou. "I called you about ten times and left heaps of messages. I even came to your house but you weren't there."

"Was that you? I was wondering who broke in."

"I was checking to see that you weren't rotting away somewhere."

"Fair enough. Grace should have been more clear that I never check my phone, only my Facebook. Thankfully, Luke here, good boy that he is, sent me a GIF about an hour ago with fireworks and we got it all straightened out in time."

"How'd you have time to make your deviled eggs in an hour?" Georgiana asked, perplexed.

"Psh, I was lying. I've never cooked a day in my life and don't plan to now, seeing as I'm so old I don't even know how old I am. I saw my neighbor taking them to a barbecue and bribed her to give them to me instead."

"What did you bribe her with?" Cohen asked.

"Keeping her secrets," Aunt Lou cackled, sitting back in the front seat. "Come on, I'm not getting any younger."

Luke held his hand out to Isla first, lifting her onto the back, and then Grace. She felt herself go clammy as he lifted her up, catching his hand on her lower back for a moment. "You girls going to be okay back here?"

"Of course," Grace said. "Bayla, you girls gonna be okay over there in the back?" she called.

"We're all good, Gracey," Jimbo said, starting the engine. "I got room for one more in the front here if anyone wants to hop in."

"Yes please!" Cohen said, running to the front as Della slid to the middle seat.

"Such a gentleman." Georgiana laughed, rolling her eyes.

"Careful with the boxes back there, Grace," said Luke. "If any of the bottles in Cohen's case breaks, he has threatened murder. And the one on top is Aunt Lou's stolen eggs. Definitely do *not* want to be covered in them all night." He called across to the other truck. "Georgiana, there's room up front with me and Lou if you don't want to sit in the back."

"You don't mind, do you, Grace, Isla?" she said. "This curly head of mine will be an absolute nest when we get there."

Isla raised her eyebrows and pointed at her own curly hair. It was frizzing up tremendously already.

Georgiana shrugged. "It suits you. But I'm never gonna find a man in this town with this crazy Einstein look."

"Go for it. Lord knows there's nobody—" Isla trailed off, staring out behind them.

Georgiana, Luke and Grace turned to see what she was staring at. Ben was standing back a bit, holding a small cooler.

"Room for one more?" he asked sheepishly.

Grace nodded. Luke stepped forward and embraced Ben heartily and they spoke for a few moments. Best friends nearly their entire lives, they hadn't really had the chance to connect since Luke had been back.

"I'll hop in the back," Ben said, as he climbed in and sat next to Grace. He and Isla looked at each other, and Grace relaxed as he watched them both smile shyly.

"I'll follow you, Jimbo," Luke said, starting up the truck. Jimbo honked the horn and the trucks slowly left the parking lot.

～

There were well over a dozen vehicles parked at Sandy Bay that Fourth of July. Some had barbecues and coolers set up in the beds of their pickup trucks. Blankets were spread out on the beach and, closer to the tree line, there were tents pitched. Some of the teenagers, traditionally, would make a bonfire after the fireworks and stay the night.

Luke followed Jimbo to the shadier side of the beach and they backed their trucks up to the edge of the sand. The girls spread a few large blankets on the beach with the coolers and beach chairs along the edge in case the breeze picked up, but the evening was balmy so far. Isla and Grace went swimming with Bayla, Mape and Georgiana. Luke and Ben played frisbee with young Leon, and Rachel ran to join in. Jimbo and Della went for a walk down the beach, hand in hand, while Cohen and Aunt Lou sat in chairs watching the goings on, drinking the French rosé he'd imported.

"This is pretty good," she said. "And I know my wine. I can get through a box of Franzia on a hot weekend by myself."

Cohen nearly spit out his wine, but Aunt Lou was chuckling. "Just joking, not done that since I was a little girl and used to steal it from my parents. I do at least try to find some nice wines to indulge in these days. Though to be fair, I've always been more of a vodka girl."

"I know, that's why I brought you a bottle," he said, pulling out the Grey Goose from his wine box and handing it to her. "Luke made fresh watermelon juice and I told him to double it up for your vodkas."

Lou nodded appreciatively, fighting the urge to throw the wine over her shoulder and pour herself a real drink. "That's why I like you, Cohen. There are probably other reasons but I can't remember them right now. That is why I've decided to help you."

"Help me?"

"Yes, I've hired your future husband to work for me."

Cohen could barely form words. "Tallulah Cleary, what on earth are you talking about?"

"His name is Tristan, how sexy is that? Tristans are always so sexy. Don't you remember Brad Pitt in *Legends of the Fall*?" she asked. Cohen nodded emphatically. "So I just knew this Tristan would be a dish. And he *is*," she said, downing the wine and quickly filling her glass with vodka. "Pass me some ice and that watermelon juice, darl, I'm empty."

Cohen did as he was told. "You are going to have to give me a bit more info than that, Lou."

"Tristan. He's my new male nurse."

"Why do you need a nurse?"

"I don't. But you need a man," she said, exasperated. "Last time I went to see my doctor in Annapolis, there was this gorgeous gay man working there as a nurse and when he told me his name was Tristan, I simply had to get to know him. So, I told him where I lived, and he said he'd always wanted to live in Maiden's Cove, and I said, well, then you will. So, I hired him."

"That's charming, Lou, but don't you think he'll wonder *why* you hired him?"

"He didn't seem to care, why do you? He moves in next week. You're coming around for a welcome dinner on Wednesday, so make sure you're free at six that evening, please."

Cohen shook his head at her audacity. He had given up on finding a man around Maiden's Cove, but had always hoped that perhaps a tourist would come by. But it was *his* dream to grow old in a cottage in this small town, not some Tristan's. And who was Lou to think that just because she met another gay man that he was right for Cohen?

"Lou, you do know I adore you, but no. I've been set up before and it's usually a disaster. What do you know of gay men anyway?"

"Heaps, darl, my husband was as gay as they came," she said.

Cohen nearly spilled his wine. "What?"

She laughed, sipping on her drink and sighing. "Oh yes, Paul was very gay. We married when I was but a child, just out of school—seventeen. Paul and I were family friends. He was sweet. A bit of work, very artistic, dreamy. I knew within the first year of our marriage where his...ah...attraction lay. But that was okay. In those days, it was very oppressive for women, you know. I was so wild and charismatic. I wanted to do so many things with my life, and Paul supported me. Our marriage gave me the freedom to do what I wanted. And my friendship gave him the freedom to do what he wanted. It was wonderful.

It was the fifties, of course. I'd like to think our world is a little more advanced now."

"Sometimes I doubt that," Cohen muttered, thinking of his own family.

"I know," she said, patting his knee. "That's why in a town like this, sometimes you need a little bit of help. Come to my dinner. Tristan will be so lonely here without new friends. Especially considering I've got no need for a nurse, which he doesn't know yet."

Cohen tried to quench the little butterflies of anticipation at the idea of meeting a man, going on a date. "What makes you think I'll even like him? Just because I'm gay and he's gay?"

"Sure, why not?" Aunt Lou rolled her eyes. "I used to hire companions for Paul, you idiot. I'm practically a dating app for gay men."

Cohen laughed but did not look convinced.

"I asked him to send me his resume. In his hobbies and passions, he lists wine, food and travel. He makes a good living, he's kind, gentle. He's gorgeous too. Looks like a Tristan—wavy gold hair and blue eyes."

"I'm listening," Cohen said, leaning forward.

"I'll find a photo, hang on," she said, putting her glasses on and scrolling through her phone. "I Facebook-stalked him, obviously."

"Obviously," Cohen said dryly. This really was too much, but he was excited nonetheless.

"Oh, here it is," she said, handing him her phone.

Tristan *was* very attractive. Cohen scrolled through a few photos.

"But never mind any of that," Aunt Lou said, taking her phone back. "I happened to walk in on him, quite by accident, mind you, while he was using the bathroom. He was very well-endowed. *Very.*"

Cohen topped up his wine. "Fine, I'll be there."

Lou nodded, pocketing her phone, smiling. "Good."

~

The fireworks were scheduled for just after 9 p.m. The girls had strewn their wet swimsuits over the side of Jimbo's truck and changed into their dry clothes. It was hot and humid but the mosquitos were terrible this year, so a full spray down of repellent was followed by light pants with socks and sneakers, and linen button-downs. Only Isla wore what she always did—a bikini, shorts and T-shirt—as she never got bitten like the others.

"Why don't you get bit by the mosquitos, Aunt Isla?" Mape asked.

"Because I'm cold-blooded," she said with a wink, taking a huge bite of her shrimp salad sandwich.

They had quite a feast. Aunt Lou and Isla drank vodka and watermelon while Cohen, Georgiana and Grace drank the wine.

The boys and Della had beers, and they all nibbled on fresh kettle chips and handmade dip, and the delicious, stolen deviled eggs. They ate shrimp salad sandwiches with macaroni salad on the side. Luke brought his little camping grill and cooked Maryland-famous Old Bay chicken wings with Ben. Dessert was a feta and watermelon salad. They ate until they couldn't eat any more and settled into their camp as the sun was setting.

"Mom, can we *please* go run up and down the beach with the sparklers now?"

"Yes, go for goodness' sake! But hold them away from your faces, and remember they burn out quite quickly. You might want to save some for when it's completely dark."

But Bayla and Mape were already gone.

"There she goes!" Georgiana laughed. "This is her first time at Sandy Bay?" she asked, and Grace nodded. "I remember my first time coming here with Monica Farthing when I was eleven years old." When no one spoke, Georgiana snickered. "Yes, yes, I was a Feather in middle school and coming here was quite the thing, you know."

"It is so hard for me to think of you as a horr— As a, uh, Feather, Georgiana," Luke said. He looked at Grace and Isla and they smiled at him. He and Ben had always been their champions in middle school and hated the Feathers that bullied them. Luke and Ben fought the entire year when Ben decided to date Monica Farthing after they'd graduated high school.

"Oh, I know, we were horrible in middle school. Like *Mean Girls* come to life. But what you have to understand about me is that I moved here when all these kids that had grown up together were starting middle school. I wanted a friend so, so badly. I'd been terribly bullied in my last school, you see. And Monica chose me to be her friend. I know it was all very childish and petty, and I'm not proud of some of the things I did, but I was so very lonely and then, suddenly, I wasn't. It was very addictive."

Nobody said anything but Grace looked at her best friend. This was the same way Grace herself had felt before she'd met Isla, like the loneliness was so great she thought she'd die of longing for a friend. Grace smiled encouragingly at Georgiana now, who continued.

"What about you, Luke?" she said. "You were so popular! And Ben, Isla and Grace, I definitely remember seeing you all here one year. When was that?"

The four of them mumbled and muttered inaudibly when Della spoke instead.

"Me and Jimbo come here every year for our anniversary and bring our family on Fourth of July," Della said, her strong voice breaking the awkwardness. "What about you Tallulah? You must've come here before?"

"I brought almost all my lovers here, thank you very much," Aunt Lou said, and they all laughed.

"Mom!" Bayla and the other kids ran over. "Look, we can write our whole names with the sparklers before they die down!"

"Super cool!"

Georgiana called out, "Oh look, the fireworks are starting!"

The "oohs" and "aahs" were raucous and filled with giggles. But as the display went on, the cheers lessened and became real, substantial, impressed. For there was something about lying on a beach, surrounded by the people you love, watching a spectacular display—something so much bigger than you that reminds you how small you really are. How insignificant. The way the sounds start to fill you up, the light starts to blind you, inspire you, make you ache with longing for life. The way it eventually goes quiet, as the lights grow bigger. The way you reach over and take the hand of the person next to you and feel their pulse as the world pulses through you.

Grace used to imagine that if there were aliens in space looking down at a beach like Sandy Bay, on the Fourth of July, they would see bioluminescence too. She'd imagined that those lights were us, our souls. That the pulsing, throbbing magic in this world that is beyond our ability to comprehend is our own energy, reverberating out when we find a love so powerful that our hearts beat together as one. The love of a best friend, of a daughter, a partner, a parent. When the loneliness of the existence we have is shared by the loneliness of the existence of the one standing next to us. And we are one, and we are alive, and we are part of something so much bigger than ourselves, this generating, living, breathing bioluminescence that is us.

Grace could feel it underneath her, in the sand where they all lay, when the silence overtook the noise. She could feel it when Aunt Lou started snoring and Cohen put a blanket over her. When Georgiana smiled at his kindness and grabbed his hand, when Mape rolled into Georgiana, when Bayla grabbed Mape's hand then reached over to Jimbo, Della, their grandkids. And when Luke's fingertips found hers, it was like magic exploded within her. Grace felt so filled with it she reached over to take Isla's hand, but she was gone.

Grace sat up, breaking the chain. She saw Ben standing on the beach staring out into the water, the last of the fireworks overhead, the lights on the sand dancing at his feet. Grace could see the slump of his shoulders as he looked out to the bay, but Isla had already left.

Chapter Twelve

Summer 2006

June passed in a haze. Isla and Grace worked at Cleary's most days and they still swam at night on occasion, but they both knew that things weren't the same between them. Until the morning of the Fourth of July.

Isla sat at the kitchen table in her oversized T-shirt, one leg propped up on the chair as she picked at some fruit, not eating anything else. It suddenly occurred to Grace that Isla didn't look very well. She'd lost weight and her perpetual tan, and there were circles under her eyes that Grace had never noticed before.

"Earth to Isla," she said, waving her hand in front of Isla's face.

"Sorry," Isla muttered. "What did you say?"

"I said we have to make sure we pack everything for the night at Sandy Bay to bring with us to work. We get off at four and Richard and Matt are going to pick us up. We need sleeping bags and a tent, and lots of bug spray and stuff. The guys are bringing beer, and Monica and her friends will come with their families and set up proper barbecues."

"What are you girls whispering about?" Ben asked.

"Fourth of July," Grace said haughtily. "Not that you would know anything about it."

"You mean Sandy Bay?" he said with a laugh, opening the door to leave. "Duh, of course we'll be there. I mean, everyone goes, right?"

"Riiiight," Grace said as the door slammed behind him. She turned to Isla, who looked like she might cry. "Since when has Ben gone to Sandy Bay? Or, like, ever wanted to hang out with anyone that I do, like, ever?"

Isla swallowed and her chin quivered. "Since he started dating Monica Farthing."

"What?!" Grace gasped, but as Isla began to cry she came to sit beside her, pulling Isla's head onto her shoulder. "Oh Isla, I didn't know. I'm so sorry, I didn't know," she said soothingly.

"My heart hurts, like I can't breathe," Isla sobbed.

"I know, honey, I know. Shhh." Grace rocked her best friend until her sobs subsided and then gave her a tissue to blow her nose. "Come on, let's have a swim."

"Okay," she said, and they walked down to the beach in their bikinis and waded in. As Grace expected, as soon as Isla hit the water she dived deep, and Grace floated on her back waiting, expecting it to be a while. But moments later Isla came up.

"Are you okay?" Grace asked.

"My nose is all stuffy," she said.

"And here I thought you had gills," Grace teased. Isla's face relaxed into a smile, and she floated onto her back too. "You know, today is the first time I've ever seen you cry."

"What? No it isn't!"

"First time I've seen actual tears. You've always been so...I don't know. I think I forget sometimes that you are a real girl, and not..."

"A mermaid?"

"Not untouchable, I guess I mean," Grace finished.

Isla sniffed. "Maybe I am untouchable, and that's why...I mean, Monica Farthing? Look, I know she's your friend, but she's just awful! Ben hated her. And yet even *she* is preferable to me."

And Isla dived again, this time not coming back up for a solid three minutes. Grace was still floating on her back, smiling.

"What are you smiling about?" Isla asked when she finally surfaced.

Grace turned her head and grinned. "Come on, let's swim back. I have an idea."

"What do you think?" Grace asked, looking at Isla's reflection in the mirror of her dressing table.

"I look weird," Isla said, examining herself more closely.

Grace had used her new hair straightener to flatten Isla's frizzy curls, and without the curl, her red hair came down nearly to her waist.

"The hair was a pretty big change so I didn't want to do too much all at once. You have the most amazing lips, like Julia Roberts. So I used one of Loretta's fancy-brand lip glosses and a little mascara. All this time, I never realized how thick your eyelashes are because they're so blonde!" Grace laughed, then hesitated, catching Isla's confused expression. "We can take it off if you want," she said softly. "You were always perfect just the way you are."

But Isla's expression began to relax as she looked longer in the mirror. "No, I think I look like maybe I could be pretty. Even as pretty as a Feather," she said.

"Ugh, those assholes?" Grace asked with a grimace.

Isla laughed. "They're your best friends!"

"No, you're my best friend," Grace corrected. She pulled Isla up by her hand. "Come on, we got this. Remember what Della always says, life goes in the blink of an eye. We need to embrace every moment—no regrets!"

~

"Dude, can you please stop scowling at Isla," Luke whispered to Ben. He had just finished his first year at college but came back to Maiden's Cove for the summer.

They were on a big blanket at Sandy Bay, Monica sitting on Ben's other side doing her hot–cold thing that Ben knew was just a game she liked to play, like a cat played with a mouse. She was simultaneously giving her sexy glances to Richard Monroe, who was giving them back when Grace wasn't looking. Ben did not like Grace's summer fling, but who was he to say anything when he was sort of, but not really, seeing Monica?

But it was true that Ben could not keep his eyes off Isla, though he hadn't realized he'd been scowling. He quickly relaxed his face and turned his gaze to the bay, glancing at her sideways instead. She looked beautiful. He'd always thought Isla was a striking girl, but tonight he realized she was beautiful. Her green eyes looked as if they were twinkling, and her lips were so full with lip gloss, shining every time she took a sip of her drink, or smiled at Grace, or licked them when she had a crumb.

Monica had scowled at Isla too, but out of petty jealousy.

"A hair straightener and a bit of lip gloss can't cover up Cove trash," she'd hissed. The crowd snickered, but not for long, because Isla did look that beautiful and everyone there knew it.

Was that why he was scowling? Because everyone else was seeing the person he thought only he saw? Or could it have been that he didn't like seeing her this way—like a real person, like a woman? She looked like Isla, but not. He wanted her hair to be frizzy like she'd been in the water all day. Her eyes murky like she could see in the dark. Her lips chapped from all the salt. He wanted her to be the person she'd always been to him, someone who was a little bit otherworldly, a girl who was not just a girl, but something more, something other. In some ways, Ben had been in love with her for years, but with a version of her that was his and his alone.

"You're scowling again," Luke said.

Ben stood up. "I need to go for a walk," he said, turning and walking toward the woods.

Once he was alone, he was able to think more clearly. To remember more clearly what had happened between him and Isla the year before. Sometimes he thought it had been a dream. But he knew it wasn't.

It was a year ago, nearly to the day. Ben had been angry at Isla for reasons he himself hadn't been able to understand. They were friends. He liked her. And suddenly he was angry at her. She looked different, felt different. She was changing, and he was too, but it didn't seem like they could change together, so he had decided to do the one thing she'd always told them all not to do—jump from the cliff.

And so he did. Ben had jumped off the highest point of the cliff. But as he hit the water, he'd realized why Isla never let anyone jump without her. The current caught him immediately and took him back under. He'd hit rock after rock and lost consciousness.

And then he woke up. But he hadn't woken up in a bed or hospital. He'd woken underwater. His nose pinched shut, his head resting in a warm hand. And Isla had been kissing him. Deep and thoroughly. It was like one of those dreams where you think you can't breathe, but then you do and you can. In his dream underwater he'd sucked the air from her lungs and they'd sat on the bed of the bay and smiled. Then she'd pressed her mouth to his again and the next time he woke up, he was in his bed, and he'd never quite looked at Isla the same after that dream that made him realize he was in love with her.

He knew it was a dream because anything else would be impossible.

"Good thing you washed up on the beach when you did," his dad said when he woke up. "Group of fishermen found you and got the water out of your lungs right in time and brought you home."

But sometimes, after that, when he and Isla were close, he could feel their breathing sync, like they were sharing the same breath.

"Ben." He shook free of his reverie of the past and turned to Isla now, on the fourth of July, her hair straight, her lips in gloss. She'd followed him from the beach.

Isla took a deep breath and walked toward him. It was as if he was frozen where he stood. When she reached him, she placed her hands on his chest and closed her eyes. Ben closed his as well, letting his forehead drop to hers, their breath mingling, and just like last summer, their breathing began to sync, like they were sharing one breath.

"Was I dreaming?" he whispered.

But she didn't answer. Instead, Ben felt her full lips press to his and she was kissing him. He'd never felt anything like it in his life. Just a sweet, simple kiss, but it was as if the world stopped, as if they were underwater and the rest was silence.

And then she was gone. And when he finally opened his eyes, the only trace of her was a ripple and splash as she disappeared into the water.

~

Present Day

Ben stared out to the water, the fireworks still going off above him. He could hear the oohs and aahs from the beach behind him as the warm water lapped at his bare feet. He'd been thinking of that summer since he saw Isla jump from the cliff at the Crab Fest. Remembering the feel of her lips on his when he was eighteen, before she ran and dived into the water, leaving him to wonder. Always to wonder.

He heard footsteps in the sand and turned to see Grace standing next to him, bringing him his shoes and sweatshirt.

"She's not gone," Grace said. "She won't leave until the end of the summer, she promised."

"Where do you think she went?" Ben asked.

"I think she decided it was time," Grace whispered. "I think she's finally gone to Henry's."

Ben walked back to Henry's place in the Cove the way he had every night since Isla had returned home. He knew it was pitiful that he was waiting for her, just waiting, but he knew in his heart that one night she would come. The way that he knew all these years that one night she would come home to Maiden's Cove. It didn't make up for his weakness. It didn't excuse that he was passive. But it did mean he never gave up hope. That he never gave up on anything between him and Isla.

He unlocked the door with the key he'd had for many years now. The house was dark. She wasn't here, at least not yet. But he had a feeling Grace was right.

He turned on a few lights and went to the deck out back. *The Maiden* was docked below. So Isla had been here to pick up and drop off the boat for the Crab Fest, but he knew she hadn't been in the house yet.

Ben turned off the light outside and sat on the old rocking chair, letting it rock him into a trance-like state as he waited.

He didn't know how long it was that he'd had his eyes closed, or even if he was asleep or still awake as he opened them. There was no splash or ripple, no sign. He simply opened his eyes and saw the crown of Isla's head emerging, as she walked slowly out of the water and up the stairs to her house, the droplets of water resting on her like they were protecting her. Ben knew he should say something, but he couldn't. He simply watched and waited.

It did not take long. By the time Isla got onto the deck she nodded and walked into the house. The current between them made the hair on Ben's arm stand up as she passed.

He didn't follow her in, not at first. Ben knew this was the first time Isla had been in her house since before Henry died. And even though their relationship was not fully understood by him, or even Grace, her attachment to Henry and grief at his passing was without question.

He felt himself waiting for her to say something, anything.

"It doesn't look the same at all," she said quietly from inside, and Ben got to his feet and walked in to stand beside her.

"I'm sorry for that. I didn't know what to do with it."

Isla turned to him. "You? You have been taking care of the house?"

"It's still yours," Ben assured her, as she began to walk around the small space. "I was so sorry when Henry died," he said quietly.

"I didn't really know how to deal with any of it. Losing a person I loved for the first time. We lost our mother young but that was different...when you don't remember, when you don't know a person."

Isla turned sharply and looked at him with an intense stare. Like she was confused, trying to gauge something she couldn't understand. "But I...you...?"

"I mourned Henry, but I never knew the kind of hole that would be inside of me when you never came back. I know I didn't come then, when you asked. I didn't know what to do. I was lost. I was young. But I longed for you, so I came here a lot after you left," he said. "Waiting for you, or something equally romantic." He laughed. She did not. "The bills started piling up. I didn't want you to lose your home."

Isla's lips parted slowly, searching for words, or air, or water—he was not sure.

"Thank you," she whispered. She walked through the little shack, lightly running her hands over furniture or surfaces that reminded her of Henry, of her youth. Ben was mesmerized by the trails that followed her hands when she touched something, like lightly glowing remnants of her being. Ben followed the trails that beckoned him, back out to the porch and down the ladder to *The Maiden*. Isla was lying on the deck, her eyes closed.

Ben lay next to her, closing his eyes, listening to the water lap against the boat, feeling the rock and rhythm of the water, the lull of the waves. He turned his head to hers and Isla was staring at him. Finally she inched closer, touching her forehead to his, as their breath went in and out of each other. And when they finally touched, the bay went black, silent. And the two lovers on the boat began to glow.

~

It was after eleven when Luke pulled up to Grace's cottage and turned off the engine. "You grab Bayla and I'll take Mape?"

"Okay," Grace agreed, something drumming in her heart.

She opened the door and went to lift Bayla up from the truck.

"Mom!" she groaned sleepily. "I'm eight! I can walk, you know?"

Luke pressed his lips together to keep his laughter at bay while Mape roused herself from sleep and the girls groggily made their way into the house.

"Left, girls," Grace called and they changed directions as if sleepwalking. "Thank god," she said. "I don't know how I would have carried that girl. She's small but she weighs a ton." Luke smiled. "I'll be right back."

Grace followed the girls up into Bayla's room and tucked them in, ignoring the fact they hadn't brushed their teeth or changed out of their clothes.

"Goodnight, my beautiful girl," Grace whispered to Bayla.

"Mom?" she called out drowsily. "Best Fourth of July. Ever."

"Mine too, kiddo," she said, kissing Bayla's forehead.

Both girls were sleeping soundly, so Grace closed the bedroom door and walked silently down to the front door, where Luke was waiting.

"Would you like to have a glass of wine?" he asked, the door half open.

She shook her head. "No." But she put her hand over his and stopped him from leaving.

"Do you want me to stay?" he whispered hoarsely. She nodded, and took his hand, leading him inside and closing the front door behind him.

⁓

A different kind of light turned on in the bay outside Grace's house that night. The light of a boat, and on it, a man, who watched another man walk into a house with his wife, and turn off the lights, and not come out.

Richard Monroe was angry.

⁓

Summer 2006

"I'm going to the cliff, okay?" Isla said to Grace.

"I'll come meet you when I finish up," Grace said. "Looks like that new boat is heading our way."

Grace went to the edge of the dock and waited. The boat was an expensive fiberglass speedboat and on it was a group of teenage boys. She recognized the boat, the *Hawaiian Tropic*. It was Matt Collett's family's boat. They went to school together.

"Yo, Matt, give the girl the rope," one of the other boys said.

Matt was a short, slightly weighty guy with red cheeks and big lips. He didn't have the style, but he did have the money.

"Hey, Matt," Grace said, catching the rope and tying it to the dock. "You guys eating in or on the boat?"

"I'll just wait till my friend Richie gets here. He's just behind," Matt said, taking some menus.

Grace heard it before she saw him, this Richie. He was on a stand-up Jet Ski, jumping the waves from the boats leaving, before pulling into Cleary's dock at breakneck speed, despite the five-knot signs everywhere. Normally Grace would be irritated. She was about to say something to Matt when she saw him. Richie.

He looked like no man or boy she'd ever seen before. He was definitely older than the rest of them, maybe nineteen or twenty, and he was wearing Rip Curl shorts that sat low on his narrow hips, his chest wide and sculpted, and he had defined abs and arms. His hair was sandy and kept short, and he wore Oakley sunglasses. When he pulled up next to the boat, causing waves and disturbance, he smirked with full lips, lowered his sunglasses and stared right at Grace, whose mouth went suddenly dry.

The way he looked at her made her feel owned, possessed, belonged to. And as though he was reading her mind, he put his sunglasses back up and smiled at her.

"Mine."

Chapter Thirteen

In Phoenix, Richard loved to take Grace shopping and buy her clothes. At first she'd felt it was really thoughtful of him. He took her shopping at places like Ann Taylor LOFT, and she always looked smart and chic in her button-down tops and high-waisted tapered pants and flats, or fitted skirts with blazers.

One afternoon when Bayla was six, Grace dropped her at school and was standing with a few "other moms." She'd never thought of them as friends, so she'd always taken to just calling them the "other moms" in her head, the same way Richard talked about them.

"Grace, I admire you. I roll out of bed and barely even have time to find a pair of yoga pants that look slightly different from my pajamas, and I usually forget to brush my teeth running around trying to get these rugrats here on time. And you are always so put together," a mom whose name she'd forgotten had said.

"I was like that when I was her age," another mom said with a laugh.

It bothered Grace when they made comments about her age, about the fact that she was so young, but they didn't mean it maliciously. When they'd met Richard in person they all agreed they'd have kept the baby if it was his too. Of course, they didn't know she'd heard them say that. Grace typically kept her head down. So it was unusual that on this particular day, she looked up instead and really saw them.

The "other moms" were all in shorts or leggings with lightweight T-shirts. They looked relaxed, comfortable. Grace looked down at herself. She looked like she always did. It was a warm day so she was wearing a sleeveless white top with a high neck, tucked into her navy blue tapered pants with navy flats. Her dark hair was parted in the middle and in a low ponytail.

She looked conservative, she realized, and she'd never been conservative when she was younger. Grace had always had a bohemian-chic fashion sense, with bold-colored sundresses and billowy skirts, shorts with cowboy boots and off-the-shoulder sweaters among her favorites. She wondered, suddenly, when her style had changed. When she'd started dressing exactly like Sandy, Richard's mother.

On her way home that day, Grace stopped by the shopping mall and walked around. She had a strange sense of seeing the stores for the first time, though she had been here often. Then it hit her. She'd never been in here alone. Instinct pulled her to the usual stores but she fought it and wandered into a little shop she'd always been drawn to called Charlotte's. On a whim, she bought a bright yellow sundress printed with big orange and red flowers. It was cinched at the waist and fell just above the knees. Grace bought a floppy hat too, and when she got home, she went through her closet to try to find her old ankle-length cowboy boots she'd had since was sixteen. She pulled out boxes, tore her meticulously organized closet apart, but still couldn't find them.

"Dammit!" she cried on her hands and knees in the closet.

"Looking for something, Grace?" Richard said from behind her.

"What are you doing here?" she breathed, her heart racing for some reason she couldn't understand. She was planning on cleaning everything before he got home from work, but that was supposed to be hours away.

He laughed. "I live here, remember?" Grace noticed he was holding the new yellow dress. She blushed, embarrassed to have bought it now. "What were you looking for?"

"My...my cowboy boots," she answered quietly.

He laughed again. "What? To wear with this piece of trash?" he asked, shaking the dress. "Is there a costume party I didn't know about? Halloween?"

"No," Grace replied.

"No? I can think of no other reason my beautifully dressed wife would ever think to dress like one of those penniless street performers, who are probably whoring themselves for money anyway," he said through his teeth, spitting a little.

His eyes were changing, the way they did when he drank whiskey sometimes. They got dark and seemed to spin, and he looked at her like he wasn't really seeing her at all, but something beyond her. His hand was starting to shake. Grace looked down at the ground and stayed very still, not saying a word, trying not to breathe lest something set him off even more. Finally she heard him take a deep breath. When she glanced up he still looked angry, but his eyes had come back into focus. Richard looked at the dress again in disgust and threw it back in the bag.

"I'll return this on my way back to work," he said, glancing at his phone. "I wouldn't suggest shopping without me again, Grace. I will know," he said pointing to the phone, where she could see the Bank of America alert. He knew that she'd bought something and came home because of that. "This mess better be cleaned up by the time I get back from work. I'll be checking that everything is hanging in its correct place then. Remember, Grace, color coordinated."

He left, and when she finally heard the front door slam closed she'd realized that she was shaking. That she was terrified of her husband.

She'd never found the cowboy boots.

When Grace returned to Maiden's Cove, she had started to unpack her clothes and put them into her closet, but stopped. She never wanted to wear those things again. So she closed the bag and threw it in the back of the closet to donate to the Salvation Army one of these days, and went out and bought herself a new wardrobe. She didn't need much. She wore the same Cleary's uniform everyone else did and that's where she spent most of her time. But she did get a couple of dresses and skirts, and she'd managed to find a new pair of boots at the Op shop. They weren't the same ones she used to have, not nearly as nice, but she still loved them. Not that she wore them often in this heat. She was usually in her work sneakers or flip-flops.

Grace finished folding the laundry in the room just off the kitchen, where she could see Bayla throwing ice and fruit into a big blender that was already nearly full.

"What are you making?" Grace asked from the laundry room.

"Homemade snowballs," she said as if it was obvious.

"Ah," Grace said, swallowing her smile. "I'm just going to throw these clothes upstairs and I'll be back down in a second to give it a try."

She heard the blender go as she made her way up the stairs. She dropped Bayla's pile of clothes onto her bed. She learned early on that Bayla liked to put her things exactly where she thought they belonged and was very particular about where that place was. Occasionally Grace tried to guess but it was never quite right, so she left them folded for Bayla to put away where she wanted.

Grace got to her room and placed her clothes on the bed and went to the closet to get hangers, but when she opened the door, she nearly screamed, her heart dropping down to her knees, out of breath. All of her old clothes were hanging in the closet, color coordinated, meticulous, perfect.

"Richard," she breathed, and quickly turned. But her room was empty. The window was open and a light breeze was blowing the curtain. Had she left the window open? She walked over to it and pulled the curtain aside, her hands shaking from fear. But no one was there. She slowly inched open the bathroom door, then pushed it open as fast as she could, pulling the shower curtain back. Still nothing.

Grace could hear her heart beating in the silence. Her head lifted suddenly. She realized that the blender wasn't going.

"Bayla!" she yelled, running out of her room and down the stairs into the kitchen.

"Yeah, Mom?" Bayla asked, pouring the concoction into two big glasses. She scrunched up her nose as she looked at them. "They don't look very nice, actually."

Grace gripped the kitchen bench and closed her eyes, taking deep breaths in and out to try to calm down.

"Are you okay, Mom?" Bayla asked, her voice suddenly concerned.

Grace was still shaking, but the oxygen was making its way back to her brain and the adrenaline was wearing off.

"I'm fine, honey," she said, forcing a tremulous smile. "Just couldn't find what I was looking for in the closet."

Bayla nodded compassionately. "Did Gloretta get to your room too?"

Grace's head shot up. "Gloretta?"

"She cleaned while she was babysitting me yesterday. Took me all night to find everything she put away and get it back to where it belonged," Bayla said, taking a sip of the snowball and making a face. "Ugh, it doesn't taste very nice either."

Relief made Grace feel weak. Loretta, of course. It would be just like her to unpack all of Grace's clothes and put them away neatly. She would have thought they were beautiful, of course, and that Grace should be wearing them. She didn't know if she should kill Loretta for terrifying her or hug her for *not* being

Richard. He was not here. He was not coming after them. He was not a danger to her or to Bayla.

"Come on, let's go to Harrington's and get someone to make snowballs for us," Grace said, slipping on her shoes at the door. Bayla's face lit up and she dumped the glasses in the trash and ran out the door Grace was holding open. She closed the door behind them and started following Bayla, but turned back last minute, and locked the door behind them.

Just in case.

⁓

"How's it looking?" Cohen asked from the doorway of the office. He must have seen the truth on her face because he stepped inside and closed the door behind him, sitting across from her. "Still in the red?"

Grace shook her head, then put her head in her hands with a sigh. "I don't know what else to do. We're busy, but not as busy as we need to be. I'm getting the bills paid, and definitely digging us out of the debt we were in, but Cleary's is a summer restaurant. We've got until the end of summer to not only get out of this, but to have enough in the bank to get us through the winter or we'll find ourselves closing the doors. Everyone is working so hard. I can't lose this place, Cohen," she said, her voice breaking. "I can't lose Cleary's."

"Summer is not over yet, honey," he said, taking her hand. "We've still got the rest of July and August. The *Food and Travel* magazine people are coming on Wednesday to take some photos and do the article, and to try the Crab Imperial dish you and Luke were working on. They've got influence. If we start filling up every day and are busy enough to open two more night shifts, we can get there. And don't forget Tommy's Cook-Off at the end of August. Luke says he's got a friend from Ocean City who's going to come and be the guest chef for the day. Big day like that could make all the difference."

"We still need to actually sell the tickets and get people here. The locals are being supportive, of course, but there are only so many of them. We need to advertise the event," she said, "and yet I have no spare funds to do it outside of social media, which Sarah is doing brilliantly, to be fair."

"Let's see if this article does anything for us. Could be free advertising, if we get it right," said Cohen. "Let's just make sure we give them one hell of an experience."

The night before the interview, Grace was too excited and nervous to sleep. The journalist, Genevieve Hull, was coming down from New York and she seemed intuitive and thorough. Grace and Cohen, along with Luke and Della in the kitchen, were going to be interviewed. The whole team had been keen to take part, but Grace was afraid someone would let it slip that they were in the red and in a summer of desperation. That was not the kind of article *Food and Travel* magazine was writing.

It was after one in the morning but the more she knew she needed to sleep, the more awake she felt. It was also so hot. One of the hottest days of the summer so far and the evening hadn't brought even the slightest respite to the bay. Grace hated closing the doors and windows because she loved the smell and sound of the bay at her doorstep, but she finally gave in and went to close the windows and turn on the air-conditioning.

"Psst," a voice called from outside.

"Isla, is that you?" she whispered, her heart racing in fear. She hadn't quite forgotten the moment she thought that Richard was back.

"Who else would be whispering at you from here? Romeo?" Isla scoffed. Grace laughed in relief. "Come on, get down here."

"Where are you?" Grace asked.

"You'll see," Isla replied, a giggle in her voice.

When Grace got to the beach, her jaw dropped. "What the...?"

"I know, right?" Isla exclaimed. "Isn't it awesome?" She was floating on the water in the bay on a styrofoam beach chair, a glass of wine in the armrest. "Bet you're wondering how it is I'm not moving with the incoming tide, aren't you?"

Grace suddenly realized that Isla was floating like she was in a pool. Like she was anchored. "I am now."

"I am so glad you asked!" Isla said with a grin, then sat up and pulled up what was indeed an anchor, which Grace realized was a cooler. Isla opened it and topped up her wine, and poured one for Grace as well, then closed the cooler and dropped it back down to the bottom.

"Come out, have a drink."

Grace laughed as she started to wade in.

"Not like that!" Isla turned and pulled an identical pool chair from the beach on a string. "Hop on, Cleary."

Grace settled into the beach chair and sighed gleefully as Isla pulled her on the string to where she was moored and tied them together. She handed her the glass of wine and they toasted and took a sip.

"Where did you get these?" Grace asked, looking down at the chairs.

"I won them, if you can believe it. Day of the Crab Fest. While you were out smooching ole *McCaaaaan*, I was exploring the festival. I passed by this big crab pot and you had to guess how many were in it. I just took a random guess and I won! Never won anything in my whole life," Isla said, smiling and taking a sip of wine.

"Hey," Grace said in mock offense. "What about me?"

Isla laughed but reached her hand out. "You were the best thing. But I didn't win you." She turned her green eyes to Grace, keeping hold of her hand. "Not a day goes by that I don't thank all the fish in the sea for the day you called me, Grace Cleary."

⁓

Grace arrived at Cleary's the following morning with Isla and Bayla in tow. Jimbo's and Luke's trucks were in the parking lot so she knew they were already here, prepping for the lunch they were going to serve Genevieve after the interviews.

Just as Grace was about to open the door, a car pulled into the lot and parked. Genevieve Hull got out, not looking like she was from New York at all. She was wearing baggy khaki pants rolled up, with a white button-down linen shirt open over a tank top and white Birkenstock sandals on her feet. Her hair was pulled into a messy bun and she didn't appear to be wearing makeup. She looked like a local.

"Genevieve," Grace said, meeting her halfway with a handshake and a smile. "Welcome to Cleary's. How was your flight down?"

"I decided to drive actually. Came down yesterday and spent the night in Maiden's Cove," she said.

"Oh!" Grace said, surprised. "I wish you would have let us know; we could have arranged a nice place for you to stay."

She smiled. "That's kind, but it's always nice to get a sense of place without everyone knowing who you are, especially in a small town."

Grace glanced at Isla, feeling nervous already. Had she heard something?

Genevieve tilted her head. "And these are?"

"This is my friend Isla," Grace said, introducing them. "And my daughter, Bayla."

"Hi, girls," Genevieve said. "I am so looking forward to interviewing you today."

"Oh, they're not—"

"Ms. Genevieve, I will not disappoint you," Bayla said confidently, as if she'd been hoping this would happen. She took her heavy backpack off and opened it, pulling out her notebooks. "I have been taking notes of the myths and legends of Maiden's Cove since I moved here in April. You'll find them very helpful, especially when you talk to my Aunt Isla here, who may or may not be a mermaid."

Isla pressed her lips together to keep from laughing as Grace's eyes widened and she gave an apologetic look to Genevieve, whose expression did not change.

"As you can probably tell even from your brief time here," Grace said, opening the delivery door to the back kitchen, "Maiden's Cove *is* a place of myth and stories, and we are very proud of it. Cleary's has been here for seventy-five years now. My grandfather built it with his own hands as a humble fisherman's wharf. Please, come inside and allow me to show you around the building. A few of the team have come to—"

But when Grace opened the door, it wasn't just Cohen and the kitchen team, but the entire staff of Cleary's waiting with anticipation.

Todd stepped forward. "Don't worry, Grace, we're all here to support Cleary's today. This is our home, and we won't let it go down. We'll make Mr. Tom proud," he said, with all the best of intentions. He was even wearing a tie.

Grace looked around to the team. There was nothing she could do now—the truth of the state of Cleary's was out. She turned to Genevieve, whose eyebrows were raised, but she forced a smile and took a glass off the tray Todd was holding, handing it to her.

"Oh Mama Colada?"

⌒

Hours later, at the end of the lunch service, Grace sat around a table with her friends as they had drinks and discussed the day.

"I guess we'll know when the article comes out," Grace said, taking a sip of her wine.

"I think it was charming," Della said. "Very Maiden's Cove. We want to be true to who we are."

Grace smiled and squeezed Della's hand. "Absolutely. Come on, let's focus on the positives. What did you guys talk about in your interviews?"

"I told Genevieve about Tommy's Cook-Off, the very first one," Luke said with a smile, taking a sip of his beer. "Day I knew for certain I wanted to be a chef, to create something like that. And now to be the one running it this year, Cleary's seventy-fifth year, in honor of him."

"Now that was mighty fine of you, Luke," Jimbo said, nodding his approval.

"And excellent advertising," Cohen said. "I took her through the wine list and gave her a few to try over lunch. Also let her know I was thinking of starting wine tastings for those looking to expand their palate. She seemed impressed."

"With me too!" Georgiana said. "I did the same with the new desserts—gave her a few samples and then talked about ideas. It's new, and different to the old Cleary's, and *Food and Travel* magazine loves to talk about innovation. Cohen, you didn't go on for *too* long about how Sancerre and sauvignon blanc are the same-same but different, did you?"

"But it's true! Luke, back me up. I mean, a New Zealand sauvignon blanc compared to this?" he asked, pushing the

Sancerre into Luke's hand. "Taste it!" he practically yelled, and Luke quickly took a sip. "Well?"

"It's like it's not even the same grape," he answered dutifully, and Cohen nodded with approval, taking his glass back.

"I talked about my family and our history with the Cleary family ever since they came up from the South on the Underground Railroad," Della said. "Added a little bit of history of the town and the Clearys, I think."

"I worked with your grandaddy when he was still alive, Gracey, so I talked about that," Jimbo said. "I was just a fisherman then. Watched this place go from a crab shack with outdoor tables to a good and proper restaurant, learned to cook, be a part of the whole team. And met my beautiful wife, of course."

Della smiled and leaned into Jimbo as he brushed a kiss to her forehead.

"Bayla told her all about mermaid lore," Isla said. "She's been writing it all down and was very excited to share it. That was my bit too, and the little stinker stole it." They all laughed. "So I talked a little about Henry and life as one of the fishermen of Cleary's. The way he thought that this place was more than just a restaurant, but something that brought the whole community together."

Grace smiled and squeezed Isla's hand.

She squeezed Grace's hand back. "And what about you, Grace Cleary, restaurant owner? What did you tell her?"

Grace looked around the restaurant and every memory of her childhood flooded back—her dad's face, Jimbo and Della, the customers, cooking food, she and Isla and their Mer-swimming.

"Everything," Grace said. "I told her everything."

~

If there is one trip you're going to take this summer, make it to the mystical town of Maiden's Cove, where the sultry heat will tempt you into the still waters of the Chesapeake Bay, where a strange bioluminescence lights up the sand, and where the mermaids are sure to lure you. And there is no place better to watch the world drift by than sitting at the iconic Cleary's Crab Shack on Isolde Bay.

Watch the fishermen bring in their catch the way they have for seventy-five years, and as the boats come in, try their classic Crab Imperial, crabcakes, or whole steamed crabs from Jimbo and Della.

Feel like trying something new? Start with an "Oh Mama Colada" cocktail and then order head chef Luke McCann's rockfish ceviche with avocado and chili. Pair your selection with restaurant manager and sommelier Cohen Bassett's selection of wines from different parts of the world. Finish with one of Georgiana Glover's infamous desserts—her strawberry shortcake being a particular winner.

This is a town filled with all the charm and magic you'd want for a weekend away, and Cleary's Crab Shack, celebrating its seventy-fifth year, is one of the best restaurants in the state. If you can only get away for one weekend, make it the final weekend of the season when Cleary's is reinstating their famous Tommy's Cook-Off celebration in tribute to the late Tom Cleary. His daughter, Grace Cleary, who grew up working at Cleary's, owns the restaurant now.

"Dad always said that Cleary's was a place for everyone to come together for good food, good beverages and good conversation. Food brings us together. I want for Cleary's to continue to share that with the world," Grace says.

And they will. Cleary's Crab Shack is a Maryland icon and one not to be missed. Tickets for Tommy's Cook-Off on August 31 are on sale now on their website.

Grace looked up when she finished reading the article out loud to the team. It was just before service, and every staff member was there, even if it was their day off. At first they were silent. Then, suddenly, they all began to cheer. Grace laughed happily, putting the magazine down and joining them all for a group hug.

"Oh my gosh, that's the best! Grace, that writer just loved us!" Sarah said enthusiastically.

"Even mentioned me and my Oh Mama Coladas," Todd said, unable to hide his grin.

"That's a damned good drink, my man," Luke said, patting him on the back, and winking at Grace.

"I'm so proud of all of you for everything you've done for Cleary's this summer, and so grateful," Grace said, hugging them each in turn. "All right, let's get this restaurant open!"

They all went to work smiling and laughing and feeling enthused. Jimbo came over to help Grace clear the table of coffee cups and Georgiana's berry strudel they'd had for breakfast.

"I'm proud of you, Gracey," he said gently. "I know it's been harder than you let on. But this is a good thing, this article."

Grace melted into Jimbo's hug. "Thanks, Jimbo."

"And now we wait," he said.

"For what?"

A moment later, the phone rang.

"For the customers to roll in," he said with a big smile.

Chapter Fourteen

"Mom, can I please, *please* come to work with you and Aunt Isla today?" Bayla asked one morning in August. After the article came out they were fully booked for nearly every service for the rest of summer. They even opened two more dinner services on Wednesdays and Thursdays.

"Not today, kiddo," she said, ruffling her hair. Grace had also started a brunch session on Sundays to help them bolster sales, and it was a day that was relentless from start to finish. "Besides, you're having such a great summer with Mape. What do you girls have planned today?"

"Mape can't play today," she said, grabbing a toaster strudel which had just popped out of the toaster. "Ouch," she mumbled, "still hot."

"Why not?" Isla asked, cutting it in half for Bayla so it cooled quicker.

Bayla shrugged. "She wasn't too sure. Something about her stepdad's oldest coming to introduce his new hussy. Mom, what's a tramp stamp?"

Grace pressed her lips together but a laugh escaped from Isla.

"It's just a terrible name for a tattoo, that's all. Which, by the way, you are never to get," Grace said.

"But Luke has a tattoo and I heard you telling Aunt Isla it really did go all the way up to his—"

"Okay, that's enough!" Grace said loudly, blushing furiously. "Isla, where's my phone?"

But Isla had slipped out the back door so she could laugh without Bayla seeing her.

"It's just here, Mom, gosh," Bayla said, handing it to her.

Grace dialed Aunt Lou to see if she could leave Bayla with her for the morning. "Come on, Aunt Lou, pick up, pick up…"

"Hello? Hello? You've got a bad line."

Grace sighed with relief. "Aunt Lou, it's me. I've got a—"

"Ha! You've reached my machine. Leave a message." Beep.

Grace looked at the phone. "Are you kidding me? That's her answering machine?"

"Is it the one where she pretends like she picked up and you have a bad line?" Bayla asked and laughed when Grace nodded.

"That was Mape's idea. We set it up before the fireworks on Fourth of July."

"Uncle Ben didn't pick up either. Shit, what am I going to do? I've got to be at work in fifteen minutes and I have no one to babysit you," Grace said.

"I'll go get dressed, just give me two minutes, Mom!"

Bayla ran past her. "Bayla!" Grace called. "You cannot come to work with me on these Sunday shifts, you know that!"

In less than two minutes, Bayla appeared back in front of her and Isla, dressed in jean shorts rolled just above her skinny little knees, and one of Grace's Cleary's T-shirts tied up in a little knot on her lower back.

Grace couldn't help but laugh. "Where on earth did you learn to do that with your shirt?"

"Duh, you and Aunt Isla. See, look, I found this. Don't I look just like Mom, Aunt Isla?"

Bayla took out a photo of Isla and Grace from the year they started at Cleary's, wearing jean shorts and white sneakers, with a white Cleary's T-shirt five sizes too big they had tied into knots around their midsection. They were hugging and laughing, Della standing behind them.

"Wow, look at how young we were then," Grace said, sitting down and smiling at the photo. Isla sat beside her.

"You were really pretty, Mommy," Bayla said, looking at the picture. "You still are, but here you look really happy too. I never saw you like that before we moved here."

Grace's heart jumped into her stomach and Isla glanced at her as tears filled her eyes. She pulled Bayla in for a tight hug. "Are *you* happy?"

Bayla thought about the question. It was one of the things that Grace adored about her daughter so much. She never answered any question without thinking it through properly. Finally Bayla nodded thoughtfully. "Yes, I am. Are you, Mom?"

"Yes, Bayla," Grace said, looking to her best friend and to her daughter. "I am now."

~

They arrived at the restaurant before service started at nine in the morning, and there was already a queue out the door.

"Oh good," Jimbo called out, a big smile on his face, "you brought free child labor."

Bayla's eyebrows shot up. "Free? I'm getting consummated."

They all laughed. "I think you mean compensated, Bayla, or at least I hope you do," Grace said. "You wanted to work, you have to work, and then you can have something to eat at the end of your shift."

Georgiana called from the back, "Got a red velvet pancake with your name on it, sweet pea!"

"That's my favorite," Bayla whispered to Della, as if it were special. "How did she know?"

"Because you tell all of us all the time," Grace said. "You can eat Gigi's pancakes later, but for now you can help where you're needed, hon. Where's she needed?"

"With me," Della said, grabbing Bayla's arm and leading her back through the door. "We got a group of regulars and they always order fourteen crab bennies. Time to make crab balls, sugar."

"Come on, I'll grab you an apron," Isla said, following Bayla into the kitchen with Della. That had been her favorite job as a girl too—rolling the crabcakes into balls. Isla winked at Bayla before heading out to the front to help the team open.

While Bayla started rolling the crab balls, Della began mixing another batch. They saved their locally caught crabs for steaming so she bought fresh hand-picked crab from a supplier who delivered tons every day—jumbo meat only for her crabcakes, the best quality. Della unpacked it into a series of large stainless bowls on the countertop. She'd been making them so long her fingers knew exactly how much was required, hand seasoning each bowl with mustard, mayonnaise, egg, Worcestershire, and salt and pepper.

"Bayla honey, throw me that box of saltines," she called, not lifting her head.

"Saltines? You mean the crackers?" Bayla sniffed, pulling a face. "I hate those things."

"You hate saltines? Who hates saltines? They're tasteless crackers," Della replied, opening the box Bayla handed her.

"It's what Mom gives me when I'm sick with the flu and can't eat anything. That and warm ginger ale." She pulled another face. "Why does it have to be warm and flat just cause you're sick? I think it's to make you puke."

Della took this in, nodding. "You got a point, honey child. But the saltines are the filler for the crabcakes. My secret one too, so don't tell nobody. We hardly use filler, but you still need a little something. Don't get all hard and crunchy but soaks up the juice and helps bind it together." Della laughed again at Bayla's wary expression and handed her a heavy mallet. "Here, want to smash them to bits?"

At that Bayla lit up. "Oh, yes please!"

And she went pounding the saltines into practical dust while Della checked her crab balls and carried the tray out to Jimbo.

"How long you need for the next lot, baby?" she called to her husband.

"Twelve seconds?" He laughed, and she hurried back inside to find Bayla wheezing slightly, her face pink but her smile bright.

"You okay, honey? You get a bit carried away?" Della asked.

"That was awesome."

⌒

Grace went upstairs between brunch and lunch service to check in on Bayla, who was eating one of Georgiana's red velvet pancakes.

"How's your pancake, sugar?" Georgiana asked.

"Soooo good," Bayla growled, her mouth full. "It's exhausting working in the kitchen. How many crab balls do you reckon I made today, Gigi?"

Georgiana went to the computer and quickly pulled up a report. "One hundred and twenty-one—*if* you rolled them all."

"Wow, no wonder I need so much substanstonas right now," she breathed, biting into her pancake.

"Sustenance, honey," Grace corrected with a smile.

"That's what I said," Bayla muttered.

They laughed. "You're going to go into a sugar coma after this, kiddo. You okay to stay up here and hang out for a while? Lunch is looking like a busy one."

⌒

Cleary's, like most crab shacks on the bay, filled with boaters pulling in for lunch, and it was always busiest on Sundays.

"Oh my god, I'm in the weeds, I'm in the weeds. I'm so in the fucking weeds."

Grace turned, surprised to hear the sweet blonde Sarah say the word "fuck." She almost laughed, but didn't, because they *were* in the weeds.

The restaurant was full to capacity with a waitlist of people sitting outside on the porch or in their boats, sipping beers, coming in for more orange crushes. Often the boaters decided to have drinks on their boats while they waited for a table—the berth was filled with such boats. Sarah was on porch and dock station, which was packed with thirsty people waiting. The bell went off at the outside bar to signify drinks were ready. Todd was back there pouring beers, orange crushes, and his now famous Oh Mama Coladas at speed.

Sarah looked desperately at Grace.

"No worries, I'll take the boats for a while as we catch up." Grace went to the bar and grabbed a tray. "Where am I going, Todd?"

"Boat five," he said. "Sorry, boss, that was Sarah's section."

"She's in the weeds," Grace muttered, taking the tray of drinks herself to boat five. Boat five, boat five.

NO.

It had been years since she'd seen *Hawaiian Tropic* on the water, though she knew Matt Collett and his family still came into Maiden's Cove for the summers. He and Richard had remained good friends all these years, but the last time Grace had actually seen the boat was the summer she got pregnant with Bayla.

Just seeing that boat she knew. Richard was here. He was here to take her, to take Bayla. To make them come back. She could feel it in every fiber of her being.

But she was tired of being scared. She was not a victim, not anymore. Grace started to turn around, take their drinks back to the bar, and tell them to leave. She could do that. This was her restaurant. *Hers.* And then she heard a familiar laugh. But it wasn't Richard's or Matt's laugh. It was Loretta's.

"Gracey! What on earth are you doing bringing us drinks?" Loretta asked with a shake of her head. "That's what you hire staff for. Look who I bumped into a few days ago—you remember Mr. and Mrs. Collett? Matt's parents. He was the best man at your wedding, remember?"

Grace turned, pasting a smile on her face. "Of course. Mr. Collett, Mrs. Collett. I've got three Oh Mama Coladas—are you waiting on anyone else?"

"No, it's just us. Matt finally got his own boat so we could take ours back for the first time in fifteen years." Mrs. Collett laughed.

Grace forced another smile and turned to her stepmother. "Loretta, would you mind coming inside for just a moment? Bayla would love to say hi. She's just upstairs."

"Oh, of course!" Loretta beamed, turning back to the Colletts. "Wait until you see the glorious little creature Gracey and Richard have. She is so beautiful. I'll bring her down to say hi."

"Maybe not today. Loretta?" Grace said forcefully, taking her hand and helping her off the boat.

The months had not been kind on Loretta since Grace's dad had passed away so unexpectedly. Loretta had been beautiful when she was young, with thick curling black hair and startling green eyes. She was still beautiful now. In her late fifties, her black hair was graying but she kept it dark in the salon. She still put mascara on every morning to brighten her green eyes, and pink lipstick on her thin lips. She kept a trim figure, dressed impeccably, and kept her shoulders back in her haughty way.

"Grace Cleary, your father would be so disappointed in you," Loretta said, as she pulled her arm from Grace's grip. "Dragging me off my friends' boat like some convict. It's been nearly a full summer and I've not been invited into my own restaurant. Tsk tsk, Gracey."

At times like this, Grace wanted to finally unleash all the things she never said when she was younger. That Loretta was *not* her mother, nor did she ever act like one. That this was *not* her restaurant. It never had been, never was, and never would be. And to never, ever *ever* call her Gracey.

And she almost did say these things, but then Grace would see a slight quiver, a smudge of makeup, a stray curl Loretta had missed, mascara only on one eye, brown tights with a blue skirt. And Grace would realize that in that big old Cleary house, Loretta was alone and she was not really dealing with it very well, and so Grace wouldn't say a word.

Loretta was lost. Her voice was forced, her demeanor had a façade of strength but with a vulnerability behind it. Grace saw it. She felt it. She felt sorry for Loretta. Which was difficult, because Loretta did not in any way make it easy to love her, let alone like her.

But Bayla *adored* her.

"Gloretta!" She jumped up when they came into the loft where Bayla was still eating her pancake.

"Be-bay!" They hugged. Loretta's mutual adoration for Bayla was obvious, but Grace still cleared her throat after a moment.

"Bayla, honey, why don't you head on down to the kitchen and see if Georgiana or Della needs some help, okay? I just need to talk to Gloretta for one minute."

Bayla tilted her head, and Loretta opened her mouth to speak but must have realized that something was amiss and closed it again quickly.

"Can I come stay with you this week, Gloretta?" Bayla asked suspiciously.

"Of course you can, Be-bay," she said, glancing at Grace. Bayla turned to her mother as well. Grace smiled a small smile and nodded. "Okay then," Loretta continued, "run on downstairs, darlin, while I talk to your mama."

Bayla gave them one last suspicious glance but went down the stairs. Loretta turned to Grace, immediately on the attack.

"What is this, Grace? I brought guests here on the boat to support you and Cleary's, and you basically give me an order to come see my grandchild and then send her out of the room the same instant. I'm worried about you. Look at you, being run off your feet like this when you should have just sold the place..."

Grace gritted her teeth at the turn of conversation and tried to get a word in but Loretta was on a roll.

"Waitressing like a right slave, and forcing your young daughter to work as well? In this kind of environment?"

Grace's patience was waning. "I hardly think—"

"You are *married*, Grace. To a good, strong man, and you belong back home in Phoenix in your own home, not here waitressing—"

"Loretta, I own the restaurant. I hardly think that qualifies as waitressing and acting like a slave."

"It's not that I'm not proud of you. Your dad loved this place so much and I know you do too. But if you had any idea how worried your husband was about you and your health—"

Grace kicked over a chair and Loretta was silenced. "Loretta, for god's sake, please tell me you haven't been talking to anyone, *anyone*, about me and Bayla."

"I would never gossip," Loretta squeaked, startled. "I happened to bump into the Colletts yesterday and they invited me out on their boat. I don't have many visitors these days and they remembered you. They wanted to catch up with the happenings at Maiden's Cove. Of course I told them about your dad, God rest his soul."

"And what did you tell them about me and Bayla?"

Loretta looked to the stairs where Bayla had just left and she looked at Grace, and for the first time in a long, long time, Grace could see that she understood. Her green eyes panicked.

"I told them that you moved back when your dad died. That you brought Bayla. That you owned Cleary's now," Loretta said, twisting the string of pearls around her neck. "They seemed quite worried about your health. Apparently Richard told them that you had a mental breakdown and disappeared with Bayla in the middle of the night." For a long moment, Loretta looked lost, drifting back into the past, and then her breath caught and she turned to meet Grace's eyes. "I'm sorry," she whispered. "They said Richard had been so worried about you and asked them to check in on us. I assured them..."

Grace exhaled loudly and sat down, her head in her hands, taking deep breaths. "What exactly did you assure them?"

"I... I don't remember. I think I said that I rarely see you. That you were devastated by your father's death and busied yourself at the restaurant. I know I said how much I love my grandchild, and how special Bayla is. But that you were both thriving and happy and that I was sure their information was wrong."

Grace suddenly knew. "Loretta, I have one last question. When you babysat Bayla a couple of weeks ago and cleaned up the house, did you unpack my bags and hang them in my closet?"

"What?" Loretta asked, perplexed. "Of course not. I just straightened up the house."

And this was the moment that Grace knew she'd been waiting for even when she thought she was past it. Richard had not moved on quietly as she'd hoped, in a better place and willing to let them go. He'd never been okay with it. He'd been biding his time, as he always did.

He was here.

A fear set in that Grace had never had before, not even when she was still living with Richard. She suddenly remembered every raised arm, every drunken fight, every bruise. She had been an abused woman. And she and her daughter were not going back to that. Not now. Not ever.

But she didn't think that Richard was going to be okay with losing his possessions quite so easily.

~

"Gigi!" Bayla flung herself into Georgiana's house and gave her a quick one-armed side hug before running into the kitchen. "What are we making? You promised a special cake. Does that mean a magic cake?"

Georgiana raised one ginger eyebrow and cocked her head to the side, giving Grace such a "Feather" look she couldn't help but laugh. Georgiana looked down at her own posture. "Oh, my god. You see, this is what calling me Gigi does to me. Why *does* your daughter call me that now?"

"That's probably my fault, sorry," she said. "Thank you for tonight. I just—"

"No explanations needed here, honey. But I would feel a little more comfortable if you'd stay too. We could make it a girl's night, just you, me and Bayla. Or we could call Isla too, if you'd like?"

"Thanks, Georgiana, but I need to be home and I need to know Bayla is safe. I'm so sorry to ask this of you."

"Well, that's not a worry, not even a little one. But I do worry about you being at that house all alone over there, especially since *he* knows you're there. I never liked Richard."

Grace turned, surprised and curious. "You didn't? Why not?"

Her eyes darted away for a moment. "He used to cheat on you with Monica those summers before she went away to college. He tried with me too, but like I said, I never liked him. I had a grandpappy that was a drunk without a soul. I knew one when I saw one."

⁓

Grace drove slowly back to Brixton Cottage and down the long drive. The house was dark, quiet. She'd never expected to get back so late and hadn't turned on any lights, not even the outside porch. It felt ominous, and Grace was afraid. But as she stepped out of the car, something caught her eye and she walked around the back of the house, releasing a breath she hadn't realized she was holding.

Isla was there on the beach, the bioluminescence glowing like a protective beacon around her home. She didn't move a muscle as Grace walked toward her, nor did she move when Grace stood beside her, their arms touching.

"You think he's here?" Isla asked. She was alert, like a hunter.

"The first time I met Richard, I remember he walked off that Jet Ski at Cleary's and gave me a look, and he came right up to me and said, 'mine,'" Grace said, and the word seemed to reverberate through the very air into the water. Hard waves began to splash at their feet. The bay didn't want him here.

Minutes passed as the bay had its tantrum, and Isla and Grace stood in unmoving silence, waiting. Finally, suddenly, it became dead calm. Grace's knees wobbled, but Isla caught her.

"I don't know what he's going to do," said Grace. "He's been dropping hints that I had a mental breakdown and took Bayla in the middle of the night, which would be kidnapping. He may be trying to get to me by taking Bayla."

"He's not going to come here tonight. If he's saying you took Bayla unlawfully, then he's going to want to do things the right way. He's got a reputation to uphold, remember?"

"But what if that isn't his plan? What if he isn't himself? What if...what if he's acting crazy?"

"Did that used to happen?"

Grace nodded. "I think I didn't realize it until recently. But I could see this look in his eyes sometimes, when it was like he was another person. Those times were the worst, for him too. Those were the times he cried in my arms afterward, begging forgiveness. I think he might need some real help."

"Do you remember the first time you had a sense that things weren't quite right?"

Grace nodded. "That last summer. The one where you didn't come home, and Henry passed. That was the last time I saw you. I only just remembered now, when Gigi told me that she'd never liked him—that he used to cheat on me with Monica."

They went up onto the porch and turned off all the lights. The bioluminescence on the sand was bright and the bay still.

"Don't worry," Isla said. "I see better in the dark."

Grace smiled sadly, remembering how they used to tease Isla. "And I couldn't even see clearly in the light."

They sat on the porch and looked out at the water.

"What else do you remember?" Isla asked.

Chapter Fifteen

Summer 2007

When Grace was younger, she used to think that she and Isla were two halves of one soul. Grace from the land and Isla from the sea. They surmised that perhaps all girls had other halves out there—a soul sister—that was different from their boy soulmate. They had to come from different elements, like Grace and Isla, and that was what made them so powerful. True soul sisters.

Grace had just graduated from high school, and at the end of this summer when they both turned eighteen, Grace and Isla were meant to leave Maiden's Cove together, to go to the Caribbean for the winter to search for Isla's family. In that first summer when they were twelve, Grace thought that Isla was going to turn her into a mermaid. The memory made Grace smile faintly and also feel a twinge of anxiety for Isla's arrival later that night.

Because the truth was, when she admitted it to herself, Grace did not want to leave this life that she was only just beginning. Isla was her best friend, her childhood friend. Could they truly be adults together?

But Isla didn't come home, not that month, nor in July. And as the weeks passed, Grace sometimes woke up thinking she could hear Isla calling her name. Or she would dream that the green light was out there, but when she woke up to look, it was always dark. But it was hard, outside of those middle of the night dreams, to think much about missing her at all, for Grace Cleary and Richard Monroe were in love.

This was the summer of Grace's sexual awakening, at seventeen. It was intense and glorious. Sometimes dark. Sometimes even a little bit aggressive. But usually that was followed by gentle sweetness. And he'd never hurt her. He loved her, of that Grace was certain. Grace was young enough and so inexperienced that she had nothing to compare it to, so, for her, this awakening was going to be what was normal, what love meant.

And she was genuinely in love. She wanted to do everything with Richard, have everything. To see him in New York City when he finished college and started with Matt's father's company. She saw their whole future in his eyes, and believed he saw the same.

⁓

One night, quite late, Grace arrived home from work at Cleary's after Tommy's Cook-Off. She was exhausted but happy. She gasped when she saw Richard on the bed.

"Jeez, you scared me! What are you doing here?"

"What, I'm not allowed to come see my girlfriend? I haven't made love to you in three days and I'm dying here," he said in his softest voice, patting the bed next to him.

Grace melted and jumped onto the bed next to him. "My dad will be home soon."

"I don't care," he said, before rolling her over and gently spanking her bottom then biting it. She laughed. He growled and grabbed the back of her hair, pulling it hard. "Are you laughing at me, Grace? Did you want to be punished?"

"Yes," she panted, biting her lip to keep from crying out. It felt like he was pulling her skull off.

Was this a game? Something sexy that he wanted to do? He'd done something before—"punished" her and brought her to her first orgasm.

He spanked her again. And then again, and again, and then again, and suddenly it seemed as if he couldn't stop, and it wasn't just her bottom. It was as if he wasn't in control of what he was doing.

After he left, Grace cried as she went to the shower. She was shocked at the bruising on her body. She feigned sick and didn't go to work at Cleary's the next day but stayed in bed with a cool towel on her head to cover the lump there. Things looked different that day, lying in bed. Like maybe their relationship wasn't as grand as she'd thought it was.

That night she cried for Isla. The pull was so strong, and somehow she knew if she was really truly calling her, that Isla would show up. Their bond was not completely gone, not yet. But it was waning. Stretching. Weakening. She wondered what would happen if a whole summer passed without her coming home. If they would be disconnected forever then. A sudden panic seized her and she opened the sliding glass door to call out to the lights, but Richard was outside on the small second-floor balcony outside of her room. She stumbled back, swallowing a scream.

"Richard," she hissed as he stepped into her room. "What are you doing here?" She quickly locked her bedroom door in case her dad or Loretta checked in on her.

"I needed to see you," he said, running his fingers through his short brown hair, his dark eyes darting around, not looking at her in the same intense, confident way he normally did.

"Grace." He moved to her, taking her face, brushing her hair aside, and she winced as he grazed the bruise near her temple, the most painful one. She stared up at him defiantly, expecting him to look pleased with his handywork, but instead he looked appalled. His eyes glistened as he pressed his lips together and bowed his head in shame.

"Richard. What…"

He pulled her to him in a hug, but he was holding her too tightly and she cried out from the bruises. He let her go.

"Take off your clothes," he said, his usually deep, cocky voice lifeless.

"No. No, not this time, not now. Please," she whispered.

"I need to see what I did to you. Take off your clothes."

Hearing the genuine desperation in his voice, she took off her T-shirt and shorts but left on her underwear. She could see his Adam's apple swallow, his eyes misted.

"I'm sorry, Grace." He dropped to his knees, buried his face in her stomach and began to cry. "I'm sorry, god, I'm so sorry. I got carried away. Never again. Never, ever again," he sobbed.

Feeling all the love pouring out of him, the genuine cry for help, she knew she was the only woman Richard needed to be the best man he could be. She was the one. Grace Cleary. She was the only one that could save Richard from himself.

"Grace Cleary, open this door this instant! Grace! Gracey!"

Grace woke suddenly at the banging on her door. She could hear her dad muttering on the other side to Loretta. "Why is the door locked? She never locks the door... What if she's hurt?"

"She probably just snuck out, Tommy," Loretta said, and Grace could almost hear her eyes roll. "You know she's seeing that boy, that Richard Monroe. Great catch."

"I don't like him," Tom muttered, trying to pick the door lock.

"What's not to like?" she asked, truly surprised. "Handsome, rich, and he's got some serious eyes for Grace, you know."

Grace was scrambling for her clothes. Richard had stayed the night, gently holding her in his arms, touching her naked body gently, softly, raining kisses on her bruises, telling her how much he loved her, how she was the one he'd been waiting for his whole life. How she excited him and tempted him and inspired him so much his emotions sometimes got out of control. Sorry. Over and over again. They slept cocooned together. Nothing sexual happened. But the bruises he'd left her with were still all over her body. She couldn't let her dad see them. So she was scrambling to find light pants and a shirt that would cover her but not make him suspicious.

"That's not important, Loretta. I need to talk to Gracey."

"Well, if that's not it, why are you banging down the door?"

"Henry. Henry's dead."

Grace opened the door, her legs exposed, her blue eyes filled, her mouth agape. "Daddy?"

Tom saw that she was safe, saw that look, and pulled his daughter into his arms. "I'm so sorry, sweetheart. I'm so sorry."

She began to sob into his arms, and he led her to the bed and sat next to her. "Let it out honey, let it out. I know how much you loved ole Henry."

Her dad held her tight as the sobs wracked her body until she felt drained from exhaustion. Finally, she stilled and she had only one thought. Nothing else existed, nothing else mattered. Only one thing. She sat up, wiped her eyes.

"Isla."

Henry's house in the Cove was dark and silent when Isla climbed up the stairs of the dock. Henry had known about the cancer for years, but he'd never said a word to her. Not once. All their neighbors, a good deal of people, had been looking in on him, Isla knew. He'd been dead less than three hours when they found his body.

Isla walked through the house, grazing her fingers along anything and everything that Henry would have touched, but there was no light, no spark, no trails. Just her cold wet hand and his empty black house.

This was her fault. He was her guardian, her father, even if not by blood. He'd supported her going off on her own, and the only thing he'd ever asked was that she come home each summer, if only for a visit. That was the responsible thing to ask of her, as a guardian, he used to say. But he'd say it with a wink and a smile, and look up at her, as she was taller than him.

Isla knew that Henry loved her. This very strange silly emotion that had her tied to Maiden's Cove not in one but in three ways. In Henry, in Grace.

In Ben.

She shook her head. The grief in her heart was so great and she had no way to release it. The tears stuck in her eyes, the scream of rage stuck in her chest, and she was lost. If only she'd come home.

If only.

She heard the gentle click of the door behind her. She didn't need to turn around. She knew who it was.

"I didn't come home. I promised I'd always come home for summer," she whispered, still not turning.

And suddenly Grace's arms were around her as she began to sob in her arms.

"It's okay. Shhh, it's okay. It's not your fault. It's not your fault, Isla."

Over and over she whispered these words, soothing, calming, until finally Isla stopping shaking, the grunting sobs from her mouth ceased.

"Can we go back to your house?" Isla asked. "I don't want to see this house ever again."

⁓

"Can you believe we're nearly eighteen?" Grace asked in the middle of the night as they lay on their backs in the water. When Isla didn't answer, she continued. "We were supposed to be leaving together at the end of the summer, remember?"

"I remember," Isla said softly, after a time.

And they both knew that they weren't going to leave together, and that things would be different now, forever.

"You know," said Grace, "when I was younger, that first summer when we used to sit and you would breathe into my mouth underwater? I thought when we turned eighteen you were going to make me a mermaid and take me home with you to meet the other merfolk."

Isla chuckled. "What did mermaid-land look like?" Then she laughed harder. "I can actually feel you blushing right now." She turned onto her front and started paddling around Grace. "Why didn't you ever tell me any of this? I feel like we told each other everything then."

"Well," Grace began slowly, "I guess because I honestly didn't know if it was true, the rumors about you and me. About you being the last mermaid and me calling you. At first I really, really wanted to believe it and it seemed to make sense. That me and you were, like, a part of each other. The breathing underwater, the bioluminescence, the way it was like we couldn't exist without each other all summer. That there must have been something really special about me that you picked me to be your best friend."

"That's one reason. And the other?" Isla said, and Grace could tell she was grinning now.

"Because you would have laughed at me."

"Well, I'm laughing now, so go ahead and tell me more about what it was like under the sea?"

Grace turned and ducked under the water, suddenly coming up next to Isla with her hands in the air. Isla laughed. "That's from *The Little Mermaid*! How unoriginal!"

Grace laughed and started to tread water. "I wasn't that creative, to be honest with you. Except there wasn't a golden castle or city. More like underground sandcastles with some caves and coves and stuff."

"And were there many of us?"

"More than I thought when we finally got down there. Wherever there is," Grace continued, smiling now, enjoying sharing old dreams and fantasies. "But we are the last of our kind, so even though there's, like, a hundred of us, that's not really a lot. It's like having a hundred fish left. So of course that's why we keep moving around through the year, from place to place. Seeing if there are any others left."

"And what about me and you?"

"Duh, we both meet super-hot mermen and get married and live side by side for our whole lives," Grace said, rolling her eyes.

Isla didn't even hold back her guffaw. It felt so good to laugh, and to be with Grace and feel more like a whole self for just a moment, even though she was not. Henry was part of what made her belong here. And he was gone. And Isla would never really be the same.

Isla had something very important to do and she knew she had to do it now, this morning, and quickly. Before it was too late. She got up from Ben's old bed where she'd been sleeping and pulled on a pair of shorts and a sweatshirt, shivering. She opened the door to Grace's room and saw she was still sleeping. She thought of leaving her a note but didn't.

She walked to Cleary's restaurant barefoot and found Jimbo on the dock ready to go out. It was five o'clock in the morning, just before sunrise.

"Hey, Jimbo," she said, her voice raspy.

"Isla, honey," he asked in a concerned voice. "How are you?"

Isla shrugged. "Mind if I come out with you today? I want to scatter Henry's ashes."

"Hop on, honey. You know where you want to go?" She nodded and Jimbo started the engine. "All right then. Let's go."

"You sure this is the spot?" Jimbo asked, about twenty minutes later when she told him to stop.

There wasn't anything special about the place that Isla had directed Jimbo to, at least not to anyone else. But Isla knew that this was where the bay became the bay and was no longer the sea. The brackish water was at its thickest, like a barrier. Isla could always feel it when they crossed it. Because underneath there was a sandbar that nobody else knew about but her and Henry.

"This is the spot," Isla croaked when they got there, and Jimbo turned off the engine.

"Do you want me to drop anchor, stay a while?" he asked.

"No. I won't be long."

The urn was heavy, and holding it and feeling its weight brought a new wave of grief to Isla. This weight in her hands, this person that used to exist, and now didn't. How could you simply just stop existing? She nearly dropped the urn, the weight too much. Jimbo picked it up and lifted her too.

"Come on, honey, we'll do it together. It's heavy. You wanna say something?" he asked.

She shook her head and Jimbo unscrewed the lid. But just before it came off, she placed her hand on his. "Wait. I'm sorry, Henry," she whispered, touching the urn.

Jimbo sealed it back tight and shook his head. "No, young lady, this isn't your fault. You got nothing to be sorry for. You don't say goodbye with regret."

"But, Jimbo," she cried, letting out her secret anguish. "I didn't come home. I was supposed to come home. And I didn't. And he died."

Jimbo pulled Isla to him, rocking her a little. "Let me tell you a little secret, honey. The biggest lie we tell ourselves is that we have control over anything. We are all just tiny little specks in a universe that don't care whether we live or die. And that might seem scary, to be so small and insignificant. But don't feel that way, honey. Instead just remember that you are a tiny part of something so much bigger than you. Henry too. Your tiny little human thoughts don't matter. You're just a little part of a big world and there is nothing you can do to change it. The only thing we can do is to love the ones we get stuck with," he said. "You love Henry?"

Tears filled her eyes. She couldn't speak, she could only nod. Yes. She loved Henry.

"And you know he loved you?"

She nodded again.

"Well, there you go. Let it go, honey. Let all that go now, okay?"

She took a deep breath and used the last of her strength to open the urn and let the wind take Henry out to the sea. His tiny, insignificant self, back into the world, somehow, somewhere. And when the last ash fell to the water, Isla looked at Jimbo and mouthed, *Thank you.*

"You need a ride home, honey?" Jimbo asked when they came back in.

"No, I'm good, I'm going to walk, I think. Thank you for today."

"Anytime, sweetie. You sure you okay to get home on your own?"

"I'm fine," Isla assured him.

She took the familiar path through the woods, and was nearly back at Grace's when she heard voices.

"Where are you going?" It was Richard.

"I'm going to find Isla," she heard Grace's voice say clearly. "She needs me."

"I need you more," he said. Isla could hear his voice start to change. "You know I need you more. Are you really going to walk away from me right now?"

Say yes, Isla thought to herself. *Just say you will.*

But instead there was a long sigh from Grace. "No."

Richard laughed and their voices disappeared into the bay.

Henry was gone. Grace was gone. Isla was feeling like she was disappearing into nothing. The sadness was too much. There was only one last hope. Ben.

Isla ran as fast as she could to the shop where Ben worked. He was there by himself, closing up.

By the time she opened the door she was breathing heavily.

"Isla?" Ben said, surprised. "Are you okay? I didn't get a chance to talk to you at the funeral. I was so sorry to hear about Henry."

She ran up to him and put her fingers over his mouth. "Come with me," she said desperately.

"What?" he asked. "Now?"

"Yes!" She laughed maniacally, tears rolling down her cheeks. "Yes now! Me and you, off to the Caribbean! Or the Philippines. Anywhere you want, we just have to go, now, and never come back."

"Isla," Ben said, his face confused. "I can't just leave. Come on, let me take you back to our house. To Grace."

"No!" she sobbed, putting her hands over her ears.

"Isla, I know it's hard, having lost Henry. Maybe next year we can go traveling? But now, let me take you home."

But Isla was in the water before he could touch her, and she didn't come home for a long, long time.

Chapter Sixteen

When Georgiana woke the following morning, it was with that feeling like she'd slept through her alarm. She jolted upright and hit her head on the sloped roof of the attic in the upstairs bedroom.

She and Bayla had spent the evening baking secret recipes Georgiana had been writing for years. Sugar cookies baked with dreams, lemon meringues whipped with whimsy. She told Bayla about her plan to open a special bakery one day from her house, when the crotchety old barber Phil, who owned the house and worked downstairs, finally retired and sold it to her. Georgiana had tried to urge Bayla to open up too, perhaps about her father, but she was quiet on the subject. It was relatively early when they went up to the spare bedroom in the attic where Bayla wanted to sleep because she was fascinated by what was called a widow's peak.

But Bayla was not here now. Rubbing her head, Georgiana grabbed the alarm clock next to her bed and saw that it was after seven already.

"Bayla!" she called down the steps to the open-plan living room, kitchen and dining area. But Bayla wasn't there either. She started feeling a panicky sensation in her gut. Without thinking, she ran down the stairs to the barber shop and opened the door still in her Scooby-Doo pajamas.

Phil the barber was outside doing his usual Monday routine— sitting outside in front of the barber shop, having a coffee with a few of his fishing buddies. They stopped talking when Georgiana appeared.

"Phil, how long have you guys been out here?"

Phil scrunched his forehead. "We've been out here since Old Donovan and Fletch came back from their morning fishing run. What time was that, boys?"

"'Bout an hour ago, I reckon," Fletch said. None of them was wearing a watch.

"And did you see Bayla Monroe come out of the house? She was staying with me last night and she's not here now."

"That Grace Cleary's kid, isn't it?" Old Donovan asked.

Georgiana nodded. They all shook their heads.

"Naw, not seen her since we been out here."

Georgiana nearly wept. She ran back upstairs, picked up the phone and called Grace.

~

Grace and Isla had stayed up the entire night talking. When the sun started coming up, Grace went and put on a pot of coffee and they sat on the porch, looking out at the bay.

"I didn't know, Isla, that you'd heard me choose Richard over you. That Ben said no and didn't come with you. I didn't know how heartbroken you truly were and I wasn't there for you. That moment is the biggest regret of my life. I'm sorry. I'm so sorry," Grace said after a long silence when they had both finished their stories.

"I'm sorry too," Isla said. "I should have been there for you. Perhaps if we would have talked about what happened with Richard, if you would have trusted me with your secrets, you wouldn't have blocked it out and forgotten about it, and perhaps you never would have married him. We were just so...so..."

"I know," Grace agreed. "So—"

"Young," they both said in unison, and smiled. Grace's phone rang.

"That'll be Georgiana," she said, hopping up to grab it off the kitchen table inside. "Probably trying to figure out why my kid gets up at the crack of dawn instead of sleeping in like a normal kid. Gigi is not a morning person, which is surprising for a baker." She laughed, looking down at the screen and seeing that it was indeed Georgiana.

"Did she keep you up all night and then wake you up at dawn, Geor— What? What do you mean she's not there? When did she leave? You don't know where she is? Oh my god, for how long?"

Isla's head whipped around and she jumped up quickly.

"Just keep looking, okay? I'm going to call Jimbo. Maybe she's at Cleary's." Grace hung up, turning back to Isla. Her breathing was shallow, she felt like she was hyperventilating. "She's not at Georgiana's house. She said when she woke up Bayla simply wasn't there. She's disappeared."

"Okay, we don't know she's not just at Cleary's. Georgiana lives on that side of the bay. She could be out exploring the Cove too. She is a kid, after all," Isla said, unconvincingly.

But Grace was shaking her head, still trying to catch her breath. "You know Bayla, she would never disappear without telling someone."

Isla took the phone. "Deep breaths, Grace. I'm calling Jimbo."

Grace nodded and focused on breathing in and out as instructed while Isla dialed.

"Hey, Jimbo, it's Isla. Is Bayla there with you or Della by chance?" Grace could hear his deep cadence through the phone but couldn't make out his words, but suddenly Isla's mouth opened. "A grease fire? At Cleary's? Oh my god—"

Grace grabbed the phone. "Jimbo! Is everyone okay? Is Cleary's okay? Is Bayla there?"

"Heya, honey. Not sure what happened, the fryer must have been left on. Nobody's hurt, and Cleary's is fine, but I'm going to put in one of the fryers from the storage instead, just to be safe. And no, Bayla isn't here, honey. Where do you reckon she might have gone?"

"I'll call you back," Grace said and hung up, looking desperately at Isla. "This is Richard, I know it. One night, when he got the crazy look in his eyes, he cut off our Internet and stole my SIM card out of my phone so I couldn't contact anyone. Whenever he was suspicious I was leaving, he would threaten me and vow he would never let me take Bayla from him. I know it's him, Isla, I can feel it, and I know he has Bayla," she cried desperately.

"I'm going to go to Georgiana's and get all the details, see if she left anything behind. Then we'll go to Cleary's and get a search party together. You stay here, call Ben and get him on the move. I've got to get out on the water. I'll go to the Cove and pick up *The Maiden*," Isla said in a rush. "We'll find her."

"I can't just stay here waiting, I need to do something!" Grace said.

"You're right, you need to call the police," she said, turning to leave. "Loretta!"

Loretta stood at the front door. "Georgiana called me just a few minutes ago. It's him, isn't it?"

"I think so," Grace said in a small voice.

"This is my fault," Loretta said. "You go, Isla. I'll stay here with Grace in case she comes home, and in the meanwhile, let's call the police."

Isla nodded, squeezing Grace's hand, then ran down the road as fast as she could.

"Here," Loretta said, handing her the phone after she'd dialed a number and pressed call. "I've called the local sheriff's department. Al Sturgess was a good friend of your dad's and he won't muck around with paperwork and red tape."

The phone was ringing when Grace put it to her ear.

"I'll make us some tea," said Loretta, walking into the kitchen.

"Sturgess here," a familiar voice said on the other end of the phone.

"Sheriff, it's Grace Cleary."

"Grace, what a surprise! Sue and I were on vacation the past couple weeks so I'm sorry we haven't been in to see all the exciting stuff you've been doing with the restaurant, but we'll be in soon. Got tickets to the Cook-Off already," he said cheerfully.

"Oh, thank you, but I need your help right now. My daughter Bayla is missing," she said breathlessly. "I don't know what to do—she'd never leave without telling someone. I'm afraid that her father, Richard, took her."

"Richard Monroe?" he said in a scathing voice. "Gotta tell you, Grace, your dad was not fond of your husband at all. You think he's kidnapped her?"

"I don't know!" she sobbed. "I just know she's missing and he's…he's…"

"How long's she been gone?" he asked.

"I don't know exactly, but she was discovered missing this morning," Grace said, taking a breath. Loretta was coming back with tea.

"Well, she can't have got far. Get your friends out there asking around to everyone you know, check everywhere she could have gone, and we'll get the patrolmen on the lookout. What's his full name and vehicle plate number?"

She gave him the details. "But, Sheriff, we lived in Phoenix so he probably wouldn't be in his own car."

"Never hurts to check. But good call. I have a friend at the airport. I'll run his name past them. Loretta there with you?" he asked.

"Yes," Grace said.

"Stay home with her and wait. It's likely they'll call."

"Okay. Thank you, Sheriff Sturgess," she said.

"Anything for Tom Cleary's girl," he said, choking up a bit. "Best friend I ever had."

Grace handed Loretta her phone back and walked down to the bay to put her feet in the water, as if hoping it was going to tell her something, give her a clue as to where her daughter was. She walked back to the porch where Loretta was and sat on the swinging chair, hugging her knees, before standing up again.

"I can't stand just siting here waiting, doing nothing."

"We are not doing nothing. Here, drink this," she said, handing her a cup of hot tea. "Al Sturgess is a good man and he's a fine sheriff. I also called Richard's parents and let them know Bayla is missing and we think she might be with him, in case he goes home, and that we're worried for his mental state. I've also called the Colletts and asked them to call Matt. I reckon if Richard has a boat, it'll be Matt's, and I'm hoping he's not so completely stupid that he wouldn't fess up when they know what I've threatened."

"What did you threaten?" Grace asked.

"Besides death?" Loretta quipped and Grace let out a breath of surprise. "I told him if he knew anything and didn't tell us, I'd have him thrown in jail as an accomplice. Then I dropped the name of a lawyer friend I knew a long time ago, and that will surely scare him. So now, we wait."

Grace took a sip of the hot tea and pulled a face, nearly spitting it out. "Good lord, what is this? It tastes like dirt."

"Mmm." She nodded. "And it might well be. I go to a Chinese acupuncturist. Doesn't speak a word of English but he's a genius. Gives me my treatment and then this stuff to drink. It keeps my nerves happy."

"I didn't know you were going to an acupuncturist. When did that start?"

"'Bout five years ago. Your dad thought maybe I should try something else for my nerves. You know, something other than the pills." Loretta glanced sadly at Grace. "I know I wasn't the best stepmother growing up. I had an addiction and I didn't realize it. There is so much I don't remember. Blank years, even," she sighed.

"I had trouble sleeping, that was how it began. My doctor gave me sleeping pills, but then I couldn't wake up properly and my work suffered, so I started drinking too much coffee. Then I got anxious from too much coffee so I was prescribed anti-anxiety pills." She shook her head. "Years of my life ruined. With an addiction fed by a doctor."

Grace was shocked to hear this admission and also that she'd had no idea how medicated Loretta actually had been, and by a doctor no less. "Loretta, I'm sorry. It must have been terrible for you."

"For me?" She laughed bitterly. "Of course it was, when I was with it. But it wasn't very nice for your dad, or you or Ben. I'm sorry," she said, taking a deep, full breath. She turned to look at Grace and took her hand. "I'm so sorry, Grace."

She pulled her in for a gentle hug. It was very awkward—she realized she hadn't hugged Loretta since the day she'd married her dad.

Loretta pulled back quickly and stood up. "Well, I'll go check up on Matt's parents and see if they've made any progress. Drink your tea, it will help." She turned and opened the screen door.

"Loretta?" Grace said. "Thank you for being here."

Her face relaxed. "Drink your tea, dear."

It had been five minutes since Grace heard Loretta pacing back and forth on the phone, yelling here, whispering there, hissing every now and again. Finally, she had popped her head out the door.

"I'll be back in ten minutes. Don't go anywhere," she said.

"Wait, where are you going?"

"Matt's new boat is called *The Nymph*, the little pervert," Loretta said. "And your soon-to-be dead ex-husband happened to borrow it for a few days. I'm just going to run up to the house and grab your dad's phone. He had a WhatsApp group that connected everyone on the water," she explained. "I'll send a message out for everyone to keep an eye out for *The Nymph*." She turned, biting her lower lip. "Would he hurt Bayla?"

"I don't know," Grace said, rubbing her temples. "I don't think so. I don't know that Richard is capable of true love, but I do know that Bayla is the closest he's got to even glancing it from afar."

"But he would hurt you?"

Grace nodded silently and Loretta took a deep breath, grasping her shoulder.

"He *did* hurt you."

It was not a question. Grace nodded again.

Loretta closed her eyes tightly and took another breath before seeming to regain her strength. She squeezed Grace's shoulder. "Never again. I'll be right back, I promise."

She stumbled slightly and had to grab the back of the chair. "I...Grace, I don't feel very well. My legs aren't working properly," she said in a weak voice.

"Loretta? Are you okay?" Grace stood to help Loretta but suddenly her own knees buckled, as though she'd lost all the strength in her legs. "What the...?"

But the words came out slurred as she held herself upright as best as she could, trying to clear her head.

Grace heard a strangled sound and looked down at Loretta, who had lowered herself to the ground. She looked up at her with wide, terrified eyes and pointed behind her, and the last thing Grace remembered was the smell of whiskey and Richard's Armani cologne, his voice whispering in her ear.

⌒

The nausea hit Grace before she opened her eyes. She took in her surroundings. The scents first. Saltwater. Whiskey. Cologne. Richard.

Then the sensations. The nausea was from a drug, she was certain. Rohypnol, she would guess, remembering that Richard had used it on her once before.

They'd been out at a party together and Richard left her side for a few minutes. When he'd come back, a young colleague of his named Tate was chatting with her. When Richard joined them, she could see the way his eyes were gleaming at Tate, at her. He'd smiled, chatting charmingly, even as he gripped her arm so tightly it bruised immediately. He'd leaned over and whispered into her ear, "Remember that all actions have consequences, Grace."

That was the last thing she remembered. She'd woken up in her bed the next morning feeling sick, with no recollection of the night before.

"Ah, my poor wife," Richard had said, looking at her when she opened her eyes. "She drank so much so quickly that I had to pick her up and carry her to the car to bring her home."

"What happened?" Grace had asked. Her mouth was dry like it had been wiped out with cotton wool. "Did you...did you drug me?"

"Rohypnol," he'd said.

"The date-rape drug?" she'd gasped.

"Date rape is such a grotesque term."

"But why?" she'd asked. Her head was still so fuzzy.

"I told you, Grace. Actions have consequences. You flirt with other men, and I will take you home, weak, helpless and humiliated. So now you know, and you won't do it again, right?" he'd said, his tone pleasant, but sinister.

She felt exactly like she had that morning now—sick, dry mouth, and terrified. The rocking back and forth didn't help the nausea. She was on a boat, obviously, and must be out of Maiden's Cove for the waves to be up on a day like this. Finally, she opened her eyes.

She was in the bedroom cabin of a fine boat that she assumed must be *The Nymph*. Richard sat at a little table across from her, watching her, sipping a dram of his favorite whiskey. She could taste some of it on her lips and wondered if he'd kissed her when she was unconscious. The thought made her feel ill.

"You were out for a long time, Grace. I was starting to get worried about you," said Richard. "That's no way to start a family holiday now, is it?"

"You drugged me," she said, no question in her voice.

"Bayla was very excited to have you on board and I didn't want you to upset her," he said. "We've been trying to figure out the very best place to take our family holiday this year. What do you think, Grace?"

She could see that the little switch had been turned in his eyes. He wasn't himself. And that made him a danger to all of them, especially out on the water like this.

"Richard," she said softly. "Where is Bayla?"

He didn't answer, but just kept staring out into a blank world Grace could not see.

"Bayla!" Grace called out.

"I'm here, Mom, I'm okay," she replied.

She did sound okay, but she was wheezing. Grace nearly cried with the relief she felt. She took a deep breath, gaining her strength.

"Richard, let me out of here, please," she pleaded. "I'm not feeling very well." He didn't answer. "Richard?" she said more loudly.

His eyes came back into focus. Grace's heart sped up and she realized she shouldn't have roused him out of his stupor. She should have run up and locked him in, gone to the radio and called for help.

"Get up," Richard said, standing and moving to the cabin door.

She stood, trying to find her balance, but the sea was not calm. Richard opened the door of the cabin and ducked through, leaving the door open for Grace to follow. Bayla was sitting on the berth. She was pale and wheezing but looked otherwise unharmed. Until Grace saw that her feet were tied together.

"You tied her up? Your daughter?" Grace yelled out. "Look at the waves, Richard!" She sat beside Bayla. "Are you okay, kiddo?" she asked gently.

Bayla nodded. "Just a little seasick, and I need my inhaler."

Grace looked around. There was no land in sight and the waves were crashing over the sides of the boat. She noticed the anchor was pulled up, so they must have been drifting for quite a while.

"What are you doing, Richard? Why have you taken us?"

He ran his hand through his hair. "You said you'd never leave me. You promised."

"You promised you'd never hurt Bayla!" she cried. "But you've tied up her feet. She's unwell, Richard, and she needs her inhaler. Drop her to shore, to Cleary's, and you and I can stay on the boat and talk for as long as you want."

"She's not getting off the boat. Neither are you," he said, walking toward the helm. "Don't you remember, Grace? This is our family holiday!"

"Okay," she said, nodding. Her heart was racing. He was dangerous at the moment. She needed to get them back to shore or at least set off a distress call. Richard wasn't a good boater and neither was she. They never should have drifted this far out, especially with a storm brewing like this. She had to try to reason with him. "I admit, I made a mistake leaving. We've been miserable without you."

Richard paused just long enough to glance back. "I don't believe you."

"It's true, Daddy! I want to come home to Phoenix. Please? We can go on a vacation first though. What about Assateague Island? I want to see the horses," Bayla cried.

"See? Bayla would love that."

Richard took a deep breath and finished his whiskey. "But what if we just had our holiday out here? We could ride the waves!" He went to the steering wheel and turned the engine on. He took the speedboat up to forty, then fifty miles per hour. He jerked the wheel suddenly and they jumped a wave as if the speedboat were a Jet Ski.

"Whoa! Yeah!" he yelled, laughing as the boat went too fast and too high.

"Richard, stop!" Grace cried, trying to get to Bayla but was thrown to the other side of the boat. "Hold on, Bayla!"

"Daddy, stop it, please!" Bayla cried, holding tightly to the side of the boat.

His eyes were wild, he couldn't see or hear Grace or Bayla. Grace tried to make her way over to Bayla when suddenly she saw another boat coming toward them at top speed.

"Isla," she whispered, relief pouring through her.

Richard slowed *The Nymph* down and turned to see the boat near them, but Isla had turned off the engine and dived into the water.

"Who is that?" Richard yelled angrily, turning off the engine. "Where did that boat come from?"

A large wave washed over their boat and Grace lost her balance, when suddenly Richard grabbed her by the hair and yanked her back, throwing her on the ground, then wrapped his hands around her neck.

"Daddy, no!" Bayla cried.

"Did you call for help, Grace? Is your new lover here to rescue you?"

Grace was struggling to breathe as he squeezed her neck, his eyes bloodshot and crazed, spit flying from his mouth. She was kicking and trying to wrench his hands from her neck, but she wasn't getting enough oxygen and she was losing her vision. Just as she thought she was going to pass out, she heard a visceral voice.

"Get off her, you monster!" Isla yelled.

Grace looked up to see Isla hit him as hard as she could with one of the large wooden oars, and he groaned as Grace felt the dead weight of his body drop on her. Isla pulled Richard off of her as Grace tried to get up.

He groaned again and touched his head, which was bleeding from where Isla had hit him.

"Are you okay?" Isla asked, taking Grace's hand. But a wave rocked the boat and Grace fell back down.

"We need to get him locked into the cabin and start back. This storm is worsening," Grace called above the sound of the waves, and Isla nodded.

They each grabbed one of his legs and dragged him down into the cabin, letting his head hit every step. He was still conscious, but barely.

"You bitch," he said, looking at Isla.

Grace punched him in the face, and his eyes rolled back in his head before they closed. They locked him in the cabin as another wave came over the boat.

"I'll get us out of here," Isla said as they ran up the stairs, but Bayla was gone.

"Bayla!" Grace yelled, looking frantically around the boat.

"She can swim, I know she can swim!" Isla cried. "Where is she?"

"Her feet were tied!" Grace sobbed. "Bayla! Bayla!"

"Turn the engine on!" Isla yelled, and then she was in the water.

Grace quickly started up the engine and circled the boat slowly. She saw Isla's head come out of the water once, twice, looking around, but no Bayla. Grace sobbed loudly, circling the boat. "No, God, please no, not my baby, please."

And then she saw them. Isla's red hair emerged from the water, and her daughter was in her arms. Bayla did not seem to be moving.

"No!" Grace cried, as Isla dragged Bayla's form onto the boat. She didn't seem conscious. "My baby!"

"Grace, you need to give her CPR. I can't tell if she's swallowed a lot of water, or whether she's hit her head or not, but either way we need to get any water out of her lungs as quickly as possible. I'll call the Coast Guard to meet us and get this boat back to shore as fast as I can," Isla said.

Grace nodded and began giving her daughter CPR, rolling her over on her side and patting her back in between attempts, to try to rid her lungs of the water that was surely there. But she didn't seem to be responding. They were not as far out as Grace had thought they were, and she could see the land was within a few minutes, but it wouldn't be soon enough if Bayla wasn't breathing.

"It's not working, Isla!" Grace shouted and Isla looked back desperately.

"Quick, come and take the wheel," she said, and Grace aimed the boat for land while Isla took over CPR.

Finally, after a moment, Bayla began to cough up the salty water.

"Oh my god, Bayla!" Grace cried.

Isla turned her over and she threw up more water out of her lungs. Grace pulled up to the beach in front of her house where the Coast Guard was waiting to give Bayla medical attention.

Jimbo and Della, Georgiana, Luke, Ben, Loretta and Aunt Lou were all there on the shore as Bayla was brought onto the beach and wrapped in a warming blanket. They checked her lungs and vitals and made sure she was okay. She wasn't actually under as long as they'd feared and was answering questions within minutes.

"The ambulance is on its way," Ben said, taking Isla's hand. "They'll take Loretta too. She got a pretty good dose of the Rohypnol as well. Bayla will need to stay overnight, they said. I think you should go too."

"I'm fine," she said, turning to Grace. "Do you want me to come with you?"

"We'll be okay," Grace said, rocking Bayla in her arms. "Thank you, Isla. Thank you for saving my daughter."

Isla glanced down at Bayla, who was looking up at her with an expression that was hard to read. "How's that little lung of yours, kiddo?" Isla asked, bending down so Bayla could keep her voice to a whisper, which was important after swallowing so much saltwater.

"Feels bigger," Bayla said, looking at her curiously.

Sheriff Sturgess arrived shortly after, and Richard did not fight when Jimbo put his big hand on his shoulder and told him to sit down while they waited for the police. Nor did he fight when they handcuffed him.

"Can I...can I say goodbye to my daughter. Tell her..." Richard choked.

Grace shook her head adamantly and wrapped her arms tighter around Bayla.

"It's okay, Mommy," Bayla whispered.

Finally Grace nodded and Richard came closer, leaning down, and Grace could see he was crying.

"I'm sorry, Bayla," he whispered, swallowing a sob. "I'll get help now. I promise."

Bayla stretched out her hand and touched his bowed head. "I forgive you already, Daddy."

Grace watched as the sheriff led Richard up toward the waiting police car.

"He's gone," Jimbo said. "Ambulance is just pulling up in a minute now, Gracey."

Grace nodded and continued to rock Bayla in her arms.

Jimbo smiled a big white smile. "There's my girls. Well then, we'll see you tomorrow. Take care, Gracey, Isla, and especially you, shrimp," he said to Bayla, who giggled and snuggled into Grace.

Aunt Lou stood after they left. "Luke, take me home," she said simply.

"Yes ma'am," he said, standing. He didn't kiss Grace's cheek the way Della had, but his finger grazed it softly. She looked up at him and smiled, her cheeks warming so much she had to turn away. "Georgiana, do you need a lift too?"

"Yes please," she said, jumping up and giving Bayla a quick hug, then squeezing Grace's shoulder. "You girls take care, okay? Call if you need anything."

"We will," Bayla and Grace said at the same time.

Isla and Ben sat side by side, not quite holding hands, but their pinky fingers linked together beside them. The ambulance pulled up to Brixton Cottage and Grace and Loretta answered a few questions while Bayla sat on Isla's lap now, looking out to the bay.

"Summer's almost over, Aunt Isla," Bayla said. "Do you think we'll see the green lights again?" She was no longer wheezing.

"Bayla, can you let the paramedics check you over?" Grace called.

"Come on," Isla said, helping Bayla up and leading her to where they were waiting.

Isla whispered into Bayla's ear then, something just for her. They smiled and Isla looked first to Grace, and then to Ben. And then she jumped into the water and was gone.

～

It was nearly sunrise. Ben and Isla lay side by side on the back porch of the deck at Henry's, naked, holding hands after making love. Neither of them had spoken a word to each other for hours, though their minds were racing after the day's events.

"Did you know that I loved you, Benjamin Cleary?"

"Do you love me still?" he asked.

"Forever," she said, a smile on her lips.

"And in between?"

Isla turned and met his eyes. "Is but a moment. The blink of an eye."

Chapter Seventeen

Though Bayla put on a brave face for everyone around her, Grace knew that the incident with Richard was not without its consequences. Bayla ended up staying three nights in the hospital so they could keep an eye on her lungs, as complications with near-drownings were common. Infections, chemical imbalances, and irregular heart rhythms could occur, not to mention that any long-term effects, they said rather seriously, could take years to fully heal. Yet Bayla was cleared a few days later and was feeling cheerful and excited to come back home and to Cleary's.

"It's my new lungs, Mom," she said as they drove home from the hospital. "I think Aunt Isla accidentally gave me one of her mermaid ones."

"Sure, hon," she said, smiling at Bayla indulgently.

"How long do I get to have a free pass and do whatever I want?" Bayla asked, grinning.

"A wee while, I think," Grace said, laughing. "How are you though, really?"

Bayla looked out the window, taking a deep breath. Despite the fact that her breathing was actually better, her throat was constantly dry and irritated from the saltwater. Bayla lightly touched her throat with her fingers now, and Grace couldn't help the tears that formed in her eyes.

"I'm so sorry, sweetheart," she said, trying to swallow her tears. "I will never forgive myself for allowing you to be in danger of your dad."

"I think he'll get better, don't you, Mom?" Bayla asked hopefully. "Where is he now?"

"Gloretta's lawyer friend helped us get your dad into a really good program near Pappy and Nanna Monroe so he's got his own family nearby. He's getting some really good help," she said.

Richard and his lawyer had asked Grace not to press charges, and she'd considered momentarily, for Bayla's sake. But then she realized that if she did that, she would be telling her daughter that it was okay to be abused. So she did press charges in the end, and went for full custody and retribution for his years of abuse. Despite the fact that he agreed to three years in therapy, Grace wasn't convinced at all that it would help a man like Richard, so the other half of the deal was a restraining order against him approaching her and Bayla, though Grace promised that after a time, she would allow him visits with Bayla if she wanted to see him, so long as they were supervised.

Bayla knew that things would be different from now on. But somehow, likely because of the familial and friend support system in place in Maiden's Cove, Bayla seemed healthy and happy. Grace marveled at her daughter's resilience.

Loretta's lawyer friend, who she'd threatened the Colletts with, turned out to be one of the most powerful and influential lawyers on the East Coast of the U.S. His name was Paton Oxford and he obviously wanted to be a little more than a friend to Loretta.

"We went to college together," she said dismissively, when he'd left the Cleary house after speaking with her and Grace. "I think he might have had a bit of a thing for me."

Grace laughed. "I think he might still have a bit of a thing for you."

"Gracey," Loretta scoffed, blushing, and Grace found that she didn't mind Loretta calling her Gracey at all anymore. In fact, it made her feel like her dad was back with her.

"Hey, if I can find love again after what I went through for a decade with Richard, so can you," she said.

Loretta glanced over. "You're right. And Luke is a good man."

"You're coming to the Cook-Off, right?" Grace asked.

"I wouldn't miss that for the whole world," Loretta said, squeezing her hand.

~

The day of Tommy's Cook-Off finally arrived and Grace had known that if they could pull off a big one this year, they could make it through. It was the ultimate celebration of her dad and everything he loved. And once the *Food and Travel* article came out, the day turned into something bigger than even they had anticipated.

Grace, Isla and Bayla walked around Cleary's setting up for the big day. Grace could not believe they'd sold three hundred tickets and left room for more to come. Jimbo had brought out all the old smokers and set them up in the parking lot. The concept of the cook-off was this: Cleary's invited a known chef, famous for a special dish, who became the celebrity guest chef for the day. Then, amateur chefs—even just a regular Joe from next door—could enter to compete. Entrants had to cook the same dish the celebrity chef was doing, but in their own style. Then Cleary's sold tickets which included an all-you-can-eat buffet of all the chefs' dishes next to Della and her team's side dishes. This year the tables were spread with Della's homemade coleslaw, potato salad, baked beans, collard greens, a fresh cucumber and vinegar salad, and a macaroni and cheese that Bayla swore she could eat for the rest of her life on its own.

"Wow, look at Cleary's! It's so cool, isn't it, Aunt Isla?" Bayla exclaimed as they walked around together.

"Super cool," she said, squeezing Bayla's shoulder.

Bayla was doing remarkably well considering the ordeal Richard had put them through and her near drowning the week before, which had turned into a great story for the local kids, though not nearly as great as the fact that she was rescued, underwater, by her Aunt Isla.

"Mape!" Bayla called, seeing Mape and some other kids from the town line up outside to wait for the doors to open. All the locals came to the Cook-Off. "Hey, guys!"

"Hey, Bayla," a boy said. "Mape was telling us you almost died. Wicked. What happened?"

She started telling them a version of the story that didn't involve her dad kidnapping them. "And then, I was surrounded by green lights in the water, and it was like I was being called down by the merfolk," Bayla said, and they all hushed. "I guess that must be when I was almost dying." They gasped. "But then Aunt Isla pulled me from the water and sucked it from my lungs!"

Grace and Isla chuckled.

"I can't believe how well she's dealing with it all," Isla said.

"I know," Grace agreed. "I keep checking in but she just says that Daddy is where he belongs right now. And so are we, and everything is okay."

"How is Richard?"

Grace shook her head. "In therapy, anger management classes and AA for drinking. Going through some pretty brutal self-reflection at the moment, I imagine. The fact that he's trying to make it all right with Bayla is what matters. I'm pleased he's doing this for her."

"And you?"

"One day I will be able to forgive him, I think. But for now, I'm just ready to be on my own journey again. Here, in Maiden's Cove. At Cleary's." She looked around with tears in her eyes. "I couldn't have done this without you, Isla. Thank you."

"What about me?" Cohen asked, sauntering over.

Grace laughed. "Without you, I wouldn't *be* here. Neither would Cleary's. And you know that. Actually," she cleared her throat, "quick pre-service meeting in the kitchen, team."

Jimbo came inside from the barbecue pit, and Luke and Della from the kitchen with Clarence and Theo. Georgiana from the baking station; Todd, Sarah, Abby and the entire front of house team, the dishwasher, the fryers, the bussers. They were a team of about twenty altogether, and Grace looked around at them all now.

"I just wanted to say thank you, all of you, for this summer, for your love of Cleary's and your dedication to making it remain a beloved Maiden's Cove destination for all. Team, we are out of the red—Cleary's is saved!"

They all cheered loudly.

"And most importantly, thank you for today." Grace took in the old signs they'd put up around the restaurant from every Tommy's Cook-Off since the first one, with a big photo of Tom right out in the front, above a table for those who wanted to leave something to his memory. "This is a true testament to my dad and to Cleary's. I couldn't be more honored. Thank you."

The team took turns hugging Grace and saying a word here and there.

"Remember the first year I started," a boy named Jay said as he hugged her. "I was only fifteen, got a job washing dishes, but he knew I liked food and wanted to be in the kitchen. So every day after work he stayed an extra hour and we made something together. Great man, Mr. Tommy."

"Thank you, Jay," said Grace.

It continued like that for a few minutes when suddenly Jimbo spoke. "Righto, team, our celebrity guest chef is here! Let's give him a proper welcome."

They all clapped and went to introduce themselves to the man who had just entered. Georgiana, Isla and Grace stayed behind for a moment with Jimbo.

"Who is it?" Georgiana asked.

"Christian Fullerton," Luke answered, falling in line with the girls. "He's a local, actually."

"A local?" Georgiana asked. "Where from? I didn't know we had a famous barbecue pit here on the bay."

"Oh yeah, he's from the Barbecue Shack, just outside Ocean City," said Jimbo. "Real authentic place. Order from the board like back in Memphis, get everything in takeaways, sit outside on benches if you can find one. Does some of the best pork butt I ever had, that's for sure."

"Is that what he's cooking today?" Grace asked.

"You can ask him yourself, Gracey, here he is. Christian, meet Grace Cleary."

Grace reached out to shake his hand. Christian Fullerton was in his mid-thirties, with broad shoulders and a small waist. He was wearing an old Cleary's shirt, rolled sleeves, with a white chef's apron covering his board shorts and chef's crocs with no socks. He wore a baseball cap and had a blond ponytail that somehow looked cool on him. His face was tanned, and his blue eyes smiled above a short blond beard with flecks of gold and gray. He was incredibly handsome.

"Grace Cleary, a true honor," he said, shaking her hand and smiling. He turned and pointed to the back of his old shirt. "Tommy's Special Smoke-off 2016. I was so stoked to be invited by your dad. He was an awesome guy. A true legend."

"Thank you," Grace said, touched. "Did you win?"

He threw his head back and laughed. "Hell no, not even close. That was the year he'd just been on *Diners* and so to celebrate, he invited only guest chefs to compete against each other. So it was an honor. But Bobbie Johns from *Memphis* came up, man. And these dudes from this shack in Austin. It was brutal! But your dad, he came up to me and said—and I'll never forget this—he said, 'Your food's good, kid. Real good. But you're young and good lookin' and the rest of us aren't, so get ready to lose. The rest of us got too much else to make up for.'"

Grace laughed. "That sounds just like him. It seems so fitting then that you came back to be our celebrity chef today. He would have been so pleased."

"I'm aiming to be one of the old ones one day where I can kick other young bucks out, so always happy to support."

"What are you making today?"

"I'm making my famous pork butt," he said, taking them over to the pit. "Figure if you're a guest chef you should bring your A game. But I'm using your dad's pork butt rub. Every dollar earned for me today is going to bottling Cleary's Rub in my shop."

"Wow, Christian. Thank you. That is so touching," Grace said, her voice faltering. Beside her, Georgiana was clearing her throat. "I'm sorry, how rude! This is Georgiana Glover. She's one of our chefs. Georgiana, this is Christian."

Grace turned to Georgiana, who was glancing back and forth from Christian to the trees beyond, not saying a word. She swallowed fiercely. Christian looked in question at Grace, who shrugged. What was wrong with her?

"Hey wait a minute," Christian said. "You're not *Gigi*, are you? From the *Food and Travel* article?"

Georgiana finally met his eyes and nodded shortly. Grace noted that she hadn't bothered to mention how much she hated the name Gigi to Christian.

"I have a confession to make," he said. "Last week I made it my life's mission to marry you."

Georgiana's jaw dropped. "What?!"

"That strawberry shortcake? Honestly. You are a genius when it comes to baking. What is your secret? As a chef, seriously, I must know."

Grace smiled as Georgiana began to speak, the electricity between them palpable.

"I suppose freshness of ingredients is the most important. But really? Food is about passion. True, complete, unharnessed passion..."

"I couldn't agree more."

The day was a complete success. Luke came out of the kitchen and spent the whole time at Grace's side, helping where she needed it, grazing her arm every time he passed, shooting shivers up her spine. He was taking it as slow as he promised, but sometimes when he looked at her a certain way, or touched her in a way that made her sweat, Grace wanted to throw all caution to the wind and lock him in the bedroom with her for a week. But then she'd look at her daughter and know that she'd been through enough this year to last a lifetime, despite the fact that Bayla seemed to like Luke as much as she did.

"Luke!" Bayla yelled. "Come tell my friends about New Zealand!"

"Duty calls," he said, tracing his thumb over her lips, which made her quiver. She loved it when he did that.

Ben arrived shortly after they opened and it warmed Grace to see him wander through the pictures of old, of their dad, of Cleary's.

"I wish I'd been a bigger part of it all now," he said, looking at a blown-up picture of Tom with Grace and Ben when they were little, in big Cleary's T-shirts. "I should have helped more after you left, not let this place get into the red like it did."

"He didn't tell you it was in trouble, or you know you would have helped. But, Ben, he didn't tell you because he knew that your path was somewhere else," Grace said, wrapping her arm around his waist and pulling him in for a side hug.

"What, at the shop renting out kayaks and boats? Some grand path," he scoffed.

"You know that isn't what I meant," she said, looking at Isla. "I remember how jealous I used to be when I'd listen to you and Isla talk for hours about all the places you wanted to see and travel to, back when we were younger," she said. "It's not too late, Ben. Don't miss out this time. Because it's all over…"

He smiled and looked at Isla. "Yeah, I know. In the blink of an eye. Thanks, Grace," he said, kissing her cheek before heading over to stand beside Isla, who lit up when she saw him.

"Well, well," a voice said from behind her. Grace turned to see Loretta, looking around with a smile. "Look at all this. I can't believe I ever said you should have sold it." She looked at the picture behind Grace. "Oh gosh, I remember that day. I'd just met your dad. Came over on a friend's boat from Annapolis. Thought I'd never met a man so sexy in my life. My friends over the bay thought I was crazy marrying him."

"Why?" Grace asked. She noticed that Loretta looked very well put-together today, but not overdone. And she looked calm, almost happy. Grace wondered if she'd had acupuncture. Or if it was just this, what they'd accomplished here this summer. The summer of their healing.

"Well, I'd always liked city life, and I didn't want children. And they all thought he might still be in love with that Alison," she said.

"Alison? You knew about her?" Grace asked.

"She was a doll—probably would have been a better mother to you two than I was," Loretta said. "But she never told him, not once, that she loved him, poor thing. And I did. I loved him. I was crazy about him. So I told him straightaway, and I made him love me back, and we had a pretty good life I think. I know I wasn't always perfect, but I always made sure he knew that I loved him. It was the best I could do given my circumstances."

"Dad always seemed really happy to me," Grace said, and she hugged Loretta, not tentatively, but firmly, and Loretta pulled her close.

"Thank you."

Chapter Eighteen

Everyone had come back to Grace's after the Cook-Off for a celebratory glass, and they talked about the summer and their success, and about the upcoming Festival Day for the end of the season.

"I'm looking forward to my first festival," Isla said.

Everyone stared at her in silence.

She shrugged, eyes wide. "What? I've never been. I thought it might be fun."

"Well, all right then," Jimbo said, "I guess we're all going to the festival. Miss Bayla?"

"Oh, yes please! And you'll come, Uncle Ben? Luke? Gigi?" she asked, looking around with hopeful eyes.

They all agreed, and the plan was in place. Grace suspected that it might also be Isla's last night in town, and she was happy that they'd all spend it together.

Everyone left around seven and Aunt Lou was the only one to stay behind.

"Good lord, what a day!" She placed a bottle of wine and three glasses on the table and flicked her wrist for Grace to pour it as she flopped into a chair, groaning. "I'm exhausted from working so hard."

"Aunt Lou, you didn't do anything but eat," Grace said, pouring her a glass. "What was so exhausting?"

"Cohen! And Tristan!" Aunt Lou huffed, taking a hefty gulp of wine. "Honestly, exhausting. It was so much easier in my day."

"I'm sure they'll be grateful for your enthusiasm one day, Lou," Isla said.

"It just takes so long. Life is too short, girls, let me tell you. Don't waste time on the boring stuff. It's annoying."

"I feel like I focused on all the boring stuff and look how long it took me to finally come back home," Isla said, looking out to the bay. "And why? Because I was stubborn? Or because I was scared? I always thought it was my fault that we lost touch, that we grew apart."

"I always thought it was *mine*," Grace said.

"Yes, well, that's always the problem, girls. We always think it's about *us*. It's usually not, you know. Everyone has a story and it's not always part of yours. But that is the curse of youth—our selfishness. Youth also has its gifts, elasticity in the skin and high libido being the two most important that I can think of."

"Aunt Lou!" Grace said with a laugh. "Surely there are more important things than that?"

"When you're my age, you decide," Aunt Lou said.

"How old *are* you, Aunt Lou?" Isla asked.

"No idea," she said, and burped. Isla and Grace stifled their laughter. "Ah, but you girls, you were part of each other's youth, each other's story, so don't worry," she said, patting their hands. "There is no bond in this world, outside of a mother and a daughter, that is stronger than the best friend of your youth, who becomes themselves as you become yourself. You are infinitely one, after that. You girls had a special bond that went beyond the myth and legend and rumor."

"What was that?" Grace asked.

"You loved each other," she said simply.

They were both quiet, before Isla took Grace's hand. "There's no past tense in this house, Aunt Lou."

"Yes, yes," she said, finishing her wine and holding her glass out again.

"Aunt Lou!" Grace cried. "You're drinking all the wine!"

"Get your own bottle," she snapped. "I brought three." She nodded to the ground where two other cold bottles sat. The girls shrugged and each poured their own.

"Of all our summers, this one has been the best of my whole life," Isla whispered, putting her head on Grace's shoulder.

~

It was close to midnight when they put Aunt Lou to bed in the guest room as she passed out the moment she finished her bottle of wine. Isla carried her. Isla was very tall and Aunt Lou kept growing tinier. They tucked her in.

"How old *is* she, do you reckon?" Grace whispered, looking at Aunt Lou's tiny form.

"None of your damned business, brat," Aunt Lou snapped between snores. Grace and Isla had to hide their laughter, and turned to leave, but Lou opened her eyes, sitting up and taking Isla's hands. "You won't leave without saying goodbye?"

Isla put one hand to her heart. "I promise." Aunt Lou was satisfied and kissed her cheek, reached out to squeeze Grace's hand, and began to snore yet again.

"What do you reckon?" Isla said, as they closed the porch door and stepped back outside. "One last swim in the bay as the mighty Gracenisla?"

She glanced up at the moon and then at the tide, finally settling her gaze on her and Henry's boat, *The Maiden*, that she'd brought over to Brixton Cottage.

"Feel like a boat ride? I've got a great idea."

Feeling freer than she had in years, Grace grinned. There was no mystery anymore, nothing unspoken or unsaid between them. They were finally free. And there was nowhere she'd rather be than with her best friend. "Lead the way, mermaid."

Isla motored them quietly out of the inlet past town into the open water, until there was more water around them than land. It was a calm night, no waves at all. No breeze either. About half an hour later, Isla turned off the engine and dropped anchor. They were in the middle of the bay, nothing around, no lights in sight. It seemed a very strange place to stop.

"We're here. Follow me, it's not far," Isla said, and jumped out of the boat, treading water while waiting for Grace.

She hesitated. She really wasn't a strong enough swimmer to be out in the middle of nowhere. But then, Isla had only just gotten back in the water again as well. She could trust her.

Isla chuckled softly. "Same ole Grace. Always overthinking it."

"Same ole Isla," she quipped, "always underthinking it."

"That's why," she said, swimming up to the boat and rocking it so Grace had to sit down, "we were so formidable as Gracenisla. Yin and Yang. Come on in, I promise, it's not far. And you're with me, remember?"

"When I'm with you, I belong in the water." Grace took off her clothes and jumped in. Isla began to breaststroke slowly so Grace could follow.

"Almost there," she said.

"Almost where?" Grace mumbled, before she suddenly felt it. Sand, like a beach, beneath her feet. Not mud or silt, but proper golden sand. Her other foot touched and she and Isla walked up the gradient. Grace marveled. "A sandbar! Wow! I had no idea there was one this far out! How did you find this?"

If someone would have looked out their window and been able to see far enough out, they would have seen two naked women who appeared to be standing on water. It seemed that way to them too. There were a few places where the sand did break through the surface, but mostly they were ankle deep. On an island in the middle of the bay, unseen. It was like they were floating. It was like they owned the water. It was like the world was theirs.

"It's only accessible a few times a year, I think. At the lowest tides. Do you remember the first day we met? At Cleary's?" Isla asked.

Grace rolled her eyes. "As if I could ever forget that day." She walked around the sandbar until she found the highest spot and sat down. Her feet fell deeper than the rest of her, but she could lay back and keep her head out of the water, on a sandy pillow.

Isla found a place using the same sand pillow so their heads were together but her body was floating on the opposite side of the sandbar. "Remember Jimbo asked where we found the scallops? We didn't know the waters then and hit this sandbar.

Henry tried to get us off, and I went for a dive. They're right under here. Oysters too, and mussels and prawns. You can tell Jimbo now. It's like the sandbar hides them. Like a booby trap." Isla grinned. "He'll know the spot now anyway. This is where we scattered Henry's ashes."

"I'll be sure to tell him," Grace said, and they were quiet for a long time, staring up at the moon and stars, floating on the water like nymphs.

"Six summers. Seven if you include this one," Grace finally said.

"Of?"

"Gracenisla. Nearly three months in a row of me and you never being apart. We explored, we swam, we worked at Cleary's. But mostly, we just never stopped talking. What on earth did we talk about all those months every year, for so long?"

"Well," Isla said, thinking. "I suppose we talked a lot about our dreams. About who we were and who we wanted to be. What we wanted."

"We talked about the meaning of life, and about our fears and what it meant to live, to really live," Grace added.

"We talked about our future selves and what we were going to become, and we'd write letters to each other as those selves."

"We read lots of books all day, often the same one, so we could talk about it all night, and analyze it," Grace said.

"We listened to a lot of music," Isla added. "The same songs over and over again."

Grace started giggling, and Isla followed, and they giggled until they laughed and they laughed until they nearly cried.

"So remind me again," Isla said, when they finally got their breath back. "What did we talk about all the time for so long that was so important?"

"Boys!" Grace hooted, starting a new wave of laughter.

Isla jumped off the sandbar and went for a vigorous swim around it until she came to float beyond Grace, who had sat up. "Isn't it so funny, we girls. The one thing you want more than anything in the world when you're younger is a best friend, someone you can grow with, bosom buddies. Remember?"

"Anne of Green Gables," Grace said and smiled. "That was our favorite the first year. How clearly Anne's desire for a bosom buddy in Diana was so true of the way we longed to find each other."

"And then as soon as you find that best friend to share everything with, you realize the only other thing you want is to find true love, and then you have someone who understands this core part of your being and desire, this teenage angst." Isla sighed with a small smile. "Did you love Richard, Grace?"

"God yes," she said, shaking her head. "I know it started as a crush, which feels like love, when you're young. But the intensity of that desire, and then, to *have* it. To have this chance to have everything you ever wanted. All those big feelings, come true. It was almost overwhelming. Does that make sense?"

"Of course it does," Isla said. "You're talking to the girl who was in love with your brother for so long she begged him to run away with her when they were kids." They both chuckled. "So you and Luke, Fourth of July?" she asked.

Grace smiled. "We talked. All night. And kissed. All night. But otherwise, I need to take it slow."

"Fair enough," Isla said.

"And what about you? You and Ben?"

But Isla didn't answer. Instead she swam away, and dived under the water and was there for a long time. Grace waited on the sandbar, where it was getting deeper as the tide came in. Isla could be under a long time. But suddenly the sandbar seemed to shake and Isla came bursting forth from the water, full *Little Mermaid* style. But her ascent was glorious. More glorious than anything Grace had ever seen. And she laughed as Isla the fake mermaid swam up beside her.

"That great, huh?" Grace said.

Isla swam up and they lay back on the sandbar. She placed her hand over her eyes and said shyly, "Yeah. Yeah, it was that great."

They stayed there until the water was too high to lie down, and then they sat until the water was too high to remain sitting, and finally they swam back to the boat and went home.

That was the night that Maiden's Cove and all the surrounding towns of the bay saw the green lights for the first time in a hundred years, coming from an unknown glowing sandbar in the middle of the bay.

⌒

"How in the hell did we miss this festival every year, Grace?" Isla said, her green eyes wide in wonder at the spectacle of the Maiden's Cove Festival.

The whole town was on parade, lit up with the shorter nights, and the carnival was back in town for the evening, with rides for all ages including the Wave Swinger, which was Isla's favorite. She'd been on three times in a row with Grace and Bayla.

"It's like you're flying!" she said, laughing as the swings spun around and around at speed.

Bayla preferred the merry-go-round with Loretta, Jimbo, Della and Aunt Lou, while Luke and Ben favored the Matterhorn which was a mini rollercoaster with loud music.

They all rode the Ferris wheel together, in pairs: Luke and Grace in one, Ben and Isla in another. Aunt Lou rode with Della, and Jimbo stayed behind with Loretta because he was afraid of the Ferris wheel, which had Bayla, who rode with Georgiana, in hysterics for at least twenty minutes.

"But you're so big and strong! How can you be afraid of the Ferris wheel?" She giggled.

"Big and strong means you fall harder and faster," Jimbo said, crossing his arms. "I'm going to win my grandkids some prizes now, you fool." And he walked off.

Georgiana winked at Bayla as the Ferris wheel took them up.

"Lou!" Tristan called up as he and Cohen took the chair in the Ferris wheel just behind her and Della. "Do you think this is good for your heart?"

"What's wrong with my heart?" she yelled down.

"It's weak, remember? And you've had two heart attacks," he said, then turned to Cohen. "Do you think she's getting dementia?"

Cohen buried his head in his arms. "I think she lied to you so you'd come be her nurse."

"Why would she do that?" Tristan asked.

Cohen sat up and confessed their conversation from the Fourth of July. "I should have told you, I'm sorry."

"Yeah, you would have saved me the trouble," Tristan said. "Trying to find ways to sneak out and see you," he said, taking Cohen's hand and smiling shyly. "I Facebook-stalked you too."

There were dozens of games at the carnival as well—bobbing for apples, guessing the weight of the pumpkin, and a balloon pop-off. Bayla wanted to try what she called her new after-almost-drowning lungs, so dragged Uncle Ben to compete with her. You had to blow up a balloon until it popped before the other teams. They came in third place.

After their share of rides and games, they all took a break together and found a big picnic table in the middle of all the food stands. They ordered hot dogs, popcorn, corn dogs, corn on the cob, big bowls of fries with vinegar, soft pretzels with cheese, and funnel cakes topped with icing sugar.

"You haven't answered my question, Grace," Isla said, biting into a soft pretzel covered in crab dip. "How on earth did we miss this every year?"

"This is the Maiden's Cove Festival," Georgiana said, reaching for some fries. "Where they call the mermaids home. Gosh, I don't even remember the story anymore, really."

"Does anyone?" Isla asked.

"I don't remember," Bayla said, "but I know it. I wrote it all down for that lady that interviewed us for the magazine. Want to hear it?"

"Definitely," Isla said.

"Ahem," Bayla said, clearing her throat and standing. "Somewhere on the Chesapeake Bay lies a very small, very peculiar little town called Maiden's Cove. It's founder, Ifan Gryphon, a fisherman from Wales, had named it Cildraeth Morwynion, but over the years the simple fishermen on whom the town was based translated it into English and it has been Maiden's Cove ever since.

"It is a very small town because it has approximately two hundred and thirteen permanent residents and it is a very peculiar town because it is said that the Cove is home to mermaids, and its history is based on Ifan's peculiar tale of having been lured into the Cove after his ship was wrecked in the Atlantic by a beautiful woman of the sea, who rescued him and brought him to a forbidden shore. She was cast out by her people for helping the human, and she became his wife on the land for many years, even producing a daughter, as the town began to build and grow with local fishermen. One night, in the year 1714, on the first of June, green lights sparkled on the bay. The whole town saw the lights but did not know what they meant, until the morning when Ifan, Isolde, and the small girl, Isla, were gone, and never returned, supposedly lured by the merfolk offshore to come home.

"The following year, on the first of June, the new mayor of the town, Ludlow Cleary, began a new tradition. He started the Festival of Lights, held on the eve of the fishing season, and the Maiden's Cove Festival at the end of the season. Every Maiden's Cove inhabitant would light a candle to bring the fishermen home, and not be tempted by the green lights that lit the water, every year, at the same time. It became known then that the Clearys could call the mermaids. History became myth, and turned into legend, and that's the story of the Maiden's Cove Festival."

Bayla took a bow, and they all clapped while Jimbo did his trademark whistle.

"Huh," Georgiana said, looking impressed. "I didn't realize there was actually so much history behind it. I always just thought it was the opening and closing of the fishing season. Well, until you showed up, Isla."

Isla laughed. "Do you reckon it was just because my name was Isla, same as Ifan and Isolde's daughter back in 1714?" she asked, and everyone stared at her.

"Um," Georgiana said, hesitating. "I think it was more like...you know, you." She blushed.

"Feral," Ben said, grinning at Isla. "Always dirty, barefoot."

"Then there was that whole breathing underwater thing," Jimbo laughed. "Don't forget that."

"And the fact that Grace called you. She's a Cleary," Luke joined in.

"You know," Isla mused, "my last night in Maiden's Cove and I find out how awesome everyone thought I was. Me, I just thought I was a fisherman's daughter, through and through."

"You'll always be just a fisherman's daughter to me," Grace said, taking her hand. "And the best friend a girl could ever have."

Isla stared at her and finally shook her head. "Hell no! I'm an awesome mermaid, that's what they said and that's the story I'm sticking with. Way cooler."

They all laughed then, and it was without the bittersweetness or the sadness that goodbyes can have, because they were all together, and they were finishing the story of the fisherman's daughter and the tale of the mermaids, here in Maiden's Cove, at the Maiden's Cove Festival, together.

It was late when they all left the festival, with long, drawn-out hugs from Jimbo, Della and Aunt Lou to Isla, who knew she was leaving in the morning. Grace, Isla and Bayla arrived back at Grace's home together later that night. None of them said a word on the way home.

Isla went to put Bayla to bed and asked to talk to her by herself.

"I'll just be a minute," she said to Grace.

Isla lay Bayla gently on her bed and pulled up the covers. She hadn't realized how much she would miss her honorary niece until this moment, brushing her bangs off her damp forehead, which she kissed. Bayla stirred and Isla stood to leave. *Goodbye*, she mouthed silently, and turned to leave.

"Goodnight, Aunt Isla," Bayla whispered in her sleep.

"Goodnight, sweetheart," Isla whispered. She closed the door behind her and went out to the porch.

Isla and Grace sat next to each other for a long time, and while there seemed like there'd be so much to say, they held hands, and said nothing.

And then it happened. Everything and nothing. The moment, where it was all just okay.

"One from the land," Grace whispered, standing.

"One from the sea," Isla said, her eyes filling as she stood too.

"Summer soul sisters, forever shall we be."

Isla pulled Grace in tightly for a brief, but fierce, hug. Finally, they both took a deep breath and Grace forced a smile.

"Are you ready?" Grace asked.

"Almost," Isla said.

"One last stop?"

"Just the one."

They pressed their foreheads together like they used to, when they were soul sisters and summer sisters and one.

And then Isla turned and left.

At Henry's, Isla cleaned everything neatly, and turned out the lights of each room, closing the door as she went.

When the house was ready, she took off her clothes, and walked down the stairs to the boat, where Ben waited for her.

Later that night they lay side by side, holding hands and staring up at the sky.

"So where to tomorrow?"

"The Philippines has always called my name," she said with a small smile. "Seven thousand islands. The diving season starts now. Octopus mating season or something like that."

"Wait, you never went to the Philippines? That was the first place we ever talked about together," he said.

"I know. And it's the place I always saved for you, if and when. The invitation is always open for you, you know?" she said, turning to face him.

He turned to her as well, brushing her hair behind her ear. "One day," he whispered. "Maybe next year, when I sell the shop."

"Maybe then," she said.

"Will you come back here next summer?"

"I'm not sure. But I leave this time with peace, knowing that I can come home whenever I feel the need, and home will be here. At Maiden's Cove. Henry's. Cleary's. With Grace and Bayla at the cottage," she said with a smile.

"And me?"

"Home should be us together, taking it with us wherever we go," she said, her voice pleading.

Ben took her palm that she'd placed on his face and kissed it. "I'm sorry…"

She sighed, rolling on her back and looking to the sky, swallowing to fight the tears threatening her eyes that she didn't want Ben to see. "Well," she said, "at least we have tonight."

"We have tonight," he said, and drew her close to him, pressing his lips to hers.

⁓

The next day they all met at Cleary's and had a long lunch on the deck. Yesterday's newspaper was strewn on the tables, which were covered in steamed crabs, scallops, steamed shrimp, sides galore and pitchers of beer. Isla had wanted a small farewell, so of course everyone showed up. It was the day after the festival and normally Cleary's would be closed, but the staff all came in to treat them like royalty and to give Isla a proper send-off. The only person missing was Ben.

"Is he not coming?" Grace whispered aside to Isla.

She shook her head and swallowed. "We decided it was best to not have a sad goodbye, and we said ours last night after the festival."

"Such a hussy," Grace said quietly, and Isla laughed out loud. They grinned at each other.

"So, Isla honey," Della said, picking a shrimp, "Gracey says you off to Asia or somewhere like that?"

"Great diving season there," she said. "I think I need to go somewhere I've never been for a job this season. Shake off that incident I had in the Caribbean."

They nodded.

"Wait, you know about that?" she huffed and turned to Grace. "Grace!"

"I didn't tell them!"

They all looked at Aunt Lou who was drinking her vodka watermelon through a straw in one long gulp. Finally she finished, burped loudly, and looked up. "What?"

"When does the season end there, Isla?" Luke asked.

"I think January, not too sure," she said. "Why?"

"Oh, well it's just my mate is getting married in New Zealand in January and he's asked me to come in for it. I thought maybe Bayla and Grace might want to join me. Bayla seems quite keen on visiting New Zealand," Luke said with a wink to Bayla. "Thought it might be a good place for you girls to meet up."

"Oh my god!" Bayla screamed. "Oh, Mom, please! Yes, yes, let's!"

Isla looked at Grace, eyes wide with a big smile.

"Well, it could be that trip we've always dreamed of taking," Grace said, smiling at Isla.

"A Gracenisla reunion," Isla said, laughing. "With a few extras," she said, winking at Bayla.

"Room for one more?" a voice said from behind them.

Ben stood at the table, his backpack at his feet, passport in hand, and looking only at Isla.

"Ben?" she breathed, standing.

He walked over to Isla, taking her hand. "Take me with you. Wherever it might be."

Isla's eyes began to tear up as she laughed, grasping his hand. "Me and you? Together? Wherever we go is where we are."

"So what do you think? Room for one more on that boat? In your life? In your heart?" he asked, coming close to Isla and wrapping one arm around her waist, cupping her face in his other hand.

"Now?"

"Forever," he said.

"And in between?" she said, a sob in her throat.

"The blink of an eye."

And then they kissed, and went off into the sunset, together.

On a planet with 195 countries and a human population of eight billion people, there are a lot of places to see and stories to tell. Sometimes those places and their stories collide, like a beautiful accident nobody ever saw coming. This collision may not cure cancer or alter the paths of most of the eight billion people. But occasionally it will alter the paths of the people it was intended to change. And this makes for a very good ending indeed.

And so ends the story of Maiden's Cove.

Epilogue

"M ape," Bayla whispered, late in the night.

Mape groaned in her sleep but opened her eyes. "What is it, Bay?"

"Let's go swimming," she whispered, excited. "Night swimming. There's no moon and it's the last night the bioluminescence will be here since the fishing boats are all leaving."

"Now? In the middle of the night?" Mape asked, sitting up, wiping her eyes.

"Yeah," Bayla said, "like mermaids."

Mape's eyes lit up. "Okay. What about your mom?"

"She won't know, and if she does, she'll understand better than anybody."

The girls quietly opened the back porch and snuck down to the beach. Bayla stripped down.

"You're totally naked!" Mape said, giggling.

"Apparently the water is always warmer naked," Bayla whispered. "I don't know why, I just heard Mom and Aunt Isla saying it one night." She walked into the water and shivered. "Oooh, still fresh though."

Mape giggled and stripped down as well, running into the water, which was much colder than it had been a week before. "So what should we do?" she asked Bayla.

"Should we mermaid-swim for a while?"

When they got tired, they came in and lay on the beach, the sand glowing only faintly at the end of the season.

Mape sat up, pulling on her sweatshirt, looking out. "Do you think we'll see it again? The real green light?"

Bayla looked out and remembered the night she almost drowned.

"Do you think we'll see the green lights, Aunt Isla?" she whispered, no longer wheezing.

They remained quiet for a long time before Isla stood and whispered into Bayla's ear, something just for her.

"No. I was the last one."

Reading Group Guide

Discussion Questions

1. When Grace realizes that her relationship with her husband is unsafe, she packs up her daughter and returns to her hometown, Maiden's Cove, to restart their lives. What kind of courage do you think that took?

2. Maiden's Cove has a strong sense of community that brings people together, which is hard to find in today's world, especially for a tourist town. What about this town do you think leads its people to being so supportive of each other?

3. Throughout the course of the book, we explore Grace and Isla's summers growing up. How did these flashbacks help to shape your thoughts about the characters as the story unfolded?

4. Isla only came to Maiden's Cove each summer, bonding intensely with Grace, but not always connecting with the other residents. How did you feel about her childhood? Do you think her life was exciting because she got to travel a lot? Or was it lonely because she didn't have one place to call home?

5. Bayla is excited to be in Maiden's Cove and see where her mother grew up, but is also at the mercy (and danger) of her parents' separation, even as Grace tries to protect her from it. What do you think Grace could have done better to protect Bayla even further?

6. Do you believe Isla is a mermaid? Why or why not?

Author Q&A

Q: Why did you set *The Secrets of Maiden's Cove* in the Chesapeake Bay area? What is the personal connection to you?

A: I grew up on and around the Chesapeake Bay and my fondest childhood memories are centered around being on the water. Fourth of July at Downs Park, going crabbing and fishing for catfish with my dad, backyard cookouts where eating crabs on yesterday's newspaper brought everyone together. I have aways lived near the water and feel inexplicably connected to it. This book is, in its purest form, a love letter to home.

Q: What about mermaids fascinates you? Why did you choose to incorporate mermaid lore into this story?

A: I got the idea for this book about twenty years ago actually! After writing *The Secrets of the Little Greek Taverna*, I knew instinctively it was time to come back to it. Once I knew the setting was going to be in my hometown, memories of my youth flooded in, and the story started to write itself. I remembered the summers of mermaid swimming in the Bay, the first time I ever saw the bioluminescence (which is incredibly rare in Maryland), the essence of being young and filled with belief and hope. I wanted to convey that sense of the possibility of magic that all girls have, and in some ways this book turned into a grown-up version of a fantasy.

Q: Food is always in abundance in your books! Why is including food something you like to do with your stories? What is unique about the seafood that Grace serves at Cleary's Crab Shack?

A: Food has been at the center of my life since I started working in hospitality when I was eighteen and then began traveling shortly after that. Food IS culture. It is such a central and essential part of who we are and how we relate to those around us, how we belong to our community. I love to eat and sharing food with others is life's greatest pleasure! As soon as food became an integral part of *Taverna*, I knew that innately food would be either a central part or at least a part of everything that I write.

Maryland's crab shacks are unique to the state and especially to the Bay. I wanted to write about food that is quintessentially Maryland seafood, but Cleary's began to form quite clearly in my mind after my dad passed away while I was writing the novel. He had a dream to have a restaurant one day and Tommy's Cook-Off is based on his annual summer parties and cooking contests at his house! He was a great source of inspiration for me writing about the restaurant and it was like making his dreams come true through words, and therefore celebrating him as well.

Q: This is your second novel. How did your process change from your first book to your second? Did you learn anything about yourself that you were able to apply to writing *The Secrets of Maiden's Cove*?

A: In some ways, my favorite part of writing became the editing process. Writing is a very solo journey at the beginning, where it's you and your characters (and a lot of Google, research and yelling out to your chef boyfriend—"Hey, what's that cooking term…?"). I found working with my editors so much fun and watching your book go from a written idea into something truly rich and well rounded is so exciting.

When writing this book, I would often have my editors in my head earlier rather than later—when I am overly wordy (I love using three words to say one thing), when I use too many exclamation marks or CAPITAL LETTERS (I love them, so very much). Probably the most useful tool I learned is that in the face of a complex issue or problem within the story, the answer is almost always to UNCOMPLICATE it and simplify it, not make it more complicated. (See, capital letters!)

Q: Why do you like to include hints of magic in your books? While never directly magical, there is a feeling that the magic could exist, which is a unique space to be in. What inspired you to write stories in this fashion?

A: I think in some ways it is an almost literal translation of what books themselves do for people—at least what they have always done for me—that you believe a story and its characters do exist. From the moment I was old enough to read I was obsessed with books. Books are *magical*. They take you to another place, allow you to be another person, to yearn and desire, to hope and dream. I love adding something just real enough and just magical enough in my stories that make them feel like they could be real, to add to the whimsy of escaping into a book that makes you believe anything could exist.

Q: For readers looking to begin their writing journey, what piece of advice would you give to them?

A: While everyone has their own process, I am an advocate of NaNoWriMo (National Novel Writing Month). In essence, it's a writing challenge to complete 50,000 words in 30 days (or your choice of a number depending on your goal and what you're writing). It's free and is basically just a way of tracking your progress on a graph that morphs and changes based on the work you put into it. It's like having a coach going "come on, just a little bit further!" And in a world that is very solo, having encouragement is key! Honestly, my entire career has come from a moment in NaNoWriMo where if I didn't write *SOMETHING, ANYTHING*, I would not hit that goal. That push, that dedication even to one hour of the day, is where magic happens. You'll never publish anything without sitting down and writing. So sit down and write!

Explore the Chesapeake Bay Like a Local

Maryland's Chesapeake Bay is the place I call home. But until I began writing this book, I didn't realize that home is not only where you're from, but who you are. It is ingrained in every memory, every moment that created you and made you who you are. While it didn't start out this way, in the end, *The Secrets of Maiden's Cove* became, quite frankly, a love letter to home.

So I invite you, my dear readers, to become a fellow Marylander, and become inspired by this travel guide (put together with the help of some local Maryland friends) that will surely inspire your next trip to the magical Chesapeake Bay!

1. Explore Maryland's Capital, Annapolis

Maryland's beautiful and historic (1649) capital, Annapolis, is consistently voted one of the most walkable historic centers in America for a good reason. From West Street and down the famous Main Street right down to the City Dock and over to Eastport, you will fall in love with the architecture, the history, and the lively food and entertainment scene!

Some of my favorite things to do in Annapolis:

- Meander down Main Street and along all the side streets filled with antique shops, book stores, shopping, and restaurants.
- Take a scenic boat trip or kayak trip from the dock. Watermark Cruises does excellent boat trips around Annapolis, to the Bay Bridge, and even to St. Michaels! Paddle Annapolis does an awesome two-hour guided trip on kayaks.
- See a live band play at the fantastic Ram's Head On Stage.
- Visit the Naval Academy.
- Eat, eat, and eat some more! Some favorites include Cantler's Riverside Inn (not downtown, but a Chesapeake Bay Icon and one that I always picture when I write about Cleary's!), Chick & Ruth's Deli, or any of the delicious waterfront restaurants from old style taverns to fine dining.

2. Catchin' Crabs

Maryland Blue Crabs are what the Chesapeake Bay is most famous for, and going crabbing is a favorite pastime. Want to try it out yourself? The season and style of crabbing is regulated but most recreational crabbers with a boat and a hand line can go crabbing from April 1 to December 15 each year. There are a few ways to go crabbing:

- On a boat with a local (or charter your own boat if you have the appropriate licensing). The old classic from when we were kids was to take your crab pots with chicken bone bait and drop them into spots in the bay with a milk carton attached with your name so you know which ones are yours when you come to pick them back up in a few hours time.
- On a professional fishing and crabbing boat. *The Marylander* is a fishing boat that does charters from the gorgeous Stevensville which is just on the other side of the Bay Bridge from Annapolis.
- Ask the locals for some tips on their favorite shallow spots, take some chicken necks on a piece of string, and walk into the water!

3. Eatin' Crabs

While eating crabs in the backyard on yesterday's newspaper, wooden mallets in tow, the table dowsed with Old Bay, and cans of beer on the table is a staple of Maryland society, not much beats having the experience in one of Maryland's Famous Crab Shacks like Cleary's in Maiden's Cove.

Some favorites of mine are:

- Jimmy Cantler's Riverside Inn (Annapolis)
- Fisherman's Crab Deck (Kent Narrows)
- Stoney Creek Inn (Curtis Bay)
- The Crab Claw (St. Michaels)

4. Fourth of July Celebrations

There's Christmas, New Years, Easter and Thanksgiving of course—but often those holidays pale in comparison to a Maryland Fourth of July spectacular. A classic summer cookout involves hot dogs, hamburgers, corn on the cob (hand shucked), potato salad and coleslaw (and often crabs, of course!). Which is followed by a walk or drive to a destination of choice to see the most amazing fireworks display.

The Fourth of July scene in *The Secrets of Maiden's Cove* is firmly based on my fondest childhood memories at Sandy Point in Pasadena—running with sparklers, watching the famous Blue Angels fly, and finally, once dark, the fireworks.

Some of the best places to spend a Fourth of July on the Chesapeake Bay:

- Downs Park (Pasadena)
- St. Michaels (Eastern Shore)
- Downtown Annapolis (Annapolis)
- An Annapolis Fireworks Cruise (by Watermark)—on a boat from Annapolis
- Ocean City (Eastern Shore)

5. Visit the magical towns of the Eastern Shore

The Secrets of Maiden's Cove takes place in a fictional small village on Maryland's Eastern Shore, but there are so many magical villages on this serene and mystical marshland. They are charming, quaint, historical, but more than anything, life in these towns revolves around the Bay, around the water—fishing, crabbing, boating. Life IS the Bay, and the Bay IS life.

Some favorite charming towns to visit on the Eastern Shore:

- St. Michaels
- Rock Hall
- Cambridge
- Oxford
- Crisfield

6. Find secret beaches, coves, and the magic of the Bay

There are no two ways about it—the Chesapeake Bay is meant to be discovered on the water. Dock Bars only reached by boat, hidden sandbars where you can sunbathe in the middle of the bay, islands that only exist in certain tides. But you can find quite a few by car as well.

Here are a few hidden gems that only the locals can tell you about:

- Wye River and Wye Island (Queen Anne's County)
- Cross Island Trail (Kent Island)
- Tolchester (Kent County)
- Dock Bar at Lowes Wharf (Talbot County)
- Tilghman Island (Talbot County)

7. A few other Eastern Shore and Chesapeake Bay favorites that shouldn't be missed, even if they are directly on the tourist trail:

- Ocean City—Sure, it's touristy. And sure, it's packed in the summer with every Marylander on family vacation. But the unique Peninsula with a solid ten-mile golden sand beach on the Atlantic on one side and the Chesapeake Bay on the other side make it one of the most unique and easy beach destinations on this part of the East Coast.
- Assateague Island—Wild horses? Check. Sandy beaches? Check. Protected National Park? Check. One of the most magical spots in the world to me? Check.
- Smith Island—for the famous cake and State Dessert!
- St. Michaels—it just really is that gorgeous.

Special thanks to Jen Browning Thomas, Kristen Duffy, Samantha Consoli Battung, Christian Battung, Casey Davis, and Andrea Phillips for their contributions to this list.

Rachel and Andrew's Ooey Gooey Maryland Crab Dip

Ingredients:

8 oz cream cheese, softened

7½ oz chive & onion cream cheese, softened

½ cup sour cream

¼ cup mayonnaise

1 tsp Worcestershire sauce

1 tbsp Old Bay hot sauce*

¼ tsp lemon juice

½ tsp garlic powder

½ tsp onion powder

½ tsp ground black pepper

1½ tsp Old Bay seasoning

8 oz block of mozzarella cheese, shredded (set aside one cup for the topping)**

8 oz block of mild or medium cheddar cheese, shredded (save one cup for the topping)**

8 oz claw meat

10 oz lump crabmeat

One 9x11-inch baking dish

Topping (optional):

10 Club crackers or Ritz crackers, crushed

1 cup cheese blend

1 Tbsp butter, melted

1 tsp Old Bay seasoning

Preheat oven to 400°F.

Combine cream cheeses, sour cream, mayo, Worcestershire sauce, Old Bay hot sauce, lemon juice, and seasonings. Use a hand mixer and mix on medium-low for 1–2 minutes, or until creamy. Fold in cheeses until blended. Fold in crab meat until blended. Spray 9x11-inch baking dish with cooking spray, then evenly layer mixture into pan. Add cracker topping IF preferred; if omitting cracker mixture, add cheese evenly on top. Bake for 20 minutes, or until bubbly.

Serve with your favorite crackers, tortilla chips, or (our favorite) sliced French bread, lightly toasted.

Making the topping:

Mix crushed crackers with butter and Old Bay until well blended. Layer lightly with cracker mixture, followed by a light layer of the cheese mixture. Add the rest of the crushed cracker mixture, followed by the last layer of the cheese. Bake for 20 minutes, or until bubbly.

*If Old Bay hot sauce is not available, any traditional hot sauce can be substituted.

**If buying shredded cheese from the store instead of shredding your own block cheese, rinse with water and pat dry with a paper towel. Preservatives added to shredded cheese affect the way it melts.

—Recipe courtesy of chefs extraordinaire, my sister Rachel Palmisano and my nephew Andrew McGlynn

Acknowledgments

Thank you to everyone at Moa Press and Hachette Aotearoa New Zealand and Australia, and to Kate, Dom, Mel, Tania, Sacha, Suzy, Sharon and Sarah for being my core rockstar team.

Kate, thank you for being my "identical hand twin"—this story would not be what it is without your insight, ideas and enthusiasm.

To Dianne Blacklock, my brilliant copyeditor—thank you for reining my characters in from laughing all the time!

Thank you to Kirsiah, Gina and Leena at Grand Central—I'm so lucky to have you as my team in the U.S.! And to everyone at Headline UK for your excitement for this book.

Andrea, thank you for letting me steal all our favorite "summer soul sister" phrases for "Gracenisla" in this tale. And

Kristen, thank you for all the many hours of mermaid swimming when we were kids.

Mom—I never believed that any dream was impossible because of your unwavering support and belief that we could do anything if we were dedicated and worked hard to achieve it. *Thank you.*

Dan—thank you for being my biggest champion. I literally couldn't be doing this without you.

To all of my family and friends in Maryland—this book is a love letter to home and to all of you. Though I had the tale of Grace and Isla in my head for many years, I began writing the story during the pandemic. I was unable to come home to Maryland for many years during that time, even when I lost my dad to the virus. In my yearning and longing for my family, my home and the Chesapeake Bay near where I grew up, I created the fictional town of Maiden's Cove and the surrounding magic of the bay as the center and heart of the story. In some ways, it was a healing catharsis, and in the end, this novel is a love letter to home.

Finally, to all the would-be mermaids out there—*never stop dreaming.*

About the Author

Erin Palmisano is the author of bestselling novel *The Secrets of the Little Greek Taverna*. She loves writing stories where her passions of food, wine and travel come together with a hint of magic. Erin is a dual NZ and US citizen and she and her chef partner live in Nelson, New Zealand, where they own and operate three restaurants. *The Secrets of Maiden's Cove* is her second novel.

www.erinpalmisano.com
Instagram: @authorerinpalmisano
Facebook: @authorerinpalmisano
X: @palmisano_erin